Thailand Honey

Leslie Cameron

authorHOUSE®

AuthorHouse™ UK Ltd.
500 Avebury Boulevard
Central Milton Keynes, MK9 2BE
www.authorhouse.co.uk
Phone: 08001974150

First published by AuthorHouse 8/21/2009

ISBN: 978-1-4490-0746-1 (sc)

ISBN: 978-1-4490-0746-1 (sc)

This book is printed on acid-free paper.

1

It was all about diamonds; always had been - right from the start. A package worth some 400k in US dollars had been stolen by Chelsea's little sister Anni. To these gorgeous Thai girls, *theft* was like *borrowing* – and the diamond scam was extra pocket money. To them, it was *Thailand Honey*: it made their life a little sweeter. To me, it was life or death.

It was Friday morning. Chelsea and I were sitting at a café table in the concourse by Bangkok's *River City* shopping mall, near the Si Phraya cross-ferry terminal. We were waiting to hand over smuggled stones to Villavito, the man who organised the scam.

Then, as the crowd of ferry users melted away, we saw him, weaving towards us like an angry cobra, ready to strike. A moment later, a snub-nosed Smith & Wesson .38 revolver was aimed at my face.

"Raphael - I have them here," and I started to open my backpack.

"*All* my diamonds, David?" Always Mr Polite.

"Most of them," I said – and pulled out the two gold pin-cushions that held the dross we'd helped to smuggle from Laos.

"And what about Rudi?"

"He couldn't come," I said.

"Why was that?" Villavito asked me.

"He tried to rob you..."

He wasn't listening. "*I warned you*," and waved his gun the way they do in cheap detective movies.

I put up my hands. "It's OK – you have the consignment..." and I pointed to the two little cushions. "And we'll soon find the missing package."

"You had your chance," he said. "Now it's my turn."

"Raphael – be reasonable!" I tried.

Too late... he raised the gun to shoulder height – changed his aim and fired twice. Both hit Chelsea – and threw her backwards like a broken doll. She hit her head on the edge of the veranda and just lay there, not moving – her blood spreading over the paving stones in a crimson flood.

Now the gun was pointing back at me. I could see his finger on the trigger. It was him or me. Which left no option. I had to kill him, there and then.... in front of everyone.

2.

How had we created this God-awful mess? Ask Chelsea - that stunning little Thai girl, with her long dark hair, deep brown eyes and the most delightful smile in the whole of South-East Asia.

I'd gone to meet her with the best of intentions. I wanted to marry her. But as the Chinese say: *It's often better to travel hopefully...*

I met her first on a scorching Saturday in Bangkok. She was working in a travel bureau in Soi Rambuttri. As I entered her shop, she was sitting at the glass-topped counter, wearing a yellow shirt and washed-out jeans and radiating a smile that could have put the *Land of the Rising Sun* on hold for most of the summer.

"Good morning - me Chelsea – how me help you?"

I was hoping to arrange an up-country tour for the following week. "Chiang Mai?" I began – but had to ask. "Why are you called Chelsea?"

"'Cos I love Diddi Logba," she told me. "He good man – he kick for Chelsea – that in England."

And I just fell for her, right there and then. It wasn't intended. It just happened. "Do you watch a lot of English football?"

"My brother, he like Liverpool." But there was more to come. "Game tonight," she said. "On TV – in here," and she waved towards the patio bar outside her shop. "You come – see game – maybe buy me drink."

That was me; down the river for a smile. I met her for the match. It cost me drinks for her, her friends and anyone who happened to be in there. After that, she put me in a taxi.

From that day on, she had me by the nuts. Did it matter? No it didn't. She was gorgeous. And when I went back home, we kept in touch, first by e-mail, then by *Messenger*.

With Chelsea, cyber-love-&-kisses had to be paid for – but in real money. First, she 'borrowed' 10,000 baht to buy herself a laptop computer. Next, she 'borrowed' for a digital camera – and more again for a cell phone. She said she needed them to send me e-mails, pictures and phone calls. This was *Thailand Honey*, big time.

Back then, she was probably my girlfriend. She liked to keep me guessing. She always told me what she thought I'd like to hear. One day, we'd hit the tits-up zone, we both knew that. Until then, she would spread the honey sweet and thick.

But her promises to *pay you back* went up in smoke when she claimed that someone had stolen her handbag, right off the desk of her travel shop.

True or false? Who could say? Who cared? She was like a business expense: if you need it, buy it. So I did. And she was worth it.

When Chelsea called me on her cell phone on that Saturday in early May, I sat up and took notice. Life is too short to ignore a beautiful woman.

"Hello, darling!" she purred.

"What's up, sweet kitten?" She was paying for the call. It wouldn't take long.

"I love you, darling," she said. It was a simple statement, quite matter-of-fact. No heart-rending emotion.

"And I love you," It was safe to use the L-word. Thais don't know much English and *love* can mean anything from casual friendship to deep and passionate devotion.

"I want to come to England."

"Why?"

"If you have to ask, I not come," Chelsea sniffed.

"OK," I agreed. "I'd love you to come to England."

"First, I want diamond ring," she went on. "My friend Patti – she get diamond ring."

I had met Patti. She worked in Chelsea's travel shop. In Chelsea-speak, Patti was in love with this German guy who ran a hotel on Gran Canaria. But a diamond ring means business. "I'd like to speak to Patti," I said. "Is she engaged?"

"Yes, she very busy," Chelsea replied. "She sending man to Laos."

I let it ride. No point in going further. I admire women with spirit and dogs that argue. But in Chelsea's case, the boundaries were often blurred. "It beautiful ring," she told me. "Only sixteen-thousand baht."

"Sounds delightful," I said.

"You send me sixteen-thousand baht?"

"Why should I send you all that money?"

"So you can buy me ring." She made it sound so logical.

"Sweetheart," I tried, "In England, a diamond ring has a very special meaning…." But I was pissing in the wind.

"You no want me buy ring?"

"Only for the right reason," I tried.

"You no want buy me ring?"

3

Time to negotiate. "My angel," I tried, "on the day you agree to marry me, I will happily buy you a diamond ring." Would it be that easy?

Not a chance. "You show me first," she said. "Then I decide."

"OK," I said. "What's your finger size?"

"52," Chelsea told me. "Small diamond – gold ring."

"But of course," I agreed. A 52 meant very little to me. But Viv worked in jewellery. All it needed was an e-mail.

"When you come, you help me fix visa?"

That would cost, but it could be worth it. "Of course," I agreed. That was something else for Viv to do. "I'll call KLM. See you in a couple of weeks."

Chelsea thought for half a second. "You bring me watch?"

According to KLM's *Holland Herald*, it can take you fifteen minutes to cross Schiphol terminal from Pier D to Pier E. But it's only an estimate. It doesn't allow for time to admire the dazzling array of goods and services on offer in the shopping plaza.

And I stopped.

Reason 1: Chelsea had asked me for a watch.

Reason 2: Chelsea had specified a *Rado* – one of the more expensive. Nice try, my love, but no cigar - and certainly no *Rado*.

"I help you, sir?" She was tall, blonde and dressed in navy blue.

"This one, please?" and I pointed to the left hand corner of the lower shelf that held the less-expensive items.

"A stony bracelet?" asked my tall blonde.

A fair description. Most of the watches in my range had diamante-style wristbands. "Good place to start," I agreed.

Before I had could finish the sentence, three bracelet watches were out of the display and lined up on the counter. "See this – and this – and this," she said in her Dutch accent.

"Perfect," I thanked her – and selected a DKNY with a silvered chain-link band that she could shorten. Chelsea's wrist was very small.

"Good choice, sir." With a smile and a Visa, we closed the deal.

Once away from the flowers, gifts, clothing, jewellery and all those very expensive cameras, I was back on course and following the big yellow *This Way* signs towards Pier E and the *Cafe Ellipse* beside Gate 9.

This little coffee shop could seat eighty people. Tonight, it was about a quarter full and it would keep me snug and dry until the *Departures* screen clicked over to show that flight KL 0877 for Bangkok was *Now Boarding*.

"I get you something?" asked a sweet little voice.

Her badge said *Marti*. And yes, she smiled a lot. But at least she could speak English.

"Heineken and one of those, please," I said. I didn't really need the *Danish,* but its topping of apricot jam was too good to resist.

Marti poured my drink from the beer-pump and used red plastic tongs to ease my pastry on to a white china plate. "Eight euros, please."

Another chance to use Visa.

As she gave it back, she read my name. "Thank you, Mr Shannon," she smiled. "Enjoy your flight."

"You're very kind," then found myself a seat on the comfortable red plastic-covered bench that ringed my side of the café. Other passengers were scattered around in ones and twos, drinking coffee or beer and (like me), just waiting for the clock to send them on their way.

I checked my watch: 19.34. Time to call Chelsea before Viv arrived. I pulled the laptop from my travel bag, plugged in my cell phone and called up *Messenger*. True, it was half-past one in Bangkok. But if madam really wanted a watch, she'd have waited up.

Shannon says: How are you? I clicked [Send] – and waited.

Chelsea says: Hello, darling – you how tonight? She was using the Vista notebook I had bought her.

Shannon says: Good morning, little squirrel.

By now, our webcams had clicked into action. For this call, she was wearing a purple sweat-shirt with *Imagine* in large white letters right across her critical features. Cheeky cat! As if I did anything else…

Chelsea says: What you doing?

Shannon says: In Schiphol, waiting for the plane.

Chelsea says: You get me diamond?

Shannon says: Don't worry, my love – you'll see it at lunch.

Chelsea says: OK – then we have party. But there was more to come. Like her wonderful *Diddi Logba*, my darling Chelsea rarely missed an opportunity. *You not forget watch?*

Shannon says: See what I can do. OK, so her watch was already in my pocket. Let her wait. No point in giving it away too early. She could have it once we were in bed.

Chelsea says: You promise?

Will do my best I replied, smiling bravely into the little camera. From there, we went through the usual farewell pattern of *Love you – Love You Madly – Pink-Pink-Pink* and loads and loads of kisses.

Although I had solved the problem of the watch, I still had to deal with the diamond.

Only a matter of time…. As I was putting away my *talk-to-Chelsea* kit, so this girl with bleached hair gelled into spikes came up to my table. She was dressed in a black leather jacket and a pair of skin-tight jeans. And she was carrying a can of diet Coca-Cola.

"Hi, Viv," I greeted her.

"Hi there, sweetie!" and she kissed my cheek as she sat beside me. "See you're on the pussy-bomber!"

"It's the only way to travel," I smiled back.

"What the fuck are you up now?" she asked. "First a ring – then a UK visa!" and she placed a small black velvet-covered jewellery box on the table.

"Sale or return?" I smiled.

"As always," Viv smiled back. "Who's the lucky girl?"

"Chelsea," I told her.

"*Thailand Honey*!" Viv replied, trying not to laugh. "As soon as you're back at the airport, she'll flog it."

"Probably," I grinned. "And thanks for the visa advice."

"Hope it works." Viv had been a mate for years. I'd met her back in the early 90s. Over the years, we'd kept in touch by e-mail. Now, she was helping with a jewellery concession in the Schiphol Plaza – and also helping Chelsea with her UK Visa application.

"Couple of weeks?" I asked her.

"Or send me a MasterCard number," Viv agreed.

3

As I pushed the jewel box into my backpack, the *Departure* screen clicked over to show that KL 0877 was ready. Next stop, Thailand.

I found seat 30C, stowed my excess in the overhead locker and made myself comfortable. Within thirty minutes, we'd been offered drinks, watched our steady progress on the TV map and received our headphones for the film or music channels, take your choice. As the on-screen trail curved down to the Black Sea, I went for *Easy Listening* on Channel 5, closed my eyes and let my mind go back to Chelsea and her never-ending search for the *Honey* in my wallet.

After many hours of music, films, red wine, water and the inevitable ham-roll breakfast, the night came to an end. KL 0877 skimmed across the Thailand countryside, lowered its flaps, kissed the tarmac with a scream of rubber and rolled up to the terminal building of Bangkok's magnificent Suvarnabhumi Airport.

Because of the amount of traffic in the city centre, it took at least an hour to reach Soi Rambuttri. Just as we were easing our way into the crowded tourist area, there she was – the girl of my dreams, looking gorgeous in a scarlet T-shirt. She was buying her lunch from a noodle stall.

"This will do," I told my driver. As he came to a stop, I scrambled out and dropped my holdall on the pavement.

"Chelsea!"

She turned and saw me. *"Darling!"* and her face lit up in a dazzling smile as she skipped across the crowded street to hug and kiss me. "You get my watch?"

"Easy, lass!" I grinned. "First, I need a beer," and I eased her through the parked cars and the endless crawling traffic to the flower-covered entrance of the Tuptim Hotel, across the road from the noodles.

Inside, the restaurant was dark and cool. It had a dozen tables, all covered by flowery red tablecloths.

"This do," Chelsea decided and picked a two-seater table at the edge of the mezzanine. In the tiny courtyard beyond the hand rail, an old black dog was dozing in the shade of a banana tree.

"OK, my love." From here, the street looked different. "Where's your shop?" I asked her.

"Not here," she answered. "Next street – I come see Pimmi."

"Your friend?"

"Best friend," Chelsea confirmed. "You see her later."

"Looking forward to it," I smiled back.

Once we were seated, Chelsea waved at a waiter. "He want a Singha," she said, showing off her command of English. "I want ice-cold glass of mango juice."

"Yes," I agreed with her, "this is fine," and I leaned back in my chair and stretched my legs. After ten long hours of confinement in Economy Class, they were enjoying the freedom. "Where shall we have the party?" I asked her.

Chelsea paused to run her fingers through her beautiful hair. "You get my diamond?" And to emphasise its promise of the future, she smoothed the creases in her T-shirt to emphasise the tempting breasts beneath the red material.

"At the party," I promised. "For once, we'll do it right."

"An' my watch?"

"All in good time, my darling."

She was not best pleased. "I want wear it tonight!"

"You will," I promised. "Where are we having the party?"

Her cell phone stopped her from answering. "My friend," she explained as the waiter returned with our drinks.

By now, it was mid-afternoon and the restaurant was quiet. Three or four people were drinking coffee or working their way through plates of sugared bread.

Chelsea closed her phone. "Anni's place," she said. "RiverSide."

"Where's that?"

"River City," Chelsea explained. "Small hotel."

"Sounds good," I agreed. "Where am I staying tonight?" If I seriously believed the question would open the door to Chelsea's bedroom, then I was out of luck. As usual, my little angel was ahead of me.

"My flat are girls only," she smiled. "Men not allowed."

Now that *was* a good one. "*Mai pen rai*," I said. "Doesn't matter - how about RiverSide?"

"What you mean?"

"Can you book me in?"

"Not now," and she held up her phone. "Want top-up."

Cheeky cat! *You can reload it yourself.* So I rummaged through the travel bag for my own cell phone. "Use this," I said.

"Will try," and she called the number from memory. When they answered, she rattled away in high-pitched Thai for a couple of minutes, then smiled with great delight: "Is OK – nice room – I fix."

"Nice one, squirrel!" I replied.

She frowned. "What squirrel?"

"It's a cute little animal with large brown eyes and a furry tail."

"I no got furry tail," she objected.

"But you're cute with large brown eyes," I smiled back. *And we can talk about your furry tail tonight.* But I hadn't finished with RiverSide. "Who runs it?" I asked. Many of Bangkok's hotels are run by the Chinese.

"Philippino," said Chelsea.

"Does he have a name?"

"Mr Raphael," Chelsea told me. "Anni no like him."

The noise from the street was getting louder. Now that the heat of the midday sun was easing off, tourists were out in droves, going though the stalls of replica football shirts, DVDs and cut-price souvenirs like plagues of locusts. Smoke from the charcoal stoves was hanging over Soi Rambuttri like a fog.

"What else does he do?"

"Trade in diamonds," Chelsea told me.

"Maybe I should have bought your ring from him," I said.

"No-no-no!" Chelsea squealed. "No buy from him – he crook!"

"You must introduce me," I grinned. "We could do business."

We finished our drinks and I paid the waiter. Then Chelsea stopped a taxi, told the driver where to take me and let me kiss her cheek. "Take care, darling," she said. "I call you later."

From Soi Rambuttri, it took some forty minutes to work our way through the afternoon traffic to River City. After we'd made a right-hand turn at the *Bangrak* sign, I saw a bank, a jewellery shop and a big blue SILVER logo. Then we turned sharp left, drove passed a row of large bronze sculptures and the Royal Orchid Sheraton until we stopped at the RiverSide Apartments.

Inside – and away from the heat of the city - it felt cold. I walked up to the Reception desk and smiled at the large Chinese woman with the pony-tail. She was wearing a navy-blue blouse with a plunging neckline.

"David Shannon - I have a reservation."

The well-built Chinese woman bowed and smiled politely. "You are welcome, Mr David – I Lucille - show me passport, please?"

Same old stuff, same old routines, same old formalities. Once she'd seen my passport, I could sign her registration card – and once she had my signature on paper, I could have a key.

Up there on the 5th floor, my room had a toilet and a shower unit, a multi-channel TV and a well-stocked mini-bar, including my favourite Singha beer. It also had a safety box to store my laptop.

Although the mattress was like an airport runway, it didn't stop me from sleeping through the afternoon. Then, right in the middle of a dream about girls-only apartments, I had a phone call.

It was Chelsea. "You like your room?" she asked.

"503 is very nice," I told her.

"You see Anni?"

"She's not in here with me."

But Chelsea wasn't into flippancy. "You no make joke!" she yelled down the line. "She very busy girl!"

By now, I was awake. "I'm sure she is," I tried. "Let me shower and I'll go and look for her." I tried.

"Why you waste time in bed?"

"Need to be fit for your party," I fired back.

"You get dressed, meet me Starbuck – one hour. We talk my friend about visa."

"Is that the one in MBK?" I asked her.

"How many you know?"

"That's the only one, my little kitten," I agreed. This was not the time to start a fight. As I put the phone down, I began to wonder how long we'd been married.

It only took me fifteen minutes to shower, dress and make my way back to the coffee shop. Nixie was on duty. (*Not too hard - I read her name badge.*) She was wearing a white cotton blouse and a light-blue denim apron. A rainbow halter kept it ship-shape, Bristol-fashion.

"Hello, Nixie."

"Good afternoon, Mr David." Although she was older than your average coffee-shop assistant, Nixie could have smiled at international level. She had been cleaning down her surfaces with a white dish cloth. "What you like?" she smiled.

There was a line of jars on her counter. I tapped the one with the Columbian label.

"You take seat?" For a moment or two, I watched her powder the beans and turn them into coffee.

"Wonderful!" I grinned.

"For Mr David," she smiled and handed me the cup and saucer. "Milk and sugar on table," she said.

Now it was Lucille's turn. She was out from behind her counter and heading towards me. "Mr David - you on holiday?"

"Yes," I confessed. "I'll be here for a week."

By now, she was beside me. "You been Bangkok before?"

"Several times," I said.

This gave Lucille her opening. "You got Thai girl!" she said.

"I'd like to think so," I agreed. "You'll see her tonight. We're having a party."

This produced a wagging finger. "Ha!-Ha!" she laughed. "Party in hotel, girl come down for breakfast!"

I finished my coffee. "I'm sure we can behave ourselves."

"You better!" Lucille was laughing. "Miss Anni no let bar girl up to your room!"

"Anni sounds like a real tough cookie," I said.

"Best girl ever," Lucille was smiling.

"Then I'll be a good boy," and I stood up to leave. "Where's the bus stop for MBK?"

"Next to 7-11," Lucille told me. "Number 36 or 93."

As Lucille had told me, it was in Si Phraya Road - a tree-lined street with market stalls and a fast-food picnic area, right across from River City.

And as I waited in the dusty heat for the 36 bus to arrive, I noticed this kid in a peacock-blue shirt. He was about fifteen yards away across the road, standing close to a market stall that sold clothing. He was partly hidden in the shadows of the trees. Maybe he was only looking for a better colour.

4

The No.36 bus was comfortably air-conditioned. For 13 baht, it took me up Si Phraya road, turned left at the Samyan market and made its way along by the Chulalongkorn University. Now although the journey was hardly half a mile, the evening traffic stretched the ride to all of twenty minutes. Eventually, we arrived at MBK.

Starbucks is on the ground floor, right at the end – near the shop that does those pastel-coloured portraits for a couple of dollars. But Starbucks is more than coffee. It's a down-town meeting place because it's easy to get to.

Chelsea was already there. She was sitting by the window, drinking an espresso and talking into her cell phone.

When she saw me coming, she closed the call. "You got my watch?" she demanded. No *hello darling* – no *can I get you coffee?* Just an up-front demand for another dip in the honey pot.

"In the morning, little kitten - when you bring me coffee in bed." Total waste of effort! It would need much more to break the seal on Chelsea's panties.

"If I no got watch, how I know what time to wake you?"

There was no real answer to that one. So I reached into my backpack and brought out the watch. "How's this?" I asked her.

"Beautiful!" and she offered her cheek for a thank-you kiss.

"Like it!"

"Love it!" and she squeezed my hand.

"What about tonight?" I asked.

Starbucks had brown padded seats by the shopping-centre entrance and pine-coloured chairs and tables for everyone else. Out in the patio area, green parasols gave shade to those who wanted to sit outside. Above the serving area, four illuminated frames listed the *Espresso* and *Frappuccino* beverages on offer. And a poster advertised: *Africa – Birthplace of Coffee.*

Chelsea took a sip of her espresso. "We meet my friend – talk about visa - then meet Anni," she said. "We have food – I get ring!"

Mai pen rai - there was always tomorrow. "Your call," I said but before I could say any more, her cell phone rang and I was back into second place. So I asked Milli at the counter for an iced cappuccino.

"It Nolli," she told me when the call was over. "She my friend – she work in gold shop near 7-11."

Could be useful. "Good," I said. "Are we waiting for her?"

"Here soon," Chelsea promised and punched the numbers for another call. "Anni…" she explained in a whisper.

Then Nolli arrived: shorter than Chelsea, a bit more rounded in the breast department and with kissable lips.

"Nolli!" Chelsea squealed.

Nolli responded with a *wai* to us both.

"This my David," Chelsea introduced me.

"Nice to meet you," I said and waved her into a chair.

"Nolli's friend have visa already," Chelsea explained and went into a long dialogue with her friend. Now and then, they glanced across the table, but never spoke to me.

Sod them, I thought - and drank my cappuccino.

In time, the chit-chat came to an end and Chelsea gave me the details. "We want a six-month tourist visa," she said. "You write letter – say how long we meet."

"Should I say I want to marry you?"

"No-no-no-no-no!" Chelsea was most emphatic. "You just invite me to visit London, see your home - and meet your wife," she added with a cheeky little grin.

Now anyone who can joke in another language gets my vote. "Love to, lass – but she'll be visiting her sister in Basingstoke."

"Be serious!" and she jabbed me with an elbow. "This important."

"OK," I agreed. "What else?"

"You sponsor me – pay all my expenses."

"Don't I always?"

"And they want your passport, see your bank book and a photo of you and me together."

"Is that all?" and I looked across at Nolli for support.

"No – they want copies of our e-mails," Chelsea added.

"They haven't got them already?"

"If you no serious, I no come," and she jabbed me again.

I ignored her. "By when?"

"By now!"

So unfair. I could fly into Thailand, fill out a landing card and get a 30-day visa, just for the asking. Why did we have to go through all this bullshit to let one beautiful Thai girl come to Britain for a 10-day holiday? But this was not the time to start a revolution. It was time to *go canny*, as the Scots would say. "Leave it with me, pussy – let me make it happen."

"You no call me *pussy*," she glared. "No nice."

"Never up, never in," I offered.

Chelsea was saved by her cell phone. "Anni waiting for us!" Without another word, she snapped it shut, dragged me and Nolli out of our chairs, pushed us through the patio door and across the pavement to the taxi rank.

Ten minutes later, the three of us were back in the RiverSide hotel, sitting at a patio table beside the Chao Phraya River and waiting for the drinks to be served. But Anni was nowhere to be seen.

"She busy," Chelsea explained. "Here soon."

While waiting for the Singha beers to arrive, we continued making plans for Chelsea's visa – or rather, she did.

"It cost you 16,000 baht," she told me. "For Embassy."

"I expect we can find it," I agreed.

"You not want me visit London?"

"Of course I do," I smiled.

"They also want to know about your tax."

Cheeky sods! "What's it got to do with them?" I asked. After all, my tax is between me and my conscience. OK, I should have told her about the visa papers. Thanks to Viv, everything Chelsea needed was in a bright green manila folder, five floors up in the safety deposit box. But as my sweet little kitten was playing *pushy female*, it could stay there until she backed-off. "They can talk to my accountant," I said, and tried to imagine Jerry's reaction to a phone call from the British Embassy in Bangkok - and how much he'd charge me for taking it.

"OK," Chelsea agreed.

All this time, Nolli had sat there, listening but saying nothing. No doubt, Chelsea would give her the nuts-&-bolts of our conversation later. But before my little squirrel could come up with *Any Other Business* for her visa application, our tray of drinks arrived – carried by the nice little man in a gleaming white shirt and well-pressed trousers.

"Mr Raphael!" Chelsea cried out.

"My darling Chelsea!" he grinned. "I so sorry - I keep Anni busy."

"We wait," Chelsea replied.

"She no be long - I bring drinks – so sorry," and he placed the tray in the middle of our table.

"And this is Mr David," said Chelsea, indicating me.

"Nice to meet you, Mr Villavito," and I stood to shake his hand. He was even shorter than Chelsea, well-built, like a little wrestler. Maybe in his forties - with a walnut face and jet-black hair.

"Please call me Raphael," he offered. "Welcome to my hotel."

"You're very kind," I said.

"Where *is* Anni?" Chelsea wanted to know.

In English? Out of courtesy - or for my benefit?

"Helping," Villavito told her. Then to me: "You like diamonds?"

"One of life's mysteries," I replied, "but I'm willing to learn."

This brought a smile to his weather-beaten face. "You come see?"

I looked at Chelsea. "May I?"

"Yes," she agreed. "You go see."

"Thanks," I said. "Look after this," and I gave her my cell phone.

"Then we will go and look at diamonds," and with a flourish of his arm, he lead me back into the hotel, past an empty Reception desk and down a passage lined with large colour photographs of Thai flowers.

"Very nice," I remarked.

"Each, two thousand baht. But for friends, a discount..."

If making money was a talent, this guy seemed to have more than his share. "Tell you later," I said. There was nothing wrong with the pictures – but as Chelsea had first-call on any spare cash, it seemed only right to let the offer ride.

5

At the end of the passage, Villavito unlocked the door to a small office. When he switched on the desk lamp, I caught my breath in surprise. On the desk, on a black velvet cloth: a dazzling array of diamonds! Thirty-three - all shapes and sizes, waiting to decorate a beautiful lady.

"You know about diamonds?"

"Not really." I looked around. It was a smallish room – a desk, a swivel chair, two display cabinets of crystals and a framed diploma. I tried to see which university, but the document was in shadow.

"Consider the shape, the weight, the cut, the clarity and the colour of each stone," Villavito explained as he swept is hand across the display. "They can be round, square or oval or even cut into shapes – like pears or hearts." Now and then, he selected an example to show me.

"They're beautiful." It was all I could think of.

"The cut is important," Villavito continued and picked up a stone the size of pea. "See it as a little tent," he said and turned the stone over so that I could see the way the base had been cut into a point. "If cut too shallow, light is lost through the roof - and the stone is not so brilliant."

"OK," I accepted.

"But if it is cut too deep," Villavito continued, "the light goes out through the windows and the stone looks dirty."

"And if it's cut properly?"

"You mean, like this one?" he smiled, picking one at random. "Then light is reflected back through the floor - and it glitters like a star!" and he placed the sample back among its buddies on the black velvet cloth.

OK so far. "What else should I know?"

"Colour is important." With care, Villavito picked out two other stones to show me. "Most of our customers prefer them to be *colourless*," he explained. "Like these," and he offered me an eyeglass to that I could see them better.

"What am I looking for?" I asked. It was an honest question.

Villavito gave me a gentle laugh. "After many years of training," he said, "you might detect the faintest trace of yellow."

"They all look exactly the same to me," I said.

"To the untrained eye, they will," he smiled. "But with a little practice…" and the two examples were put back on the cloth.

"So when it comes to buying a diamond?" I asked.

"Cost depends on weight," he told me.

"Is it controllable?"

"She will choose her ring by shape and shine," said Villavito. "But if you can guide her to a stone that suits the delicacy of her finger…"

"Wishful thinking," I said, hoping that Chelsea hadn't been on one of his diamond seminars.

"But if you were to buy a small selection…." and he waved his hand across the velvet cloth, "you could build the ring of her dreams – and sell the rest to cover the cost."

He made it sound so simple. "What are we talking about?"

Villavito paused for effect. "Here, we have fifty-four carats of good quality stones," he said. "You can weigh them if you wish."

"I'll take your word," I said.

"If you were to buy them on the Amsterdam market, they would cost you – let's say $400,000."

Now let's play at being serious. "And here?"

Villavito sighed as if making a deep and costly decision. "I could let you have them for…. maybe $200,000….?"

Was this for real? "Then what?"

"I send them to your home – you sell them one by one – and make a nice little profit!"

I saw the figures dancing in my brain: two-hundred thousand dollars… profit! There was only one problem. Would Visa raise my credit limit to the asking price? "Can I think about it?"

Villavito smiled. "For as long as you want!" he said. "I'm always here - your Chelsea can always find me."

As he showed me out of the office, I saw this guy waiting in the passage. He was dressed in casual clothes and looked like a middle-aged tourist.

"Can you find your way back to the patio?" Villavito asked me quietly. "I need to speak with this gentleman."

"No problem, Raphael," and I left them to it. But as I passed the Reception desk, there was still no sign of anyone who might have been Anni.

When I got back to our table, it was getting dark. Large white globes gave the patio an easy-going light – and on the river, the illuminated floating restaurants were on their evening routines. One said: *Long Live the King* in golden lights.

Chelsea was using my cell phone. As I approached, I clearly heard her say in English: "You call back – he looking at me," and closed down.

"I wasn't *looking* at you," I tried. "I was looking *at* you."

"What difference?"

"Who cares," I said. "I was only admiring your beauty."

It was enough. "Anni busy," she said. "We see your room," and the two girls headed for the Reception area. At the desk, they stopped and Chelsea collected my key. "You better hurry or you miss the fun!" she teased me.

We took the lift and made our way to 503. Inside, she helped herself to the mini bar, choosing Coca-Colas for herself and Nolli and making free with the nuts and crisps.

"You want Nolli give you massage?" she asked.

This, I was not expecting. In Bangkok, the *massage* means a whole lot more that it does back home on the National Health. "Why not?" In for a penny, as they say.

"Take off trousers," Chelsea told me. "Get on bed."

So I did as she told me.

"On back," came Chelsea's order.

As I turned to lie on my back, Nolli climbed on to the bed, gripped my right foot in both hands and started to manipulate each and every bone, joint and muscle she could find.

It was bloody marvellous! Once all moving parts in my foot had been re-aligned, she started on my leg, along the calf, around the knee and up to my thigh with a delicacy of touch that most men only dream about in truly wild fantasies.

Now, she had my leg on her shoulder and was working ever so carefully towards my groin. I caught her eye – and dared to laugh.

At this, Chelsea decided it was time to referee the contest. She slipped out of her chair, crossed over to the bed, pulled down the sheet and climbed in.

"At last!" I grinned.

"You better off with Nolli," Chelsea grinned. "She got six kids – she know how to fuck you good!"

I guess it pays to advertise - but before I could come up with an appropriate reply, her pretty pink phone began to sing.

"It my mam," she said. "You speak…" and gave it to me.

I paused for half a second to check the score. My girlfriend was lying in my bed. *Her* best friend was making free with my groin – and now I had to speak to her mother on a cell phone.... "Hello," I said, trying to keep the sexual frenzy out of my voice. "Nice to talk to you."

Chelsea's mum giggled down the phone and spoke in Thai.

"I sincerely hope we get to meet," I said.

Chelsea's mother said something else in Thai.

"Maybe we could meet for lunch?"

At this, Chelsea reached out and took the phone. "She no eat lunch," she said. "But maybe she cook you dinner – if you nice to me."

"Wonderful," and just lay back to let Nolli make merry with my other leg, my arms, neck and shoulders.

"What you think she worth?" Chelsea asked me when the job was done. She was still lying in my bed – but showed no sign of inviting me to slip in beside her.

"A thousand?" I suggested. "She's amazing."

"OK," Chelsea agreed – and she lifted my wallet off the bedside table, took out a 1000-baht note and gave it to Nolli. "We go now," she said, slipped out of bed and finished her can of Coca-Cola.

"I'll see you down."

"Thank you," said Chelsea, emphasising the 'you'.

Outside in the corridor, she pressed the DOWN button for the lift and waited. As its door slid open, two Scandinavian tourists – a man and a woman - got out. And there I was, with a Thai girl on either arm, looking smug and satisfied.

I caught his eye; he looked envious.

Then I looked at her. She was tall with very long legs - and dressed in white ski pants and a white semi-see-though blouse. And she was taking a very keen interest in Nolli.

Tough luck, I thought. *She's my masseur….*

But to their everlasting credit, neither Chelsea nor Nolli said a word – not until we were safely in the lift, the doors had closed and we were moving downwards.

At which point, we all burst out laughing.

"Her face!" I said.

"*His* face!" said Chelsea with a wicked laugh. "But *she* really fancied Nolli – should we offer her a massage?"

"Then she'd really have something to smile about," I agreed.

6

Next morning, I was awake by eight – had a shower, put on an orange T-shirt and hit the street. My first job was to walk along New Road to find the Bank of Ayudhya. In the end, I found its bright yellow door buried under signs and logos for a brigade of silver merchants.

It was a typical small-branch bank – a counter, yellow seats to wait on – and a ticket machine. First, I had to take a ticket and wait until summoned by the little red numbers on the display board. So I drew a ticket, found a seat, picked up a copy of the Bangkok Post and waited. In time, 072 came up on the display.

"Twenty-thousand, please," and gave my Visa card to the girl behind the counter.

First, she filled out an application form and swiped my card. "You sign?" she smiled at me.

I scrawled my name.

"You show me passport, please?"

Then she took my card and my passport, photo-copied both and stapled the copies to the cash-withdrawal form. Last of all, she counted twenty thousand-baht notes from her till, placed them neatly in my passport and handed back my card. "You have nice day!" she beamed.

But as I was back in the street, my cell phone rang. It was Chelsea.

"Morning, little kitten!"

"You see Anni for breakfast?" she asked.

"Couldn't say," I said. "I don't know what she looks like." Perfectly true, but not very smart. Yes, we'd waited half the evening for Chelsea's sister, but she'd never shown up.

"She my sister," Chelsea growled. "Look like me."

On a good day, so does half of Bangkok, my little angel. "OK," I tried again, "I didn't see anyone who looked like you at breakfast." At the time, I was trying to find a gap in the New Road traffic so that I could sprint for the orange-juice cart on the other side. "Why?" I asked.

"Because she no come home."

A click in her voice stopped me dead in the middle of the screaming traffic. A hundred squealing sirens screeched as they swerved to avoid me – until a narrow gap between a green taxi and a tuk-tuk sent me dashing for the safety of the other pavement.

"Say that again?" and I used my free hand to screen out the noise.

"Anni!" Chelsea shouted. "She no come home!"

"Have you asked around?" She could have worked late and stayed over somewhere.

"I call RiverSide – but nobody help me."

She seemed more upset than annoyed. "I'll go and ask," I said. No doubt Lucille would throw some light on the problem.

"Love you!" and she sounded like she meant it.

I was in luck. Nixie was in the coffee shop. "Hi, Nixie," I began, "Need your help."

"Mr David!" she smiled. "You want coffee?"

"Good idea -" then added: "Is Anni on duty today?"

By now, Nixie was deep into her coffee-making routine. "Anni not here," she said without even looking at me.

"Do you know where she is?"

Nixie didn't have a chance to answer. Lucille was there beside us. She did not look happy. "Miss Anni," she snapped. "You see her?"

"No I haven't," I said casually. "But my friend is asking for her."

"*Who your friend?*" Lucille was now standing in front of me, her eyes blazing. "What friend want *thief*?"

"That can't be right," I protested.

"It right," Lucille insisted. "She make plenty trouble – for me an' you – an' for everyone!"

"Oh come on, Lucille," I protested. "Last night, she was your brave little soldier. What's gone wrong?"

I asked – so Lucille told me. "Miss Anni very bad girl," she said. "She steal from hotel."

Chelsea's sister? Fingers in the till? "Surely not?"

"Surely yes," Lucille replied – and then explained: "Man pay bill – she no have change – she promise to credit his account."

"And did she?"

"*No she not!*" Lucille snapped, going red in the face. "She keep money to pay the poker debts of sister's boyfriend."

"Is that right?" I hit back. "And which sister would that be?"

"Call herself Chelsea!"

Like an idiot, I had to answer. "But *I* don't play poker!"

And Lucille was ready for me. "*You not her only boyfriend – **and** she married!*" And she turned away, face glowing red with satisfaction.

Chelsea? Married? Other boyfriends? It didn't add up. "Jealous cow!" I muttered, trying to hang on to my English reserve. I needed help. But there was only Nixie with my cup of Colombian.

It was black. "Any cream?" I asked her.

"I get for you…" she offered. Then: "You know 7-11?"

"By the bus stop?"

"You meet me fifteen minutes," she said quietly. "I tell you Anni."

In Si Phraya Road, I waited under the trees across the road from the 7-11, standing by a stall of large, expensive-looking watches at very silly prices. Nearby, a boy in a peacock-blue shirt was also looking at the watches…

I paid him no attention. My mind could only hold one thought: Chelsea with a *husband*! But Thais don't talk like Europeans. To them, *husband* could easily be another word for *boyfriend*. And *married* could be their word for *going steady*.

Would Chelsea give me a straight answer? Would anyone give me a straight answer? Did I deserve one? And had I ever been promoted to the rank of *boyfriend*? Not that I knew of.

Then I saw Nixie. She was hurrying through the crowds around the fast-food barbecues and making her way to the 7-11. I let her go inside, then skipped my way through the rat-run of taxis and tuk-tuks to reach the pavement on the other side.

"You want taxi?"

"All day – hundred baht…"

"Anywhere – forty baht…"

I waved them away and pushed the door. It opened with a heavy-duty *clang*. Inside, I found myself in the cramped surroundings of a general-purpose grocery shop.

7-11's are wonderful oases - and this was just one example of these all-night Aladdin's Caves that keep us *farangs* in drinks and doughnuts long after the bar girls have finished with us.

Aisle 1 dealt with personal cleanliness: soap, shampoo, conditioners and toothpaste.

Aisle 2 had sandwiches in plastic wrappers: plus biscuits, cakes and the Thai equivalent to the mainstay of the Euro-diet, the strawberry-jam tart.

Then we had rotating displays with postcards, CDs and DVDs. And the back wall had pens, pencils, writing pads and envelopes.

Next, I found the coffee machine and the doughnut-heater. In the heat of a Bangkok night, many have been saved by knowing where to find hot food after 3am.

Last of all, I found Nixie. She was in the corner by the cold drinks cabinet. As well as Heineken and Singha and the usual Cokes and Fantas, there were at least a dozen varieties of water.

"I'm here," I said. "What did you want to tell me?"

First, she placed six bottles of ice-cold water in her basket. "French café at River City?" she asked.

"By the pier…?" I said.

"You go – I come," she told me. "Now you buy water…."

She made it sound like an order, so I took a single bottle out of the fridge and went to the counter to pay for it.

The checkout girl was dressed in scarlet. "That all?" she asked.

"Thank you, yes."

"Fifteen baht…"

And when coins were safely in the till, she wrapped my ice-cold water in a red-&-green 7-11 carrier bag and gave it to me. You could almost hear the warning: "*Don't drink it all at once*".

"Thank you," I smiled.

I found the café. It sits at the side of the precinct, just before you reach the cross-river ferry. Dead opposite, the River City shopping centre waits for tourists with unlimited credit. I have been there, but only to look. Everything it sells is *very* expensive.

But the French café – as Nixie called it – is there for everyone to use. They call it *French* because it sells croissants. But as it also carries a large number of pastries, they might just as well call it *Danish*. Its coffee is good, but I prefer the way that Nixie makes it, just for me.

Karina was on duty. She was dressed in black.

"Two cups of coffee, please – and two of those…" and I pointed to the plate of pastries.

While Karina was preparing the coffees, I watched a stream of shoppers making their way to the pier. On the other side of the river, the Klongsam market would be waiting for them. Many were wearing the canary-yellow shirts they use to honour the King.

Nixie arrived. Now that she was away from her coffee counter, I could see that she was taller than your average Thai. Her long black hair was held back in a scarlet butterfly clip. She was wearing a black T-shirt and a matching pair of tight-fitting ski-pants.

"Where would you like to sit?" I asked her.

The Croissant Café cares for two kinds of customer. First, there are those who'll take a coffee and a *Danish* on their way to work or to the markets. Then there are people with time

23

to spare, who prefer to sit and pass a quiet moment in the River City precinct. There's always something or someone to watch.

It's a passing place. Ferry-users are always coming or going. Bangkok people sit around to meet their friends, eat a crispy-fried supper – get cosy with a girl friend or smoke a cigarette. *Like that boy in a peacock-blue shirt over there by the Sala Thai restaurant.*

For those who like the shade, the Croissant Café has a small veranda with neat little chairs and tables. Sun-worshippers can use the larger aluminium tables on the edge of the precinct.

Nixie chose a table-for-two on the veranda, sniffed at the coffee and nibbled her *Danish*. Then she spoke. "You ask about Miss Anni?"

"I want to find her," I said.

"Why?" Nixie tried the coffee. It was not to her standards, but it was good enough.

"She's Chelsea's sister," I said. "She's asked for my help."

Nixie tried her coffee again – and nibbled a little more of her pastry. "Today, Lucille not like her," she said.

"I got that impression," I smiled. "What did she do?"

Nixie thought it over for a second or two. "How I know you friend of Miss Chelsea?"

No easy answer to that one. I pulled out my cell phone and gave it to her. "Give Chelsea a call," I suggested. "Ask her yourself."

A wave of ferry-users from the Klongsam side swept past the Croissant Café and hurried along to the taxi-ranks or bus stops by the 7-11. Many were carrying bundles of clothing.

Nixie didn't use the phone. Instead, she picked at the pastry while thinking of her answer. "I know Miss Anni for six months," she said. "She always good to me….she my friend."

"She worked on Reception?" I tried to prompt.

"She good to customers," said Nixie. "She never cheat *anyone*!"

"What was Lucille on about?"

Nixie shook her head. "I not know, but Mr Villavito not happy."

"Did Anni annoy him?"

Again, Nixie thought about the question. "He not say," she said, almost in a whisper. "Last night, he call her to office – lot of shouting – then Miss Anni is running out."

"Did she say anything?"

"She come to me – *he want to kill me!* she say. Then she run."

"Villavito - did he mean it?" I asked.

Nixie shook her head. "He bad man," she said. "But maybe no."

"Was there a reason for the shouting?"

Nixie shook her head. "She not say."

"Was it anything to do with that missing money?"

Again, Nixie shook her head. "Not Miss Anni," she said. "Three hundred baht she make in tips no problem!" and she smiled at her own command of the English language.

"Did Lucille make it up?" I asked.

"I don't know," said Nixie. "Yesterday, they happy – then today, she hate her."

I took a sip of coffee. "What went wrong?" I then decided it was time to ask my supplementary question. "What about Chelsea?"

"I don't know Miss Chelsea," Nixie explained. "But Miss Anni never say about other boyfriend."

"No," I agreed. "She's never mentioned it to me, either."

Well fell into silence for a moment, sipping coffee and nibbling our pastries. Then Nixie she opened her purse and handed me a piece of paper. It had three cell phone numbers.

"You call first two – maybe help you," she offered.

"Are they expecting me?"

"They sit by," Nixie nodded and stood up to go.

"And number three?"

"Is mine," Nixie smiled. "I want help you."

I nodded my thanks. "One more question," I said. "Is she OK?"

"Oh yes," Nixie promised me. "Miss Anni – she OK."

She knew more than she was telling me. No point in getting heavy, so we parted with a smile and a *wai*. As Nixie made her way back to the hotel, I decided to hang on for a minute and enjoy another coffee - but when I looked across to the *Sala Thai*, Mr Peacock-Blue had moved off.

Fair enough. He'd finished his cigarette and gone for the ferry. It was nothing to worry about. But Chelsea was definitely someone to worry about – so I picked up my phone and selected her number. I'd hardly got beyond "Hello!" before she'd cut across me.

"*You find her?*"

"Not yet," I said. "But people are talking to me."

"*What they say?*"

"First, that she stole some money…."

"*She maybe borrow – but she not thief…*"

Now for the killer blow. "And she did it to pay your boyfriend's gambling debts."

Chelsea didn't even catch her breath. "Who tell you all this?"

25

"Lucille," I said.

"It all lies!" Chelsea snapped. "I thought she like me."

"Well, she doesn't now," I said. "But I have a couple of numbers."

"Numbers?" Chelsea demanded. "Who give you numbers?"

"Nixie from the coffee shop," I said. "Lovely girl."

"She not lovely – she not like me either."

"Leave it for now," I said. This was not the time for a cat fight. "Let me call these numbers. We can meet up later."

"You bring my ring?"

"I might," I said, "if you'll let me leave it under your pillow."

"I not prostitute!" she fired back. "You give because you love!"

"Oh come on!" It was time to try the off-the-wall approach. "It's an honour to be invited to share an Englishman's bed!"

But she didn't get the joke. "You think that?" she said. "You just want girl to share your bed?"

Oh no – too much, too soon. "Sweetheart," I tried again, "if I can't have you, I don't want anyone."

Too late. The damage had been done. "You wait, see what you get," she warned me. "You be *very* sorry. Now go find my sister!"

"OK," I agreed. What about the *fury of a woman scorned*? Let it ride. I had a call to make. "Let's rattle a number and see what happens," I tried – but there was no way back. She had closed the call.

Oh yes – Chelsea had spirit. She could fight her corner any day of the week. Maybe she did have another boyfriend. Who could blame her? I could only get to Thailand twice a year – and you couldn't expect a beautiful girl to *sitby* and knit sweaters. Well not in Thailand, anyway.

I picked the first number from Nixie's list and punched it into my cell phone. It twittered twice – and then:

"Hello?"

"Hi," I said. "I'm Dave – Nixie asked me to call you."

A two-second pause – and then: "Risa – want meet me?"

"Yes please," I agreed.

"You come now?"

"If you wish." I checked my watch – it was almost ten o'clock.

"You know *Tha Tien?*"

The pier for *Wat Arun.* "Yes," I said.

"You come by boat – I wait," Risa told me.

"I'm wearing an orange T-shirt," I said.

"Me in lime green," she replied.

7

As Risa had told me to use the ferry, I made my way along to Si Phraya and waited. I like the river - and stop No 3 is a good place to sit and enjoy it. For a start, the pier has comfortable wooden benches, a solid roof and a marble floor. And there's a breeze to keep it cool.

This morning, there were eight or nine other passengers. Some were Thai, some were European – and we all sat and waited patiently until the regular ferry chugged up to the pier and came alongside. At this point in the program, the pilot was guided by the shrieks of the whistle-man as he worked the engines to keep the boat against the landing stage. Then we all scrambled aboard and hunted for seats.

A Chinese girl took the row in front of mine – and started taking pictures of absolutely everything.

"Nice camera," I said. It was a compact Canon IXUS 860.

"Thank you." She seemed eager to talk. Maybe she wanted to practice her English. "My mother wants to see where I visit," she added.

"Just like a mother!" I said. "Where are you from?"

"Hong Kong," she told me. "Have you ever been?"

If only! "No," I smiled back. "Not yet."

After that we enjoyed some fifteen minutes of general chit-chat along the *have-you been their-either?* lines that took us all the way upstream to the dreaming spires of the *Temple of Dawn*.

"Is beautiful!" She seemed genuinely impressed.

"Even better when you go inside," I told her.

"How I get there?"

"When we stop at *Tha Tien*," I said, "catch the cross-river ferry." And had it not been for a date with a girl in a lime green shirt, I might have offered to escort her.

"How much it cost?"

"Three baht," I said. "There's a ticket desk on the pier."

I was so busy chatting to the Chinese girl that I almost missed the boy in the peacock-blue shirt. He was near the front of the boat, but by taking pictures of the temple's majestic pagoda, he seemed to be watching me as much as the scenery. Perhaps he was wondering about me and the Chinese girl. And that made two of us.

By now, we were closing in on *Tha Tien* and it was the whistle-blower's turn again. Through a series of short sharp blasts, he was able to guide the pilot forward or back until the boat was bouncing off the line of old lorry tyres that were chained to the pier. Then a crew man jumped ashore and looped his mooring rope around a convenient bollard. While all this was going on, Miss China and I had worked our way to the on/off deck at the back of the boat. Once the boat had been secured, we grabbed the safety rails and swung ourselves over the shock-absorbing rubber and onto the floating pier.

"You come with me?" It was almost an invitation.

"Sorry, no," I said – and pointed to the little Thai girl in the lime green shirt who was standing in the shade at the end of the gangway. "She's my date for lunch."

"Then you enjoy!"

"Do my best!"

I let the Chinese girl go first – and as I followed the other passengers over the rocking metal gangway and into ferry port No 8, I was closely watched by a full-length portrait of His Majesty above a corrugated lean-to roof. It was comforting.

As the *coming-&-going* point for two major temples and the Grand Palace, *Tha Tien* is always busy during daylight hours. First, you have the regular up-down river ferry traffic and the cross-river boats that serve *Wat Arun*. Then you have the private-hires, the long-tail boats that make a fortune out of tourists who want to visit a floating market or a snake farm. Anyone with half-an-hour to spare can always relax at a shady table in the little café and enjoy a steaming bowl of fish-ball soup along with rice and seafood - plus tea, water or an ice-cold drink.

My date in the lime-green shirt was waiting for me by the ticket office for the ride across to the *Temple of Dawn*.

"You Mr David?" She had watched me cross the gangway.

"Risa?" She was maybe five feet tall, with long dark hair and deep brown eyes. "Thank you for coming," I said.

"Miss Nixie asked," she smiled. "Me know Anni – what wrong?"

"That's what I want to find out."

"She go missing?"

Although we doing our best to move away from the pier, there were so many either coming or going that we seemed to be swimming in a tide of washed-up passengers. "Could she have gone to see her boyfriend?" I suggested. This was *easy-question* time; the hard ones would come later.

"I help if I can," Risa offered.

By now, we had managed to escape from the pier and were now making our way along a narrow passageway and into a street of shops that sold dried squid, mackerel and fish that looked like kippers. "What can you tell me?"

Halfway along, a hand-written sign offered:

Thai Original Massage

Body Massage

Foot Massage

Oil Massage

By expert from What Pho

But the illustration of the patient having his leg turned inside out by the *expert from Wat Pho* did not encourage me to make an appointment. From this point on, it was Nolli - or no-one!

"How much?" I asked Risa.

"More than it worth," she smiled. "My friend Daffy – she good."

Could anyone ever be as good Nolli? "Then let's go meet Daffy."

"We meet her soon," Risa promised. At the end of the Street of a Thousand Fish Shops, she guided me through a gateway and into the grounds of *Wat Pho* – the *Temple of the Reclining Buddha*. A pencil-thin Thai girl in a light blue dress was waiting for us. "This Daffy!"

Daffy greeted us both with a delicate *wai*.

I returned her greeting. "Nice to meet you," I said and offered her a handshake. "Why Daffy?" I had to ask.

"She like Daffy Duck," Risa explained.

Was this the time to ask another stupid question? "Why do you all change your names?" I asked.

"So evil spirits not find us," Risa explained. "If they know us, they can haunt us."

"A bit like our nick-names," I said. "We also use them to keep out of the devil's clutches!"

Risa smiled. "Yes," she agreed. "We say nick-names, too."

"They don't always work," I said. From experience, Old Nick could find me anytime he wanted.

Just inside the gate, we found this large brown board with information for mystified tourists. It had four categories:

(a) Tickets

(b) Information

(c) Please Dress Properly

(d) Guide

To get the ball rolling, I gave Risa a 1000-baht note for the tickets. "Will we need one of those?" I asked and pointed at item (d) on the board.

"No," Risa replied. "Daffy is training to be tourist guide – she want to practice on you."

For once, it was hard to say *No thank you*. "I'm at your mercy," I agreed and smiled at Daffy.

Risa cut me off at the pass. "Daffy have Swedish boyfriend," she said. "Soon she go live with him."

"Handy for IKEA," I smiled.

Risa bought the necessary tickets and lead us into the temple. On the way, we came to a giant waterfall and rock formation, right in the middle of the compound. It should have included two large phallic sculptures, there to help barren women get pregnant. But today, they weren't on view. "What happened to the magic pencils?" I asked Daffy. As a tour guide, she should have known.

"They go," she said.

"Removed for re-erection?" But she didn't get it.

At the temple door, we removed our shoes. Inside, it was cool and dark. And as my eyes adjusted to the light, I noticed we were standing by these feet – enormous feet, covered in mother-of-pearl icons.

"They represent the signs of the true Buddha," Daffy told me.

"And what do they tell us about Anni?" I asked. Chelsea could call at any minute and I needed answers.

"If truly believe, you find her," Daffy promised.

Was that a clue, an answer or a promise of the future? "So push me in the right direction," I replied.

We were walking towards a line of bowls. A woman in a red sari was taking money for the ceremonial candles, lotus buds, joss sticks and saucers of coins.

Risa paid for three sets of these coins; gave one to Daffy, one to me and kept the third for herself. "We will now offer our riches," she said and began to drop her offerings into the bowls.

I followed on with Daffy just behind me. "Help me," I tried again. "Anni is missing and her sister is worried sick."

"You mean Miss Chelsea?" From the tone of her voice, she did not seem to think Miss Chelsea was the worrying kind.

"Yes," I said. "Miss Chelsea is my girlfriend." Optimistic? Probably, but I needed a little street-credibility.

We were halfway up the line of bowls. On my right, the giant figure of the Reclining Buddha, hard to see in serious detail through the line of square pillars. "Miss Anni was afraid of

Mr Villavito," Daffy admitted. "I hear that Miss Chelsea borrow money to pay for mother's time in hospital."

I scattered my remaining coins across the nearest four bowls. Job done; riches offered. "Any idea how much?"

"No," Daffy told me. "But when she not pay back, Anni have to work for Mr Villavito."

Blackmail – Thailand style? "What did she have to do?"

"Help him in hotel," said Daffy.

"By doing what?" Was he running a brothel? I looked straight up into the golden face of the enormous Buddha.

"She help with his business," Daffy told me.

I sighed and stared back at the massive Reclining Buddha. The benign expression seemed to understand my frustration. As a Private Eye, Humphrey Bogart could always ask the right question - but I was swimming in a bowl of porridge. It was time for a new approach. I was hot, I needed fluid. It was an ideal opportunity. "Fancy a drink?" I asked.

"Good idea," Risa agreed.

"You come," said Daffy and lead us back to our shoes.

On the way to the soft-drinks department, Daffy steered us into the *Wat Pho School of Massage*. If it was hot outside, it was sweltering inside - and incredibly popular. There were twenty beds, all crammed together in one small room. Each bed had a victim – and each was being handled by a masseur. And each masseur had a pupil.

As I watched, it seemed that every part of the human body was being taunted, teased or tenderised, according to the specific routine.

"They come all over world to learn," Daffy explained.

"And who are the patients?" I asked.

"Anyone who pay," Daffy told me. "You want to try?"

I saw the mass of sweaty bodies on display. I heard the *smack* of hand on flesh. I felt the pain that had to follow violent manipulation. I looked at my watch. Midday: Chelsea would be wondering. "Maybe next time," and we returned to the world outside.

Risa laughed. "It not hurt one little bit!" She promised.

"You go first and I'll watch," I offered.

The soft-drinks bar was shaded by dark blue parasols. We ordered ice-cold Pepsis and talked about this, that and visiting Thailand.

"Anyone hungry?" I asked.

I think the answer was YES because Risa ordered three plates of *Pad Thai* – noodles, prawns, bamboo shoots, peanuts and banana flowers.

"Looks good," I said when it came.

"It is," Daffy confirmed. "I save some for my dog," and she hunted in her purse for a Tesco bag and scooped in a handful.

"What kind of a dog?"

"I find him in telephone box," Daffy admitted.

"That's very sad," I smiled. "So what's his name?"

"He called *Hello*," Daffy replied.

You couldn't argue with that - but before I could make any comment, Risa's phone began to sing.

"Excuse," she said and took the call, chatting busily in Thai.

So while she was talking, I brought the subject back to Anni. "How long has she been working in the RiverSide?" I asked.

"Five months – maybe six," said Daffy. "I not sure."

"How did she help Mr Villavito?"

Daffy thought about my question for a second or two.

Then Risa broke off from her call and chipped in. "I have call about friend," she said. "She called Catti - she work in massage parlour."

"As what?" I asked.

"Maybe waitress – maybe bar girl – what it matter?" and she shook her head. "But she know a lot about *Anni*."

"Where can I find her?"

"*Chao Phraya 2*," said Risa. "You go at six - I call you."

8

Once we had finished our lunch, I walked my tour guides back to *Tha Tien* and watched them safely onto a down-stream ferry. Then I called Chelsea.

"I'd like to see Mr Villavito," I told her. "Can you fix it?"

"I try," she promised. "You see more girls?"

"Possibly," I admitted. "I have a meeting in a massage parlour."

She didn't even catch her breath. "When?"

"Tonight."

"I come with you." It was a promise.

"Nice," I agreed. Maybe the storm was over.

"You ever go to massage parlour?"

"No," I said. "Never needed to."

"Good boy!" Chelsea purred. "I look after you."

"I'm sure you will," I replied. "Now – Villavito?"

"You wait – I call," she promised.

Within two minutes, she was back on the line.

"He see you two o'clock," she said. "You better hurry," and she gave me the address of his office.

I found Villavito's office block at the far end of Mara Phrutharam, the road that runs beside the *Phadung Klong* - the canal that flows into the Chao Phraya right by River City. With a long-tail boat, I could have saved myself the taxi fare.

However, before you can enter Mr Villavito's kingdom, you have to be validated. And on this occasion, main-gate security was sitting on a stool beneath a big brass VILLAVITO sign on the left-hand side of the big double gate.

"Who you?" When the guard stood up, he was taller than he should have been – and immaculately dressed in a US-style khaki uniform with very shiny boots. He was wearing enough gold braid, tassels and medal ribbons to have been a Brigadier.

"David Shannon," I smiled politely. "Here for Mr Villavito."

That cut the ice. "He wait for you," the duty officer confirmed. "I take you – come with me."

Almost hand in hand, we walked together through the forecourt until we came to a very tall building with a single glass door beside a goldfish pond. Behind the door, there was a lift.

"You go 8," he told me.

"Eight it is," I thanked him, went inside, closed the door and pushed the button. With a swish from the motor, the lift shot up until it stopped at the 8th floor. There, I found myself in a long, narrow waiting area with red-leather benches all down the right-hand side. At the far end, there was a *Reception* window. I rang the bell.

Within two seconds, my call was answered by a young girl with an orchid in her hair. "I help you, please?"

"David Shannon. Mr Villavito is expecting me."

"He waiting," and with a very expensive *swish*, a door beside *Reception* opened sideways to invite me into Mr Villavito's private offices.

Miss Orchid escorted me along this light and airy corridor – white walls, laminate floor and ash wood doors. Now that I could see all of her, she was tiny, hardly more than a wisp of smoke - but nicely dressed in a Dulux-white blouse and a navy-blue skirt. My little flower girl was so light on her feet that her sandals hardly made a whisper as she ghosted her way along the floor.

"We are here," and she delicately knocked on a door marked *Raphael Villavito*.

It was opened by a secretary. "Please come in."

Today, Mr Villavito was using the *Please excuse me – I'm a busy man* approach. To start with, he was sitting behind his desk. Second, his shirt could have enjoyed a ten-minute one-to-one with a steam iron – and third, he had his jacket off to show these bright green braces.

OK, point of order. I don't care about bright green braces - but if you choose to wear them, keep your jacket on. I'll give him one thing, though. When he stood up to greet me, he had the decency to put his cigar in an ash tray.

"David!" he grinned, "Good of you to come - you like a coffee?"

Ms Secretary offered me a chair, nodded to her boss and left.

"Very kind of you, Raphael," I replied. I looked around. Along one wall, three glass-fronted cabinets were lit by the clear white glare of halogen spotlights. Inside each, black velvet trays displayed the most amazing set of gems of every colour, size and shape.

Villavito noticed. "Come and see," he said – then took me over to the nearest cabinet. "Sapphires," he said.

"Amazing colours," I said, just gazing at the stunning shades of blue and green and yellow. "I'd only ever seen blue," I said.

"Because the others are so valuable," he said and moved me on to the next cabinet. "Rubies…" and pointed to a round stone with a criss-cross pattern. "Know that one?" he asked.

"No," I replied.

"It's a star ruby," Villavito explained. But the third cabinet was the best of all.

"Diamonds!"

"You're learning," Villavito smiled and steered me back towards his desk and recovered his cigar.

I took the hint and made myself comfortable. "It's about Anni," I said. "She didn't get home last night – and Chelsea is really concerned."

At this, Villavito put his smile on hold. He gave his cigar a really enthusiastic draw and blew a mushroom cloud at the ceiling. "I never wish to hear of her again," he said in a very quiet voice.

That took me by surprise. "What did she do?" Last night, she was everybody's favourite. "Why do you want to chase her out of town?"

"Because she steal my diamonds," and sadly shook his head as though he found it hard to believe. "Right from out of my pocket!"

"From out of your office?" I asked.

"From out of my safe," he told me.

"How many?" *One, two, five – all of them?* "Or how much?"

"The whole four-hundred-thousand, Mr Shannon."

Nice one, our kid. "So let me help you." Well, why beat about the banana tree? He'd lost his goodies: I needed money. Let's see if we can sing along together.

"Help me?" and he raised his arms in a gesture of a man who owns a fair proportion of the world. "Please tell me why…"

"You've been good to Chelsea," I said. (*OK - one more porkie won't make that much difference at the Final Judgement.*) "Let me help you get them back."

While he thought of an answer, he tapped the ash from his regenerated cigar and gave it another draw to see how it was coming along. "And what's in it for you?" he asked, giving me his cold-eyed stare.

"Ten percent – or a handful of diamonds," I replied. Why piss about? We were both in it for the money.

At that moment, the secretary returned with two cups of thick black coffee – with cream and sugar - on a silver tray - with a small plate of biscuits. Without a word, she set the tray on Villavito's desk, gave a cup to him and one to me. Then she placed the cream, the sugar and plate of biscuits on his desk. Job done, she slipped away as easily as she had appeared.

"Help yourself to cream and sugar, David."

I stood up, leaned over the desk and checked the plate of biscuits. Four were chocolate – and one had a bright yellow smiley face. I'd played this game. It's an interview technique. It's used to separate the sheep from the wolves:

Do you have the nerve to take the yellow biscuit?

Too bloody true! I placed the smiley yellow biscuit in my saucer, helped myself to the cream and those wonderful brown sugar crystals – and sat down again.

Villavito didn't show he'd noticed. Instead, he returned to the concept of a search for Anni. "And you could find them?"

Them? Not *her?* First job in any contract is to decide where we want to go. "Which comes first," I asked him, "Anni or the diamonds?"

Villavito returned his cup to its saucer and gazed into space for a couple of seconds. "For forty thousand dollars, I want both," he said.

"Dead or alive?"

Now we were back in the land of the cold-eyed stare. "Don't be dramatic, Mr Shannon," he said. "Just find my diamonds."

9

By the time I had made my way across the city to Soi Rambuttri, it was pushing four o'clock. Chelsea was in her shop, dealing with a drunken Brit who wanted to sail to Phuket.

"Not possible," she told him.

"It's OK, darlin'," he tried again. He was getting redder by the second. "I know the bloody boat can't pick me up from the street, but you get me to Phuket, OK?"

"Not possible," Chelsea repeated – and opened a map to show him that the seaside town of Phuket was on the wrong side of the peninsula. From Bangkok, a boat would have to go round Cape Horn to get there. "You want to fly?"

"No-no-no!" and he slammed his hand on her desk. "Can't you fuckin' wogs speak English?"

And that upset me. Tourists drink, we all know that. Some can hold it. Others can't. Now I don't care if a guy gets drunk and falls in the gutter. And I don't care if a guy gets drunk and throws a rainbow warrior in his sleeping bag. But I hate a guy who drinks too much and takes it out on a Thai who is trying to help. And *no-one* ever calls my girl a WOG...

So I hit him. One clean swing to the side of his jaw – and down he went, spewing his guts all over the tiled floor of Chelsea's office.

"Sorry, sweetheart," I said.

"Fuck you!" came a weak little voice from the floor.

So I kicked him, hard: once in the belly and once in his jewel box. After that, he stopped moaning.

"Police? – or shall we dump him in the street?" I asked her.

"No need," said Chelsea, all business-like and on the ball.

Two of her buddies from the taxi rank had seen the drunk go down and were now in the doorway. Chelsea spoke to them in Thai, gave the orders – and the two lads grabbed hold of the trembling legs, dragged the body out of the shop, bumped it down a small flight of steps and bundled it into a taxi.

"Where are they taking him?" I asked.

"Out of town," said Chelsea. "Long walk back." Then she phoned her friend in the Four Sons Reception to borrow their cleaner for a couple of minutes. It was like a well-drilled operation. I got the feeling this was not the first occasion.

"No-one speaks to you like that," I said.

"You not have to hit him," she said - and there was a look in her eye that made me think I'd got it wrong. "You not here all time - what happen when he bring back friend?"

"Call the police," I said.

"This happen every day," she said. "Bad for shop. If he tell boss, I get fired."

"But he was rude to you," I said.

She was not a happy little squirrel. "He not first *farang* who call me WOG," she said, standing tall and totally defiant.

"No-one speaks to you like that," I tried again in my own defence.

"Is OK," Chelsea smiled – then she remembered our six o'clock appointment. "Go Four Sons – have wash – have beer. I come soon."

With Chelsea in that kind of a mood, it was better not to argue. "Yes, love," I said, looking away. "I'm sorry."

At this, she mellowed and offered me her cheek to kiss. "Is OK," she said. "But not again."

"You're the boss," I said and left her to the clean-up. I found the Four Sons washroom, splashed my face with a lot of cold water, went back outside and ordered a Singha.

Fifteen minutes passed before I saw her walking across the hotel patio. Oh my God... how she could walk! Happiness is watching Chelsea walk towards me.

"Ready, Mr Englishman?" she asked, half smiling.

"When you are, Miss Thailand," I said.

"Let's go find your new girlfriend!"

Chelsea called one of the taxi drivers, gave instructions and we settled back to enjoy the ride across town. Being late afternoon, the traffic was in stop/start mode, close to gridlock – but once we'd made the right-hand turning by the Royal Turf Club, the hold-ups disappeared and we began to make progress. But for the fifty minutes that it took to make that journey, Chelsea never said a single word to me. Instead, she seemed to spend most of the time chuntering into her cell phone.

In time, we reached Chao Phraya 2. It was like a block of flats, but without windows. Up on the roof, a large neon sign said *Bath and Massage*. Our taxi dropped us by the entrance.

"How much?" I asked the driver.

"Hundred baht."

Seemed reasonable, so I paid – and followed Chelsea up the flight of steps and in through the big glass door.

"Good evening, sir," came a voice in a suit.

I smiled back. Inside, it was rather like the concourse of a small airport. Half-a-dozen people were just milling about. Down the right-hand side, there were benches and tables for those who wanted to eat or drink.

"You want another beer?" Chelsea asked me.

"Why not?" I replied.

The most important feature was a plate glass window that ran the full length of the left-hand side. And behind that window: a dazzling array of girls in flowery dresses or colourful T-shirts. Each had a wristband with a number. I wasn't unduly worried. Risa's friend could have worked as a waitress. All we had to do was sit and wait for the phone call.

"Mango juice?" I asked as we headed for the comfortable seats.

"No," said Chelsea. "Just food." She was still in a bit of a paddy.

"OK." We sat at one of the tables and called for a waiter.

When he came, Chelsea ordered prawns and rice. I would have given anything for egg-&-chips. In the end, I settled for a bowl of fishy soup and a large bottle of Singha, which we shared.

"Any idea who we're looking for?" I asked.

"She your contact," Chelsea reminded me. "When your Risa calls, you find her."

Later, I realised I'd never given Chelsea anybody's name. If I'd been concentrating on her – instead of keeping an eye on the rows of half-dressed sex machines in the window only half-a-dozen yards away - I might have seen it coming.

We were not the only body-watchers. Every few minutes, another customer would walk through the big glass door, make his way across the concourse and wander up and down, checking the talent on offer. And as the client walked across their line of sight, so the girls would smile and wave and try to attract his attention.

If one of the girls took his fancy, he'd trot over to a little man who seemed to be running the show and give the number. Then he'd be taken to the cash desk, cough-up the baht and get to meet his partner for the entertainment.

"Go ask him," Chelsea offered. She had noted my curiosity and wanted to improve my Thai education. "Ask what happen."

"OK," I said, "I will." Purely out of academic interest, I made my way over to the little floor-walker and asked the relevant questions.

"How does it work?"

"For here," and he pointed to the left-hand end of the window, "is 1900 baht," he explained.

"And what do I get for my 1900 baht?"

He smiled and went into salesman mode. "These lovely ladies will give you body-body massage," he said. "Then bath in baby oil."

"What's body-body?"

"She rub her lovely titties all over your body," the MC explained.

It sounded far more fun than bingo. "All over?"

He nodded. "All the way over."

Fair enough, chief. "Is that it?"

"Oh no," the little man replied. "You also get one go of sex – with condom," he told me. "It all take ninety minutes."

"And I only have to pick a number?"

He hadn't finished with the sales pitch. "But up here," and he continued his patter by waving his arms at the rest of the ladies, "you get massage and bath – and then blow-job."

No holds barred, it seemed. To fuck or not-to-fuck – that was the only question. "Same price?"

"Oh no – these are only 1400," he said.

So: 1400 baht for the standard treatment – plus 500 for the wick-dipping service. "What's upstairs," I asked.

"Big bath!" he grinned. "A blow-up mattress and bed!"

Food for thought, indeed. "OK - what time do you close?"

"Last man up at eleven."

"I have a beer to finish," I said. "Then I'll come and find you."

"This me," and he gave me a business card with his name hand-written on the back. No doubt he was on commission.

I went back to Chelsea.

"You not come before?" she asked.

"It's a whole new world," I said. "Fascinating."

"Want to try?"

She was joking, surely? "Thank you, no – you're quite enough."

"How you know?" and she gave me a naughty little grin. "You never had me!"

Good point. Now that she had mentioned it, would they let me take her to a bedroom, dunk her in the bath and romp with her on the mattress? Then my cell phone called me back to Planet Earth.

"Hi – it's Dave," I said.

"This Risa – you want Catti?"

"Yes, I do," I said. Which waitress would she be?

41

"Catti Number 12," said Risa. "She give you everything."

That took my breath away. Here I was, in a Bangkok massage parlour – with my girlfriend – and being told to go and book a session with a prostitute. Not exactly what my mother would have wanted.

"What she say?" Chelsea asked me.

One deep breath – beer finished in a swallow – eyes fixed firmly on the window. "Catti is Number 12," I said. Suddenly, it didn't seem quite so funny.

Chelsea looked me straight in the eye. "What now?" she asked.

"I have to talk to her," I said. "But how can I do it from here?"

"You go rent her," Chelsea explained.

Rent her? Are you for real? "Don't you mind?"

"If you get my sister, why I mind?"

"Fair enough," I said. "England expects..."

I found the master of ceremonies over by the cash desk. "Number 12, please," I said and gave him a couple of thousand–baht notes.

"Good choice!" he said and gave me back a hundred. Then he made a call on his buzz-through box. "She come," he promised.

And within fifteen seconds, this rather good-looking girl in a low-cut salmon-pink dress was standing beside me.

"Hello, handsome!" she smiled.

I checked her over. She was maybe 5' 4", with long black hair that came halfway down her back. As she spun around to show me what I'd bought, I could only stare in wonder at the firmness of her delightfully sculptured butt. And as she came around full circle, my eyes could hardly tear themselves away from the wonder of her well-filled breasts. How much was in play… and what was out of bounds?

"Good evening," I said. "And you are?"

"Me Catti," she confirmed.

At least we were still on track. "Nice to meet you, Catti," I said. "Where do we go?"

She took my arm and steered me over to the elevator door. Another man and woman were already waiting for it. He and I exchanged glances. It was enough. After all, what do you say to a brother client? You can't really offer the old-time favourite: "Don't fancy yours much, John!" He might take offence… and so might she.

Never mind, I'm sure the girls swapped glances as well.

Our ride stopped in the 5th floor – and all four of us got out. They went to the left, while we turned right. It was a long hallway, mostly in shadow – so the punters couldn't see each other, I suppose.

On either side, shelf-loads of towels waited to be taken to the rooms. Lime green plastic baskets (not unlike the ones you get in Tesco) were filled with packets bottles of bath oil and packets of condoms.

Then we came to a narrow passageway that took us along to the actual bedrooms. It was all quite exciting. You don't get facilities like this in Kentish Town – well, not that I know of.

Catti had the key to 517 – and as she unlocked the door, a maid slipped in front of us to check that everything was in order.

We followed. The room was in two sections: the wet-play area with a simply magnificent bath and tiled surround – and the dry-play zone with the bed, a sofa, a coffee table and a TV set.

I looked around. The bath area was spotless and the bed had been re-made with a clean cover. And there were mirrors absolutely everywhere – around the walls and on the ceilings.

Catti switched the TV on and clicked through half-a-dozen channels. We had a choice of Thai or Chinese game shows and a music channel. But there wasn't any sport.

"You want drink?" Catti asked me.

"I could take a beer," I said.

"Me have coffee," and she told the maid what we wanted.

I sat on the sofa and Catti sat on the bed – and she swished her legs in a re-make of the well-known *Sharon Stone* routine. But Catti as did it nice and slowly, I got the full-frontal of a dark, luxuriant Epping Forest, just waiting for the hunt to begin, right there in the folds of her dress.

When the maid came back, she placed my beer and Catti's coffee on the table and dropped a clean white rubber airbed next to the bath. Last of all, she turned on the water.

"You give her two hundred baht?" Catti asked me.

No problem. At which, the maid gave me a bouncy little *wai*, put the money in her apron pocket and closed the door behind her.

Now Catti was off the bed and kneeling in front of me. "We take off shoes," and she untied my laces and removed my shoes and socks.

"What about Anni?" I asked.

"You wait, lovi-lovi – you get lots an' lots of *anni*!" Then as she stood up, she caught sight of herself in a mirror. "Is far too big," she complained and she tapped her rump.

Which was little short of an invitation. "Not from here," I said, stood up and placed both hands on her sweet little butt. Too big? No chance! Firm and round, yet tender to the touch. "Seems OK from this side," I said and gave it a playful slap.

With this, she stood up sharply, shimmied her hips a couple of time and let me gaze in admiration as her dress slithered down her delicate body, all the way to her ankles.

She was absolutely naked.... and those breasts! I have never seen anything quite like them, anywhere, on anyone. Like Jaffa oranges, they were – firm and round, sweet to the tongue and hard to the touch. If they were implants, they were good. And those nipples...! Acorns – dark and proud and waiting to be given the licky-licky treatment.

OK, I thought. *If this is how we play the game, let's do it.* Or as Nelson might have signalled to the fleet: *"Drop your drawers and run out the hardware!"* In two seconds flat, I was naked, too – my clothes in a rather untidy heap on the floor.

"You come," and she took my hand and drew me into the bathroom zone and coiled up her long black hair. "You lie on mat?"

And so I did – on my back – and waited.

From her lime green shopping basket, Catti removed a bottle of bath foam, splashed some on my back and whipped it into a creamy lather.

"You like black girls?" she asked.

"I don't care about colour, creed, race, religion or nationality," I said. "So long as they can fuck!"

"Then get ready for a real fuckie-fuckie!" and she turned me on my front, took my leg, raised it on to her shoulder - and slid her body under mine. This was even better than the *body-to-body* in the sales pitch...

Catti used her magnificent foliage to massage every possible inch of my legs, bum, back and shoulders in a sea of foam. It was everywhere – all over my body, in my ears and in my eyes. But somewhere up above me, there was Catti, straining every ounce of her body to give me the ultimate experience in sensual pleasure.

"Up!" and there was a resounding slap on my butt. I turned over, ready to enjoy a re-run of the entire routine – only this time, tit-to-tit. For this part of the game, those magnificent breasts would be mine for the taking! So I brushed away the foam from my eyes – and opened them...

Oh Jesus Christ Almighty!

No - it wasn't Catti who was standing over my pelvic region. It was Chelsea! Bright-eyed, smiling – and wearing a skimpy blue bikini.

Without a word, she reached out and took Catti's hand – then slipped the other arm around the girl's naked body.

"Darling Englishman!" said Chelsea, straight-faced and with a steady voice. "We are honoured that you let us share your mattress!" And they both collapsed in shrieks of laughter.

What could I do? This was worse than being caught with my trousers down. This was almost a *dick-in-fanny* crime.

"Now have bath," Chelsea ordered. "Give Catti lots of money."

Game over – so I gave Catti a thousand-baht note and shooed them both out of the bedroom.

Once they'd trotted off – still gigging like schoolgirls – I enjoyed a luxurious bath (thanks to Catti's collection scents and oils) and spent some twenty minutes or so soaking the embarrassment out of my system. Then I used as many towels as I could find to dry myself – and then got dressed.

When the lift brought me back to earth by the cash desk, I found Chelsea waiting for me.

"Tell your friends, Mr Englishman?" she asked me. "Tell them me an' Catti – always very good!"

Then I saw the joke. "You set me up," I said. "This had nothing to do with Anni."

"We teach you lesson," Chelsea laughed. "You get smart – I get smarter." She was enjoying herself. "You no piss me off again."

Game, set and new balls to the gorgeous little Thai girl. "No I won't," I said. "Anything happen while I was away?"

"Yes," she said. It was all done and dusted. Back to business. "Mr Raphael say he meet you seven tomorrow morning – at my shop."

Now what could Villavito be wanting with me at the crack of dawn? "Do you have a coffee pot?" I asked. "I can't face Raphael on an empty tank."

"Lucky boy to still have tank," said Chelsea, making the most of an easy target.

10

Next morning, I was up by 6am and packed my survival kit (and the green manila folder) in my backpack - along with the diamond ring. Then I walked along to the Royal Orchid Sheraton to find a taxi. Being early, the streets were quiet and I was on the patio of Chelsea's office well before Villavito.

"Any chance of a coffee?" I asked her. We were sitting on either side of the desk: she at her PC, me pretending to be a client. Outside, the street was totally deserted. Even the taxi boys hadn't clocked in.

Chelsea's office was at the very far end of Soi Rambuttri, just to the left of the Four Sons hotel. Large glass windows to the front and side made it look like an aquarium, but with one very pretty little fish.

In the street-side window, a TV screen played this never-ending diving video, over and over and over again. After watching its reflection in the glass for twenty minutes, I knew the storyline by heart – and was ready for the menace of the moray eel as it glowered at the camera from its lair in the reef.

Chelsea was lucky. It faced away from her desk and she didn't have to watch it.

"You want espresso?"

"Please," I said.

So she opened the office door, called to the girl on the hotel Reception desk and told her what I wanted. "Mr Raphael let you finish it," she promised.

"Why at this time?" I wanted to know.

"Go see Anni's boyfriend," she said. "Thai boxers train early."

"Then you've just got time to check this over," and I gave her the green folder with the paperwork for her visa-application.

She didn't need to speak. Her smile said it all. "You naughty man! You have this all time!" Two points to me – but she still slipped an arm around my waist and hugged me.

Villavito arrived just after 7am. He was wearing a light blue polo shirt and white slacks with knife-edge creases. His white Mercedes had been washed and waxed that very morning.

"David!" he beamed. "How is the search for our Anni?"

I wasn't ready for a cross-examination so I played for time. "Making progress," I lied. "Too early to comment."

Villavito paused as if thinking. "So many diamonds," he said, almost to himself. "She cannot sell them."

Why not? On the night of Chelsea's party, he'd suggested they'd be easy to shift. "Perhaps she doesn't want to," I said.

"Then where was the point?"

I remembered what Daffy had said about Chelsea's debt. "Is there anything she wants from you?" I asked.

"It's not the way to get a pay rise!" he laughed.

"Nothing you would trade?" I pressed.

Villavito was not in a negotiating mood. "Let us not argue," he smiled. "Let us go and see my boxers."

"You coming?" I called to Chelsea.

"Who see to shop?" she replied.

"OK," I said. "Should be back for lunch," and started walking towards Villavito's car.

"No," she said. "No lunch – I go shopping."

"Fair enough," I agreed.

"Need five thousand baht," and she held out her cute little hand.

As a wise man knows when he's beaten, I gave it to her. "Enjoy!" I said. Admit defeat and pass the honey. It's the English way.

"I win again!" she laughed and skipped up the steps to her office.

"She's a very lovely girl," Villavito smiled as we pulled out of Soi Rambuttri. "You want to marry her?"

"Provided she isn't married to anybody else," I said.

Villavito stopped, mid-stride. "Why do you say that?"

"People keep suggesting I'm second in line," I said.

"There is only you," he said. "I see it in her eyes."

"She sees me as her credit card," I said. "All she has to do is tap my keypad."

"No-no-no!" Villavito laughed. "You couldn't be more wrong!"

"But she's always asking for money."

By now, we were away from the Khaosan area and heading for the city centre. At a set of lights, Villavito made a right-hand turn and eased his way into a stream of slow-moving traffic.

"David," he said, "you must understand – you are Mr Moon."

"And he is?"

"Like Santa Claus," Villavito explained. "You make her happy."

"Is that so?"

"Every time you give her money, you get another star!"

"Two more payments and I'll own the Milky Way," I said.

Twenty minutes later, Villavito turned into this narrow street off Soi Ladprao. Down one side: parked cars, apartment buildings and trees. On the other, a long white wall and a pair of blue-&-gold gates – with a twin-revolver design. A large blue sign said: *Sasiprapa Gym*.

"This is it," Villavito announced as he parked beside the long white wall. "Are you coming?"

"With you all the way," and I scrambled out of the car to join him by the gates.

"My boxers use the cooler part of the day for their training," he said as he showed me into the gym.

To my left, a boxing ring had three sets of boys working together in pairs. They wore gloves, some had helmets – and they were all bare-foot. Even at this early hour, they were covered in sweat.

Above the ring, the flags of a dozen nations hung in the still air.

In the centre of the hall, several other boys were working the really heavy punch bags. To my right, others were getting personal tuition from a coach, either one-to-one or with a full-length mirror. As I stood and watched, this little man in a red vest came out of the crowd.

"Mr Takoon!" Villavito smiled. "Please meet Mr Shannon – he from England!"

We exchanged broad grins and bowed to each other.

"Mr Takoon is manager," Villavito explained.

"Pleased to meet you," I said.

"He make champion boxers!" Villavito went on.

There were small brown Thais, tall white Europeans, large tanned Europeans – and this frail-looking Chinese girl in a pink leotard.

"Where are they all from?" I asked.

Villavito pointed to a well-tanned heavy-weight with a pony tail. "He from Spain," he said. And then to a tall thin boy in blue: "Singapore."

Mr Takoon smiled proudly as Villavito identified the boxers.

"How many nationalities - altogether?"

"See the flags," said Villavito.

So I did. Korea, Eire, Australia, Greece, Spain, Denmark, USA were only some of them. "World famous?" I asked. Until today, Thai boxing had been little more than a late-night program-filler on some minor sports channel.

"They come from everywhere," Villavito told me.

Mr Takoon just kept on smiling proudly.

In one corner, a tall, thin white boy in yellow shorts was dancing on a lorry tyre. "He's from Scotland," Villavito explained. "He work hard – Takoon turn him into champion!"

"Lucky boy," I said and tried to catch the boy's attention, but he was deeply engrossed in his balancing techniques.

All around, the trainees were swapping punches, aiming feet at all parts of an opponent's body or practicing their kicking and punching routines on a variety of padded bags.

Then a bell rang. Everybody stopped and went for water, either drinking or splashing it over their glistening bodies.

"Having fun?" I asked the Scots boy.

He was taller than me and looked extremely fit. "Hard – but worth it," he smiled.

"What do you eat?" I asked him.

"Rice," he said. "Pots and pots of rice."

"Is that the food of champions?"

"Supposed to be," he grinned. "But I'd kill for beans-on-toast!"

"See what I can do," and I watched him walk over to a bag and practice kicking at its head.

Villavito had returned with this little guy in dark blue shorts. He had bandages around his wrists and ankles and his upper body was a mass of intricate tattoos.

"This Little Tiger!" said Villavito. "Anni's boyfriend."

"Pleased to meet you, Little Tiger," I said.

Little Tiger smiled back and gave me a very polite bow.

"When did he last see her?" I asked.

Villavito translated – both for him and for me. "Two weeks ago."

"Has she phoned him or sent any messages?"

Little Tiger shook his head.

"He says no," Villavito reported.

So what were we doing all the way out here? "If she does, can he let us know?"

"Of course he will," Villavito promised and sent Little Tiger back to a training mat to practice double-kicks at his opponent's chin. He was fast and very accurate.

"Sit and watch," said Villavito and he gave me a bottle of water.

At the back of the training area, there were a couple of stone benches and a table with a chess-board inlay. The Chinese girl was a couple of yards away, adjusting the bandages around her very shapely ankles.

It was hot and steamy in that training hall and so I hunted in my backpack for anything to wipe away the sweat. As I raked around the bottom of my bag, I came across the piece of paper that Nixie had given me. I still had a number to call. So I pulled out my cell phone, punched-in the digits and waited.

Seconds later, a cell phone rang hardly six feet away. And the Chinese girl reached into her training bag to answer it. "Hello?"

"Nixie asked me to call you," I said. "It's about Anni."

"Who is this?" she asked.

"Dave Shannon," I said.

"Kallie," she said - and looked around until she saw me. Then turned away and waved to someone across the hall. "Can't speak here," she said. "You know Dusit Palace?"

"Yes," I said. "I'll find it."

"Eleven o'clock – ticket office by Elephant Museum," and she snapped her phone shut, dropped it into her bag and danced across the floor to buddy-up with one of the other boxers. Seconds later, they were kicking buckets of bell-oil out of each other. But they seemed to be enjoying it.

The giant Spaniard with the pony tail came to sit beside me. "Is hot!" he said, noticing my attempts to mop the sweat with a spare sock.

"You here to fight?" I asked.

"Never fight," he said. "Just train."

"Why?" I asked.

"Discipline," he explained. "Good for the soul," and he flexed his biceps to show me what he meant. Impressive, yes - and as I looked around and watched them practicing their kicking and punching, while ducking and diving, bobbing and weaving, that I began to see that there was more to *Muay Thai* than merely whacking someone's head.

"You want to stay or go?" Villavito was standing beside me.

I checked my watch. We'd been here for an hour. Plenty of time for breakfast and a trip to Dusit Palace. Chelsea could wait. She had a shop to run.

"Can you drop me at the RiverSide?" I asked. "Have more enquiries to make."

"Of course, I am heading that way," he agreed. "And tomorrow, I pick you up at ten o'clock and take you to Om Noi."

"What's at Om Noi?"

"*Muay Thai*!" Villavito smiled. "Big event – on TV!"

"Can Chelsea come?"

"I fix it with her boss," he promised.

"Then it should be a good day out," I agreed.

As we left the Sasiprapa, I made a point of saying goodbye to Mr Takoon and picking up some of his business cards. Somehow, and soon, I'd have to get a tin of beans to that starving Scots boy.

11

The Dusit *Ticket Office* was a small square building screened by trees. While Thais could get in for 75 baht, *farangs* would have to pay a full one hundred to go in and look around. There was a list of times when Thai and English-speaking guides would be available.

Notices in both languages warned that the *Ananda Samakhom Throne Room* would cost extra and that the display of Thai dancing had been moved to the *Sanan Chandra Palace* in Na Korn Pathom Province.

Close by, a coloured map of the Palace Gardens showed where to find the silks, the silverware and a collection of old state carriages. In front of the *Royal Elephant National Museum*, a boy was using a petrol lawn mower to cut the grass. They had thought of everything.

Then Kallie arrived. She had changed from the pink gear to a yellow T-shirt and a pair of ragged jeans.

"Thank you for coming," I said.

"No probs," she grinned. "Anni was my friend - what's she done?"

"Wish I knew," I replied. "She didn't go home last night."

"Says who?"

"Chelsea."

"That's her sister, right?"

"Right."

"Odd," Kallie frowned. "That's not like Anni."

"Known her long?" I asked. As we were talking, so the boy with the petrol-driven mower kept on zapping at the grass by the *Royal Elephant National Museum*.

"Since I've been here..." Kallie began.

"Which is...?

"Six months - she was always in the gym, watching Little Tiger."

I had to ask. "Why is he called Little Tiger?"

"Wait till he springs at your throat!" Kallie laughed.

"I'll remember not to annoy him," I smiled back.

"He's a pussy-cat," Kallie promised. "Out of the ring, his tattoos keep him safe from evil forces."

"Lucky boy!" We were still by the ticket office. Seemed only right to look big and pay up. "How much?" I asked her.

"Give me the money," she said. "I look local."

So I gave her a 1000-baht note and watched her neat little body walk up to the window and buy our tickets.

"Keep the change for the tea room," I smiled.

"What a nice kind man you are!" she grinned. "Chelsea must be chuffed to monkeys!"

"You speak amazing English," I said.

"For a Chink?" she smiled.

"For anyone," I replied. "Where are you from?"

"Camden Lock," she said.

"Jesus Christ!" I laughed. "We're almost neighbours."

"My mum runs a restaurant."

"How original…. the *Golden* what?" I asked. Most of the Chinese restaurants I know are called the *Golden* something or other.

"*Dragon*," Kallie admitted.

Again, how original. "How long are you staying at the gym?"

"Planning on a full year," she said.

"Why?"

"'Cos I've got a boyfriend, dick-head!" she laughed.

"Does you mother know?" I smiled back.

"And you'll be telling her?"

"I'll slip a short, sharp note into one of her menus," I threatened. "I'm not into suicide!"

Kallie smiled and thought about it. "Wouldn't work," she finally decided. "She's far too busy finding wives for my brothers!"

"Glad to hear the old traditions are alive and kicking," I said.

We were walking along this stone-built path that was lined with palm trees and luxuriant purple flowers. We were heading towards this elaborate pavilion. In front, a multi-jet fountain was filled with a swamp of scarlet lilies. According to the map that came with the tickets, this pavilion contained an exhibition of Thai handicrafts.

"Take a look?" Kallie asked me.

"Why not?" I said. "It's cool inside and we can talk about Anni."

Handicrafts was right; the ornate pavilion was all about the exotic silks and textiles that are developed, created and woven in the provinces of Thailand. We weren't the only people in there – but it wasn't crowded and we had all the time we needed to look at the wonderful fabrics.

"You gotta give 'em points for style," Kallie remarked.

I had to agree. As I moved my head around, the intricate patterns returned a variety of colours and shades. It was like watching a kaleidoscope in real-time action. "Smart," I said. "But what about Anni?"

"I'll tell you outside," said Kallie softly. "Keep it casual till we get to the exit."

It was then I noticed the boy in the peacock-blue shirt.

Once outside, we strolled along calmly enough – not quite arm-in-arm, but in a very sociable manner - past a small display of old-time military cannons and across a little bridge where brilliant orange and yellow iris flowers turned the stream into a roaring fire.

To make us look like tourists, I took a couple of pictures – then we wandered along until we reached this little wayside watering station.

"What do you want?" Kallie asked. "Water or Thai Green Tea?"

"Green Tea, please," and I sat under an orange parasol and waited.

"Yes, master – may it be cold enough!" she grinned.

"Tell me about Anni and I'll stop the whipping," I promised.

Kallie took a long hard draw on her straw.

"OK," she said, "I'll tell you – but you won't like it."

"I'm a big boy now," I said. "Sock it to me, sweetie…"

"Call me *sweetie* one more time," she laughed, "and I'll sock you right in the sweetie-box!"

"You make it sound like an optional extra," I said.

"One kick from this little Chinese girl and you can forget your *extras* – optional or otherwise!" But she was still laughing.

I took another suck on my straw. Green Tea is delightfully refreshing on a hot Thai morning. "Anni?" I reminded her.

"We did part-time bar work in the RiverSide," she began. "I was new, she looked after me – found me a room, that kind of thing."

"Good of her," I said.

"In a way, it was," Kallie went on. "Through Anni, I met Raphael – and Raphael introduced me to Takoon at Sasiprapa."

"Did you box before you came?"

"Yes," said Kallie. "But here, I can train with the best."

"At Sasiprapa?"

"Takoon coaches the Thai national team," said Kallie. "And you can't find better – anywhere!"

"What about Raphael?" I asked.

Kallie paused to take another sip of her Green Thai Tea. "Glad he's not *my* boyfriend!" she grinned.

"Who's boyfriend is he?"

But Kallie dodged the question. "Your Chelsea knows him better than me," she said. "Ask her about his jewellery business."

I could hear the menace in her voice. "Is he bent?" I asked.

"As a bloody corkscrew!" Now, she wasn't laughing.

I thought back to the diamonds. "He showed me some stones," I said. "Wanted me to buy them."

"And did you?"

"Not at those prices!" I laughed.

"But think of the profit…!" and she dropped her voice and a party of Japanese tourists ambled past, clicking at everything with their Nikons.

"Think of the risk," I said.

The Japanese had moved on. She was back into normal-speaking mode. "You were right," she said. "It was a scam."

Did I really want to hear this? No choice. I was now in the loop.

"It was a scam from start to finish," Kallie went on. "Rich tourist is introduced to the highly-respectable Mr Villavito – who shows him a selection of quality stones."

"OK so far," I said. "I had the ten-baht tour."

"Mug likes them – smells the profit – pays in cash – and the stones go into a packet which is sealed and signed by both parties."

"Are these really quality stones?" I asked.

"Oh yes," she said. "Any jeweller would sign 'em off as kosher."

"So where's the scam?"

"You really want to know?" We had finished our drinks and Kallie was keen to be moving along.

"That's why I'm here."

"OK," Kallie agreed. "But don't throw up in the bushes."

"I won't," I promised.

"Before the packet got sealed and signed, he'd call someone into the office as a witness."

"So far so good," I said.

"Hold hard, sunshine," she smiled. "The best is on its way."

We were approaching these large silver-painted iron gates that protected the grounds of this magnificent white palace. It had a large bay window and a dome. A notice pointed to the *Ananda Samakhom Throne Hall* and a set of little icons warned us not to think of using cameras, videos, mobile phones (or even having a smoke).

"So what's the bottom line?" I wanted to know.

"Some kind of a distraction – coffee spilt – a can of coke knocked over – or a call to the victim's cell phone…"

"And then?" Although I could see it coming.

"They switch the packets – and the dick-head gets to sign for the sub-standard merchandise."

"And what happens to the duff package?"

"Villavito tells you that his shipping agent will get it through your Customs," she said. "Not that it would matter – what's inside ain't worth the postage money."

"And he doesn't complain?"

"What would he say?"

I could see what she meant. Jewel smugglers don't have a union. "So where's the vomit-maker?" Trust me – I had to ask. I could have let it ride. But no, I had to ask.

"Anni makes the switch," said Kallie.

Holy God! "Was that the price she had to pay for Chelsea's debt?"

Kallie just laughed. "And what debt was that?" she asked me.

"For her mother's hospital bill," I explained.

"Don't believe everything she tells you," said Kallie. "For all I know, *she* could be Villavito's girlfriend."

Now that hurt. But what's the first rule of man-on-woman combat? Never let them see the pain. "Anything is possible," I said.

"I could be wrong." said Kallie as she took my arm. "She's always been a bit of a wildcat."

"Women with spirit," I smiled weakly. "And dogs that argue."

"Brave little soldier!" she grinned and gave me a consoling hug.

"So Anni switched the goods and nicked the real diamonds?"

"If she did, he'll kill her."

"Really?"

"Don't expect him to thank her," Kallie warned me.

We had given up the idea of visiting the Throne Hall. It was now midday. It was also very hot.

"Is that why he wants her back?"

"If you find those gems, he might let her off with a beating." said Kallie. "But I wouldn't bet on it."

"Nor me," I said. We were just meandering along, admiring the flowers, looking at the trees and wishing we could paddle in that fountain. "Do you know where she is?" I asked.

Kallie took a step of two before answering. "No," she said. "But I know how you could speak to her."

Sounded better. "Got a number?" and I took out my cell phone.

"Oh no," said Kallie. "Far too easy to trace."

"So how does it work?"

"Uses a dating agency," Kallie smiled. "Calls herself *BoxerGirl*."

"Web address?" and I pulled the notebook out of my pack.

"Just for you, lover boy!" she grinned and wrote down the www-etceteras for the *Let_ Me_Love_U* website. "Call yourself *BoxerBoy* and she'll know you're for real."

It was different, I'll give her that much. Better than a message in a bottle. One more question: "Could she sell the diamonds?"

"Wouldn't dare!" said Kallie.

Then God tapped me on the shoulder and whispered in my ear. "What if I sold the diamonds?"

Kallie looked horrified. "Are you mad?"

"For two-hundred K in sterling?"

And when Kallie realised I wasn't joking, she could only see a mountain of dollars. "Are you cutting me in?" she asked.

Got you! "Twenty percent – and no risk." I promised.

Kallie stopped walking and looked me dead in the eye. "Can't help you with the selling," she said, "but I know a girl who might…" and she borrowed my cell phone to make a call. She spoke for several minutes in Thai – and then explained: "She's a jeweller, calls herself Ronni."

"Where do I find her?"

"*Temple of Dawn*, by the Warriors – two o'clock."

"And wearing what?"

"A red T-shirt," Kallie told me.

12

We said our goodbyes by the display of old State Carriages. While she went to the *Ladies*, I took half-a-dozen shots of the exhibits, then drifted out of the gate and waved-down a taxi.

"Uh?" he asked. (*You get a lot of those in a Thai conversation.*)

"RiverSide," I said, "near River City," and I emphasised each syllable. First, I had to get my laptop out of the safety box.

"Uh," he promised.

At ten minutes to two, I found myself back on the pier at *Tha Tien*, waiting for the cute little cross-river ferry that would take me to my meeting with the jewellery girl. I'd paid for my 3-baht ticket and was standing in the full glare of the afternoon sun, watching the incoming craft as it wallowed in the wake of an upstream express boat.

Three ranks back in the crowd behind me, some kid was wearing a peacock-blue shirt. A mid-summer fashion? The must-have colour for the season? Just had to be. They were everywhere.

When the ferry arrived, we all scrambled aboard, found seats and hung on tightly as the little vessel ploughed across the wash of the passing river traffic until we reached the temple's pier.

I waited my turn, then hopped ashore with the other passengers. I've always enjoyed visiting *Wat Arun*. It's on the west bank of the Chao Phraya, and being away from the city, it seems to have a special feeling of peace that I've never found in *Wat Pho* or *Wat Traimit*. They get too many visitors, I guess.

As promised, my date for the afternoon was waiting for me by the giant War Lords who guard the temple entrance. She was slightly over five feet tall, with a slim little figure and the most engaging smile. And she was wearing red - but not just any ordinary shade of red. She was wearing RED! It was a glaring, blinding tone of red that could have scared an entire herd of fighting bulls.

"Love the shirt," I smiled.

"Thank you, David," she replied. "Ronni's lucky colour."

"It's enough to frighten the soldiers," I said.

"They not scare easy," she said. "They good fighters."

"Do they get much practice?"

Ronni stopped and looked up at the figures as if to apologise for the ignorant *farang*. "*Tha Tien* – you know?" she asked me.

"Yes," I said. "It's over there," and pointed back across the river.

"It mean *broken place*," she said. "Two more giants live there –always fighting."

"And *Wat Arun* is still untouched."

"Shows how good these two are," Ronni laughed.

"Nice one, boys," and I waved at the one with the green face.

"Yes," she agreed. "Now we have coffee."

Lesson over – time to go – and I followed Ronni out of the temple area and into a little side street. A large red and blue sign offered:

Palmistry
can help you obtain
accurate answers about yourself

"Could it help me find Anni?" I smiled.

"You find diamonds – you find Anni," Ronni promised.

Further on, we came across a 4x4 that was transporting two black Buddha figures to a new location. A sign on a white-walled building said *Temple of Dawn*.

"Where monks live," Ronni explained, then crossed the street towards this tiny little eating place. It had four plastic tables, plastic crates for seats and a cold-cabinet for the waters, colas and fizzy drinks. "You want water?"

"Iced, please," I said.

Ronni spoke to the old woman in charge and chose the table away from the street. It was nice to be out of the sun for a moment.

"These diamonds," I asked. "Where do they come from?"

"China," said Ronni. "First, he bring them to Laos – then he get man to carry them to Bangkok."

"Are they any good?"

"Some - yes," Ronni confirmed. "Others – no."

Our drinks arrived and we paused to sip them. "Are the good ones worth the money?" I wanted to know.

"Good ones, yes." Ronni sipped again. "But Villavito work scam."

"I've heard about the switch," I said. "But why are they sealed in the envelope?"

"So you can't check with real jeweller," she said. "Once in post, you no get money back."

No such thing as a freebie, even in the *Land of Smiles*. "And Anni has the good ones?"

Ronni smiled. "She clever girl!"

"Could she sell them?"

Ronni shook her head. "Be very hard," she decided.

"Could I sell them?"

"Even harder," Ronni told me.

Which only left one option; I looked her straight in the eye. "Could you sell them?" I asked.

She didn't even blink. "For twenty percent," she agreed.

From *Tha Tien*, I took the up-river ferry as far as Phra Arkit and walked through the alley with the tailoring shops. Once into Rambuttri, Chelsea's shop was hardly more than a hundred yards. But in that heat, carrying the laptop didn't make it any easier.

As I turned into the Four Sons outdoor café, she came running down the flight of steps to meet me. Then she saw the laptop.

"You go shopping?" To Chelsea, spending money on anyone but her was only half a point below adultery.

"No," I said. "I brought it with me. It will help me find Anni."

That was better. "Good," she smiled. "I get you drink – come in office - more private." Not that it would have made any difference. Although there must have been some twenty people having afternoon tea, not one of them had even noticed us – *except for this kid in the peacock-blue shirt.*

Once inside her office, the air-conditioning took over and I began to cool down. A shower would have been nice. I should have had one at the RiverSide.

I had an idea. "If I moved in here, would you mind?" and I waved an arm in the general direction of the Four Sons Reception window.

"No," said Chelsea. "Why me mind?"

"Was only asking," I smiled. "We call it being 'English'."

"Oh," said Chelsea, not at all interested. "You want me ask?"

"Please."

"OK – you want water?"

"Please…" After a day in the scorching sun, my throat was far too dry for chit-chat.

She asked, got me a room and dipped me for a 500-baht deposit. Then she found me a bottle of ice-cold water. Pure magic!

"Now what Mr Raphael say?"

So I told her about the Sasiprapa – and about Little Tiger.

"I not see him. What he like?"

"Small, brown and cute," I said.

Chelsea thought about it. "She not bring him home," she said.

"He seemed OK," I said. "Looked hellish fit!"

"What you mean?"

"He could kick your butt before you could blink," I explained.

"Why he do that?"

Never mind, my angel. "And I called the second number from Nixie," I said. "It was answered by one of the other boxers."

Chelsea usually found it cold in the shop and today, she was wearing a long-sleeved navy-blue cardigan. "What he like?"

"Who?"

"Other boxer."

"It was a girl," I said. "A Chinese girl from London."

"London?" and she narrowed her eyes, like a cat with a mouse. "She old girlfriend?"

This was Chelsea having a joke. "No, my love," I said quietly. "London is a very big city."

"Then how you know her?" While we were talking, she picked up her cell phone and was punching numbers.

"She used to work with Anni at the RiverSide."

"What she say?"

I had to tell her that I knew. "That Anni helped Villavito with his diamond scam." Next, I'd have to cover what they'd been saying about Chelsea. That would be tricky.

She saw it coming. "Why you need laptop?"

"Anni is using a website," I said. "It's the only way to reach her."

"Did Ronni tell you that?"

"Yes, she did," I said – and glanced across with that *who told you?* look in my eyes. I hadn't mentioned Ronni.

But Chelsea gave me her win-win smile and held up her cell phone. "Nixie," she said. "She my friend!"

Not what you told me yesterday, my little laughing pussy. However, the bit about the meeting in *Wat Arun* and the offer to buy the diamonds was strictly between Ronni and me. And the fewer people who knew about it, the better chance we had of keeping it secret.

"When I've finished my water, I'll have a look for Anni," I said. "Can I use one of your sockets?"

"OK," said Chelsea and went on whispering into her cell phone. "Now you help me fill in application for visa?" and she waved a small yellow form at me.

"Give it here – I'll take a look," I said.

It was the all usual bullshit – name – age – DoB – where born (town/country) …. And then we had this really interesting question…

"Are you married?" I asked.

"Why you want to know?"

"It's on the form – are you single, married or divorced?"

"Three husbands and eight children," Chelsea said, poker-faced.

"Wonderful!" I grinned. "I *love* children! – shall we call it *single*?"

"Why not?" Chelsea replied. "It true."

"I'm not arguing," I said. "And your date-of-birth?"

"19 November, 1975," she told me.

"You're not seventeen any more?"

Chelsea just smiled softly. "Give here," she said. "I finish it."

I gave it back to her. If she claimed to be *single*, I had no reason to dispute it. Thai words and English words don't always match. And sometimes, *marriage* can mean anything you want it to.

"As a matter of interest…" I asked. I had opened the laptop and clicked my way across the IE browser until it settled like a weary homing pigeon on the *who's available* pages of the *Let_Me_Love_You* website.

"What you want?" Chelsea was still in cell phone mode.

"What does Anni look like?"

"She my sister – look like me."

"Of course she does," I agreed. "But a picture would help."

"You mean like this?" and from her desk drawer, she produced this postcard-sized print of a Chelsea look-alike.

In this, Anni was a long-haired girl, younger than Chelsea, and with the sweetest smile. She was on a beach with her back to the sea. And she had this white T-shirt with smiling cartoon tiger and *Laughin' Pussy* right across her bouncy little breasts.

"Why the advert?"

"She mad about tigers," Chelsea told me. "Have poster over bed."

"Especially little ones," I said. Then eight clicks down, I found *BoxerGirl.* As part of her introduction, she had invited the world of cyber-sex to *stoke my fur and make me purr…*. And as her entry was supported by the self-same picture of the *Laughin' Pussy* T-shirt, at least some of what Chelsea had told me was right.

I answered: *Hello BoxerGirl – can I count your stripes? Os & Xs – BoxerBoy* and left it open.

Then a couple of Chelsea's friends came in for a girly-talk session – as women do, of course. One was Nolli, the friend who gave visa assistance and in-bedroom massages.

"Say hello Nolli," Chelsea told me.

"My legs have never felt better!" I said, giving her a *wai*.

"You want her do it again?" Chelsea asked.

"Nice idea, but not in front of the children," I said.

"She make good girl friend," Chelsea teased me. "Nolli always keep you happy!"

"I'm sure she would," I agreed. "But if I can't have you, I don't want anyone," and gave her my *love-you* look to let her know I meant it.

But Chelsea let it pass. Instead, she introduced me to the other girl. This one had blue-streaked hair in a pony tail. "Say hello Pimmi."

Pimmi seemed a little older. "Nice to meet you," I said and while I went back to my search for Anni, Chelsea organised her in-house party. For this, she ordered enough food and drink to satisfy the Household Cavalry on a four-day exercise. Then held out her gorgeous little hand.

"Five-hundred baht," she demanded.

No choice: pay up and let them see that Chelsea had fallen on her pretty little paws again. "Save a chicken leg for me," I said.

"You want?" Chelsea asked, offering to let me share.

I looked at the spread: eight plates between three girls. It didn't seem right to leave them short. "Maybe later," I smiled and went back to *Let_Me_Love_You.*

To begin with, the girls were gabbling away in Thai and working their way through a copy of *Cosmopolitan* that Pimmi had brought along. When they hit the fashion pages, they all screamed into overdrive.

"You buy me this?"

I looked up. It was Chelsea in her very best English. She was waving a page of the glittery tops that girls wear at parties.

"What is it?" I asked. When girls get on to clothing, it's best to be ignorant. Knowledge can be dangerous, often leading to a *how-you-know-this?* interrogation.

"Bright and sparkly is best for me!" said a very excited Chelsea.

I couldn't let this go, now could I? "Why do you prefer the bright and sparkly?" I asked.

"So everyone look at me and no at them!" she laughed – and all three girls dissolved into a fit of the giggles.

At least they were enjoying themselves - then my laptop gave a *ping* to say I had a message.

BoxerBoy – let's play ball – call me – BoxerGirl and her cell phone number came in brackets after her call sign.

BoxerGirl – will do – BoxerBoy I replied – then disconnected my phone from the laptop and punched in the number. It rang twice.

"David?"

"Anni?"

"You know O'Reilly's?"

"Top end of Patpong?"

"You wait – I come – I wear shirt," she said and closed the call.

Chelsea stopped drooling over the pictures of the party-wear and looked across the desk at me. "What wrong?" she asked.

"Nothing at all, my little darling!" I smiled. "We're in business."

"What you mean?"

"We've just found Anni!"

13

Chelsea insisted on coming to Patpong and got shirty when I tried to stop her. In the end, it was easier to give in. Not my best-ever decision. She spent the next fifteen minutes on her cell phone, telling everyone and anyone. In the end, I had to get tough. "Stop it – now!"

"What you do?" She was pouting; a sure sign of trouble.

It was time to act tough or go under. "I'll toss it in the river…" and tried to sound as though I meant it.

"Then you buy me new one," she snapped. Still defiant, she punched in another number.

"NO!" I said. "Every call puts your Anni in more danger."

That, she didn't understand. "How you mean?"

I gave it to her, chapter and verse. "Your sister is running around with pocketful of diamonds – and a lot of Villavito's people would like to find her," and I drew my hand across my throat in a slitting motion.

Suddenly, she looked sick. "Mr Raphael no hurt Anni," but I'm not sure if she believed it. However, it stopped her from making any more phone calls. When it was time to spread the news, I would spread it - good or otherwise. Until then, my little kitten, stick your cell phone where it won't see daylight.

We took a taxi and enjoyed the stop/start/stop thrills of driving through the city on a Friday evening. We tested the clutch along Phraram 4 until the sharp right-turn by Jim Thompson's Silk Shop put us on the pavement within easy reach of the Night Market….. and all those damned clothing stalls.

These two streets are more that just an outlet for fake designer-gear. Patpong is just one example of the *fuck-me* entertainment that Bangkok has to offer. They may be only side streets, but you have to be there to believe them.

You have the girlie bars for eating, drinking, watching and whoring, private rooms for *Pussy Writing*, *Pussy Smoking*, *Pussy Whistle* and *Pussy Ping-Pong*. And it's not too hard to find a live sex show. Plus, for those who like home-decorating, they also do body-painting.

It was busy, it was noisy. It was expensive. Patpong traders charge tourist prices, plus a mark-up for overheads.

"You give me thousand baht?"

Who else? That was Chelsea – and believe me, it's a far better bet to cough up the cash, on the nail, right there and then and get it sorted. From experience, I have learned that something like – *"No love, you choose and I'll pay"* - will end up costing three times as much. So I opened my wallet and gave her the money.

"I love you!" and she offered her cheek for a kiss.

"Enjoy!" and I aimed as close to her lips as I dared.

"No allowed!" and she jabbed me with her elbow.

God forgive me, but these cultural problems drive me crazy. Some of the *keep off the grass* books that help *farangs* make-out with Thai girls warn that it can take a couple of years before we're allowed to hold hands in the street. Open-air kissing takes even longer – and you can forget leg-over land. It's so far out of town, it's not even on the bus route.

"Worth a shot," I smiled.

"Worth new jeans," came her predictable answer.

Was I surprised? Chelsea and clothes are like pigeons and corn – no such thing as *enough*. By the time we had worked our way through the crowds around the heaps of not-quite Levis and Wranglers the replica football shirts and the dubious Cartier, Swatch and Tissot watches (and don't forget the Gucci and the Rayban look-alikes and all that imitation perfume), my thousand baht was long gone and forgotten.

Other traders were offering pirate software - and if you wanted movies, you could have stocked your bookcase on DVDs that were still in Hollywood, waiting on a release date.

Further along – the food stalls. From what I could see, there wasn't much they couldn't cook. If it had legs, they fried it – and if they fried it, you could eat it. Every little pavement kitchen in the *Soi* had customers. "You hungry?" I asked.

"No," said Chelsea. "I want new watch."

Was it worth a protest? Probably not – but why make it easy for her? "What about the one from Amsterdam?" I said. We'd already bought three pairs of jeans, two replica football shirts - *Barcelona* for herself (she liked the colours) and *Liverpool* (for her brother) – and a pair of Armani sunglasses, most of which she had carefully stowed in my backpack.

"That my best watch," she explained. "Need cheap one for work."

Why fight it? "Small or large?" I asked.

"Big and chunky," she grinned. "Like my *love-you* boyfriend!"

There were dozens on display, copies of every make in the universe. If I didn't jolly her along, we'd still be here at midnight. Not that there was any need to rush. Anni was on Thai-time – and that allowed her all the leeway she could possibly need. But I didn't want to hang around too long. In Patpong, any form of *time* costs *money*.

"OK," I agreed. "Close your eyes and pick one."

So she did – and found a Ladies Boss with a plain silvery band.

"A thousand," said a boy who seemed to be running the business.

At this, Chelsea slammed the watch back on the table and told the kid his fortune in a very loud voice. After an exchange of opinions, she grabbed my arm and ordered: "Give him five hundred – that all it worth!"

So I did – he took it – and everyone was happy. Well, except Chelsea, that is. As we walked away, she hugged my arm. "He think I born in coconut!"

All my fault, of course. So I kissed her cheek again, just to say "Sorry!" for screwing-up. Only this time, she didn't jab me.

Instead: "You want food?"

We'd wandered along as far as the lottery tables. Books of tickets were laid in neat little rows and columns – and men of every age and size were checking for their own specific lucky number. It was a very slow and deliberate process.

"Wouldn't mind," I said.

"OK, I fix," she agreed. "Very cheap!"

I had to smile. Up till then, I didn't know she knew the word – but as there's a first for everyone, I followed her into this very noisy bar.

It was a typical Patpong *sex-for-sale* screwing shop. In this one, the navy-blue walls made it seem darker than usual. A dozen or so teenage girls – all dressed in flimsy white bras and micro-skirts - were up on a catwalk, gyrating slowly to the raucous music and using their imagination to tempt us into a quickie in the courtyard.

"Where are they from?"

"Village girls – care for their families," Chelsea told me.

"And nobody minds?"

"Treated with respect," said Chelsea. "They make sacrifice."

"It's a whole new world," I said quietly.

Although the bar itself was bright enough, the only lighting for the dancers came from UV strobes that swished a criss-cross pattern over the catwalk and gave each girl a ghostly, iridescent sheen. As my eyes became used to the conditions, I was able to count some twenty or so punters, just standing around in groups, with bottles of Heineken, watching the girls.

"You like?" Chelsea asked me.

Good question. She was pointing up at Number 17, a tall (and very agile) girl with long black hair that came right down to her butt. "She's a bit scrawny," I said. "But I've seen worse."

Chelsea laughed. "OK," she said, looking round for the *mamasan*. "I buy her for you – want it now or later?"

"Later, please," I said. "I have a date with someone's sister."

"Sister wait two minutes," Chelsea promised.

"You can really boost my ego!" I grinned.

We found a table-for-two down beside the catwalk and Chelsea ordered something from a tall, thin beanpole of a girl who was also dressed in the standard *if you want it, ask me* uniform. But this girl was wearing high-heeled sandals that were strapped half-way up to her knees. She had fixed her top so that a third of each chocolate nipple was clearly on view. Who could ever forget *her*?

"Does she also cook?" I wanted to know.

"No," said Chelsea, missing the joke. "She get it from café."

We were not the only diners. I counted five other tables in use – but there could have been more on the other side of the bar. "It's popular," I said.

"And lot of other bars," Chelsea agreed. "All up street."

If only I had the nerve to open something like it in Brighton... But how long would it take them to jail me for doing so...?

We were halfway through our plates of crispy-fried duck - with salad and rice, of course – when my cell phone jingled in my pocket.

It was Anni. "Where you now?" she wanted to know.

"In a bar – with Chelsea – having dinner," I confessed.

"O'Reilly - thirty minutes."

"See you there," I said. At least we had time to finish the Singhas.

"That Anni?"

"Yes," I said.

"I want talk!" and Chelsea made a grab for my phone.

"Too late," I told her. "Anni gone - we'll see her in a minute."

"How you know it her?"

Good point. "Because she called from the same number," I said and showed her the *Caller Log* to prove it.

"Mean nothing," said Chelsea. She was now in a mood. My fault again. I should have let her speak to Anni. "She not come."

"Why not?"

"She not know you," Chelsea argued. She was determined. She was right and I was back on her hit list. "She keep away."

"But you'll be there," I tried.

"But she not trust you."

"You watch too much TV," I said as I finished my beer. It wasn't all that clever, but it stopped the bickering.

It took ten minutes to walk from our girlie bar to O'Reilly's. To get there, we had to shimmy our way through a mass of window-shopping tourists, all the way along this narrow footpath, in between two lines of those *once-in-a-lifetime* market stalls that tourists go for.

Some sold the bangles and bracelets that you find in any temple gift shop. Others went for little resin ornaments of Buddhas and Indian gods. We found any amount of woven handbags and leather ware. Luminous tapestries of temples, tuk-tuks and elephants playing football were selling quite well – as were those horrifying weapons that everybody has to carry in a martial-arts movie.

It was little short of a miracle that Chelsea kept going. "Watch wallet," she warned me. "Indians come to steal."

"I'll be careful," I said and checked the zip-up pockets on my backpack.

O'Reilly's is an ex-pat paradise. Apart from real draught Guinness, it also stocks a range of Irish whiskies. And for those who never want to see another grain of rice, it serves real, genuine, Irish food - like Irish stew, steak pie and smoked salmon.

Inside, it's been decorated like an old-style Victorian pub – snugs on the ground floor and a private dining room upstairs. For those who like to sit and watch the world go by, there is an outside veranda – with waitress service and a Sky TV that shows the English football games.

"I think we should sit outside," I said.

"OK," and sat where we could both watch the street.

I sat beside her and waved at a waitress in an emerald green apron. "Two Singha, please," I said.

"Then you drink both," said Chelsea. She was still in a paddy over the phone-call incident. "Me 'n Anni want cocktails."

"You said she wasn't coming."

Chelsea corrected herself. "If she come, she want cocktail."

"What kind?"

"*Sex-on-Beach*," said a wide-eyed Chelsea, daring me to criticise.

"Now you're taking the piss," I told her.

We were so busy arguing, that I hardly noticed the boy in the peacock-blue shirt as he slid into a seat at the far end of the veranda.

The waitress brought our beers and we sat in silence, almost enjoying the stillness of the moment. Some describe that silence as the very truest form of all true love. But to those who've been there, seen it and stitched-up their wounds, it's just a lull in the battle, where both sides reload their rifles for the next attack.

I tried a compromise. "Would you like to see the ring?"

"No," said Chelsea. "Wait till Anni come."

"Suit yourself," I whispered into my Singha.

Across the street was a massage parlour, and judging by the numbers going in and coming out, it was a successful massage parlour.

The street itself was a mass of coloured signs: *Nareerat, Club Disset, Albatross, Three Seven* and the inevitable *Coca-Cola*, stretching into the night in a rainbow of colour. It was crowded – in every corner, tourists checking posters in the girlie-bar windows, reading handbills for the sex shows or talking to the bouncers.

Then I saw this kid in a white T-shirt. She was coming towards us at a steady pace. To get a better look, I used my camera to zoom in close. And there is was: *Laughin' Pussy* – right across her buffer zone.

"Yes!" I whispered to Chelsea. "She's here!"

At which, the world went crazy. Suddenly, a black-sleeved hand shot out and tried to grab my camera. But as the strap was firmly wrapped round my left wrist, the would-be thief was thrown off-balance by the jerk as I snatched it back.

On instinct, I was on my feet and swung a punch that caught him right in the teeth. He went down - the table went over – glasses shattered as they hit the floor - and beer splashed in an explosion of foam and spray.

The waitress screamed – two women at a nearby table screamed – and anyone within twenty feet of our table jumped up and tried to scramble off the veranda. It was instant chaos.

The right-hander must have caught his lip. In seconds, there was blood everywhere, dripping over everything.

"Darling – you OK?" Chelsea took my hand and kissed it.

The kid was on his knees, sobbing loudly and trying to staunch the blood with a paper napkin.

"Why you hit so hard?" she wanted to know.

Before I could explain about hitting people, a small policeman in a khaki uniform was there in front of me – right out of the magic beer bottle, like the genie in Aladdin. (*Three wishes? Not a chance!*) He had one hand on the butt of his .357 Smith & Wesson – and did not look happy.

"*You - stand still!*" he said in English.

I turned to Chelsea and pushed a thousand-baht note into her hand. "Sorry, love," I said. "No shags tonight – the party's over." and I tried to ease her away from the battle zone that had once been our table.

"*STAND STILL!*" our policeman shouted. By now, his even smaller friend had appeared. "She is witness!"

I tensed and looked around, ready to run. But there was no way out. We'd been well and truly nailed.

With an apologetic smile, our policeman took the thousand-baht bank note and gave it to the waitress. "For beers," he said. But when he turned back to me and growled: "When they let you out of jail, you pay for damage, OK?"

I sensed that he was starting to enjoy his Friday evening. "I want to call my embassy."

My policeman smiled. "And girlfriend?"

"She would like a solicitor, please," I said, trying to stay calm.

I thought he was going to smack me. Instead, he gave my backpack and camera to his buddy and gripped my arm above the elbow. "You come," he said. "No fuss – OK?"

By now, there were four of them – all in khaki – all with Smith & Wessons. All willing to restrain a drunken *farang*.

"Resistance in useless!" I smiled. There was no point in fighting – not against four of them. So I took a deep breath, let myself relax and allowed him to arrest me. "No fuss," I promised.

He led me to his car. His side-kick followed with Chelsea and the other two took charge of the would-be mugger. Ninety seconds, start to finish. Then O'Reilly's got back to the eating and drinking. Last of all, there was Little Mr Blue-Shirt, still in his corner, making free with his cell phone. But when I glanced back down the lane, Anni had vanished.

Then I remembered Chelsea's comment about the bright and sparkly party-wear… "*They look at me – not at her!*" So while I'd been watching the Blue-Shirt boy for the past couple of days, who'd been watching me?

14

"Where are we going?" It was a comfortable car. OK, so I was in the back behind the wire guard, but he hadn't used the handcuffs and I was able to stretch out and put my feet up.

"Bangrak," my policeman explained. "Mr Sam waiting…" but that was all. He ignored all further questions and just carried on through the evening traffic.

I looked behind, but there was no sign of Chelsea's police car. "My friend?" I asked. Waste of effort. He was not in a chatty mood.

In time, my driver slowed to walking pace, made a left-hand swing onto a forecourt and eased into a parking space. This was *Bangrak Police Station*. As we came to a halt, two more policemen came out of the shadows to welcome us.

"You – *get out!*" said my man.

Why argue? So I allowed all three to escort me through a side door, along a well-lit passage and into a small square room. It had dark grey walls, a single lamp, two of those bum-numbing aluminium chairs and a well-worn trestle table. As one of the chairs was for me, I sat down and tried to look harmless.

One minute later, the smaller cop arrived with my backpack and gave it to the man who was about to book me. Then he stayed behind to witness my interrogation.

"My girlfriend?" I asked.

The little guy gave an encouraging smile. "She fine."

That was something. "Thank you," I nodded.

My man sat in the other chair and emptied my bag, placing each item on the table as if laying out a chessboard. First, he opened my passport.

"Is yours?" he asked.

"Check the picture in the back," I said. "If it looks like me, it's probably mine."

He ignored the sarcasm. "You like Thailand?"

"Yes, nice food - nice people."

"Nice hitting?"

One up to him. Now it was my turn to say nothing.

Next, he inspected my travel documents. But as these modern down-load versions don't look anything like the old-fashioned air ticket, he had to read each piece of paper several times. In the end, he returned the KLM paperwork to its neat little plastic folder and opened the ring box.

"This for her?"

"If she'll have me," I said.

"She like man who hit boys?"

Come on, son, don't flog it to death. You made your point, now leave it alone. "I have to show her that I care," I said.

"Mr Sam not happy," he said and returned everything to my backpack. "You want coffee?"

Surprise! Thumbscrews, yes - but not a coffee. "Very kind," I said. "Milk – no sugar."

"You have black..." and told the smaller man.

"Uh!" the smaller policeman agreed – went out – and was back in a couple of minutes with two plastic cups of hot, black coffee. He placed them on the trestle table, one in front of each of us.

"Very kind of you," I said.

"Mr Sam see you in minute," he promised.

Would that be a Thai minute or a British minute? Who could say? So I sipped away and wondered just how quickly they would bump me onto the next available flight to London.

After some ten of *our* minutes, my man received a phone call. First, he gave my backpack to the smaller guy - who scuttled out the door and scampered up the passageway.

One minute later: "Now *we* go," and he waved me to the door.

"Mr Sam?" I asked.

My man just smiled. "He not happy."

The office was only a dozen steps along the corridor. My man stopped at the door, knocked, waited a second – then marched me in.

Mr Sam was sitting at his desk. In his well-starched uniform, he looked more like a soldier than a policeman.

It was just a basic office - a desk, a swivel chair and two filing cabinets. The wall behind the desk was dominated by a very large sepia-toned picture of the King. On the desk: a clean white desk pad, my travel backpack – with his black-handled 9mm Colt right beside it, in a well-polished leather holster. It looked just right for Clint Eastwood.

The stage was set and we were ready…

"Mr David Shannon," he began, quietly. "Please sit down."

In front of his desk: a cushioned chair – and I gratefully accepted the invitation. After the aluminium special down the hall, this was a treat. "Thanks," I said – and tried to look relaxed.

Mr Sam deliberately emptied my backpack onto his desk and checked each item in turn. As before, he began with passport. "You are an English man?" he asked me.

"Guilty as charged," I replied.

He turned the pages one by one and counted my entry visa stamps. "I have never been to your country," he said. "But you have been to mine six times."

"You ought to come," I suggested. "Everybody welcome."

"To go round hitting people?" he asked.

As we'd been down this trail before, I decided to head him off at the pass. "I was afraid he might attack my girlfriend," I said.

"How English," Mr Sam smiled. "And was this the first time?"

What's the golden rule of cross-examination? Only ask the questions if you know the answers? "No," I confessed. "On Thursday evening, this British guy called her a WOG – so I dropped him."

The policeman shook his head. "Are you a boxer?" he asked.

"No," I smiled. "I'm a Londoner."

He ignored the comment and moved on to the next point on his agenda. "Mr Shannon," he continued. "You keep interesting company."

"Yes," I said, "I think she's terrific."

Mr Sam replaced my passport on his desk, sat back in his chair, folded his arms and fixed me with a black-eyed stare. "Mr Shannon," he said in a very low voice, "we can do this here - or we can do it in the privacy of a padded cell. The choice is yours."

It was the way he said it. On TV, they rant and shout and wave their arms about. But with Mr Sam, it was his way or the sin-bin. Time to play ball; there was Chelsea to consider. "OK," I said and held up both hands. "Your game – your rules."

"Thank you," Mr Sam smiled. Then he introduced himself. "I am Lieutenant Samran," he said, "but you may call me Sam."

"OK, Sam," I agreed. "I'm David - how can I help you?"

Mr Sam went back to my passport, turning the pages and counting the entry-visa stamps. "What brings you back so many times?" he asked.

"I only come to see Chelsea," I said.

He picked up the little square box, opened it and inspected the ring. "You are hoping she will accept this?"

"That was the plan," I agreed.

"Now you are not so sure?"

I clasped my hands behind my head, crossed my legs and tried to adopt a casual appearance. "It was all going so well," I said, "and then her sister went missing."

"Miss Anni?"

"Yes," I agreed. "Little sister Anni."

"And this is why you've been keeping interesting company?"

"Depends on what you call 'interesting'," I replied.

Sam laughed. "You find Raphael Villavito boring?" he asked.

I sat up sharply. "Not at all," I said. "He has his moments."

Sam let it go. "How many times have you seen him?" It was an odds-on bet that he knew already.

"Three," I said. "Once in his hotel – once in his office – and again when he took me to Sasiprapa."

"You know what he does?" Sam asked.

"He runs a diamond scam," I admitted.

"Well done!" he smiled. "You have some amazing contacts."

"Anni has a lot of friends," I explained.

Sam moved the papers around his desk until he found a list of names. "So it would seem," he remarked. "A coffee girl, a part-time tourist guide, a Chinese boxer…"

"She's from London," I said. "I probably know her mother."

"… a girl in a massage parlour and a Bangkok jeweller," Sam finished. "Have I missed anyone?"

"Not that I can think of," I said. "Who's the tail?"

Sam laughed. "He likes peacock blue – we call him Alfie."

"But he was easy to spot," I complained.

"Yes," Sam agreed. "But the others weren't."

Another point to the man in the khaki uniform. To make a little space, I eased myself forward in the chair and flexed my shoulders. It had been a long day and I was tired. Right now, that padded cell was beginning to whisper to me. "Why were you following me?" I asked him.

"You were beginning to interest me, David," he said. "From being little more than a Singha-drinking friend of Miss Chelsea, you suddenly became Mr Villavito's very best buddy."

"It wasn't intentional," I said. "Anni works there – Chelsea is my girl – and we were celebrating her birthday."

"You booked in to his hotel," Sam observed.

I could see where this was leading – but I couldn't see any benefit in telling him it had been Chelsea's idea. So skipped over that and carried on with my *Anni-and-the-Party* story. "And because Anni was busy, he carried the beers to our table and introduced himself."

"How very convenient..."

"Then he showed me his diamonds," I said.

"The stones that disappeared with Anni?"

"As far as we know," I confirmed.

"And you offered to recover them?"

"For ten percent of their value," I said.

"What about Anni?"

"He wants her, too," I said.

Sam made a note on his desk pad. "And will you deliver her?"

"Not if I can help it," I said.

Sam sat back in his chair and rocked it from side to side. "What about the diamonds?"

Good question! "Let's just wait and see!" I grinned.

Sam shook his head in mock sorrow. "When we fish you out of a canal," he asked me, "do you want to be cremated or repatriated?"

"Just park me in the corner of my favourite bar and let the Singha breathe me back to life!"

Sam just shook his head again. Then shuffled his papers back into order. "Villavito," he said. "When are you hoping to see him again?"

I checked my watch. It was close to one o'clock – and well past my bedtime. "Later this morning, he wants to take me to Om Noi," I told him. "It's your call." After all, he had the cell keys.

"Yes, it is," Sam told me.

"I'm in your hands," I said.

"Yes, David – you are in my hands." For a moment, Sam gazed up at the ceiling as if planning a strategy. "Let me put your little ducks in a nice straight line...."

I had to smile. "Good English," I said. "Where did you learn it?"

"At St Andrews," Sam replied. "Where I studied girls and golf – and did a little medicine in my spare time."

"Nothing like a good education," I said.

"My father was of the same opinion," Sam agreed. "But that doesn't help us with my immediate problem."

Duckie line-up time. "Which is?"

"Your involvement with Villavito."

"It seemed like an easy way to cover my expenses," I began.

Sam picked up a pen and started making notes. "Go on."

"As you can see from the ring, I want to get serious with Chelsea – but she's expensive."

"*Thailand Honey?*" Sam smiled. "But you love her....?"

"Probably," I confessed, "We'd almost got to the *how-about-it* speech, when Anni went missing."

"Then you volunteered to find her...." Sam finished it for me.

"You got it," I agreed. "If I could find Anni and those bloody diamonds, the forty-K would just about pay for everything."

Sam leaned forward, put his elbows on the desk and looked me in the eye. "Consider this," he said. "Chelsea could have set you up."

Ouch! "For what reason?" I asked.

Sam paused for a second or two to frame his answer. Then he changed tack. "In your recent travels around our beautiful city," he began, "has anyone mentioned *trekking?*"

"Sounds like hard work," I tried. "What is it?"

"It's how they smuggle diamonds from Laos," Sam explained. "It starts from a Country-&-Western bar near the border."

"What's that got to do with me and Chelsea?"

Sam was in full flow. "They run a hands-off operation," he told me. "They only touch the stones at the start and finish of a run."

Intriguing. "How do they operate?"

"Freely and with impunity," Sam replied.

"And where does Villavito fit into the picture?"

"He's the artist," Sam explained. "He finishes the canvas."

"And who provides the paint?"

"A number of South Africans," Sam revealed. "They organise the *trekking* run and Villavito finds the outlets."

"Why not pick them up and deport them?" It seemed a simple way to solve the problem.

"Because they are clever."

"In what way?"

"They use couriers," Sam explained. "First, the diamonds are delivered to contacts along the border – and then his mules trek them into Bangkok."

"Why can't you stop them?" It seemed a simple question.

"Because he never uses the same courier twice," Sam explained. Then he stopped, mid-thought. "Forgive me," he smiled. "Can I get you a drink?"

"Water would be nice," I thanked him.

"Good idea," Sam agreed and used his phone to send the order. Fifteen seconds later, I was sipping ice-cold bottled water through a straw.

"So who are these couriers?" I asked.

"Back-packers in need of drug-money," Sam told me.

"How does he find them?"

"Sure you want to know?"

I could see it coming – but I couldn't stop it. "Chelsea?"

"Through her travel shop," he said. "European kids on holiday – run out of money – she sends them along to our good friend, Raphael."

"Not good news," I said quietly. "Is she is in trouble?"

"Just about as much as you are, Mr David," he smiled. "But in a different way."

"How come?"

Sam eased back in his chair and stretched himself – then he folded his arms and stared at me across his desk. "Who introduced you to Mr Villavito?"

Oh shit! "You think I'm next in line?"

Sam leaned forward and fixed me with his black-eyed stare. "I'm sure it isn't personal," he said. "She's only trying to save her sister."

As the words hit home, I could only see two options: (a) to run like a frightened rabbit for the airport – or (b) play the Sir Galahad role and rescue the Big Sister from the Villavito dragon. And being Mr No-Brains, I chose the one most likely to cause me bother.

"Is it possible to dig her out?" I asked.

"It all depends on you, David," Sam said. "Provided Chelsea hasn't already delivered a victim for June, I'm fairly sure that Villavito will take you on as a courier."

"Oh Christ!" I said. My one-way trip to the canal was getting closer by the second. "Then what?"

"We can arrest him when you deliver the consignment."

"Why not nail him now?"

"I need to catch him with his nose in the trough - as you English like to say." Sam reshuffled some of his paperwork. "Remember, he never touches anything in transit."

"So how does he keep out of trouble?" I asked.

"He has a number of influential friends," Sam reminded me.

Fair enough. Villavito likes to mix it with the suits. "You mean he pays them off..."

"I never said that, David."

"But you're not denying it."

"And I'm not denying that I like my job," Sam said quietly.

I thought it over for a second. There was no point in asking if I had a choice. "If I agree?"

"You and Chelsea can live happily ever after!" he laughed.

"You believe in fairy tales?"

"I believe you can keep her out of the *Bangkok Hilton*," he said.

That made it easier to answer. "What's the plan?"

Sam didn't answer. Instead, he picked up my camera. "Is Canon an expensive item?" he asked.

"They cost enough," I said.

"But not the most...?"

"God no!" I said. "But I can't afford a Nikon."

Sam turned the camera in his hands, pushed the right buttons and displayed the last photo. "And who is this?" and he handed me the camera.

It showed a girl in a white T-shirt with the *Laughin' Pussy* logo. "It's Anni," I said. "She was on her way to meet us."

"Did your mugger try to steal the camera?" Sam leaned back and stared at me. "Or was he there to see if she was still alive?"

Good question. "Can't you ask him?"

"He's Burmese," Sam explained. "He won't speak Thai."

"Want me to smack him again?"

"No thank you, David – not in my police station." Then he stood up, walked around the desk and asked me: "Can you reach Anni?"

"If she needs me, she can find me," I said. Did he know about the *Let-Me-Love-U* website? Was he aware that we had a cell phone link? If he did, he kept it to himself.

He gave me back my phone. "Call me - anytime," he said and gave me a number.

"Alfie?" I asked, adding Sam to my list of *special friends*. "Could we have a change of colour from the peacock blue?"

"I will ask him," Sam smiled. "Now – I believe you have booked a room in Rambuttri?"

"Correct," I agreed. Why argue? He seemed to know, anyway.

"Go there – meet Raphael tomorrow – and enjoy the boxing," he said. "Just keep in touch."

"What about Chelsea?"

"Alfie will watch her," Sam promised.

"What about me?"

"Play each ball as it lies, Mr Shannon!" he grinned.

If only he'd stuck to medicine....

15

Sam repacked my bag and gave me my camera.

"What about the mugger?" I asked him.

"Not your concern," Sam replied. "Now let's find Miss Chelsea," and he opened the door and took me back to the grey-walled interview room – where she was waiting for me.

"OK?" I asked her.

"Nice way you treat girlfriend!"

"Wasn't what I had in mind," I said. "What now?"

"I go home – you go bed – be at shop for ten."

I checked my watch. It was almost two o'clock as we walked away from the Bangrak Police Station. "No problem," I said and waved at a passing taxi. (*It's one of the plus-points – in Bangkok, you can always get a taxi, any time, day or night….*)

"I drop you first," said Chelsea. "Two hundred baht….?" She held out her hand to take the fare money.

"How far are you going?" I asked.

"I Big Sister," she reminded me. "Family need breakfast."

Next morning, I was up at a reasonable time – organised a coffee, cleared my room and settled my bill with Lucille.

"Problems back home," I told her.

"You come again?" She hadn't heard about Bangrak.

"I will."

Then I used a tuk-tuk to take me and my kit to Si Phraya – and caught the express ferry to Phra Arkit. It gave me thinking time.

Where were we? Lieutenant Samran had me by the balls. He knew about Chelsea, he knew about Anni – and what he had yet to learn about me wouldn't take long. Now we had a minder. Sodding little Alfie…

It gave me an idea. I pulled out my cell phone and called Viv. Even though it was still early morning in Amsterdam, she answered within three rings. "Hello, big boy!" she squealed. "Has she dumped you yet?"

"No, my little lipstick-lesbo – not so far."

"No taste!" Viv laughed. "She needs talking to."

"And you're the one to do it!"

"Is she open to offers?"

"No, my sweetheart, she isn't – but I am."

Viv changed from *frivolous* to *serious*. "Who's nicked your nuts?"

"Too long for cell phone chat," I said. "Need backup."

"All expenses?"

"Cash on arrival – and I'll book you in."

"Bell you when I get a flight," Viv promised.

Although it's not all that far from Phra Arkit to Rambuttri, I was feeling the heat by the time I reached the travel shop.

This morning, Chelsea was wearing a brand new pair of jeans and a bright yellow shirt. "Why you not use taxi?" she wanted to know.

I didn't have the breath to give her an answer.

Chelsea just laughed at my stupidity and spoke to the girl behind the hotel's *Reception* window. There was a fair amount of girlie giggling – then I was given a key.

"You lucky," Chelsea told me. "Room not used for long."

"I'll try not to think about it," I said. Then this cute little boy grabbed a bag in each hand and sprinted up the stairs.

"You give him twenty baht!" Chelsea called after me.

Room 302 was backpacker-friendly: a large bed, TV, a wardrobe and a shower zone, complete with a flush toilet. The water was warm and the towels were fluffy.

As an added feature, the room had a balcony that overlooked the street. From here, I could watch the tourists and the taxi drivers – and see what everyone down on the patio was having for breakfast. Fruit seemed popular – as were omelettes. And almost everyone was having coffee.

Fifteen minutes later, I was in full working order. Life was wonderful again – and it was only half-past nine.

"You want espresso?"

"Why not?"

"You sit," and she waved me away from her door and into the patio of breakfast tables. "Hotel get it – now you guest."

To keep her happy, I sat at a street-side table and watched the tourists wandering along Rambuttri and being hustled by the taxi drivers:

"Anywhere you like – fifty baht!"

"See all temples – forty baht!"

"Want good shopping?"

"Thank you, no - I just want peace and quite." I spent the next few minutes trying to connect with Anni through my laptop. *BoxerGirl* was still on the *Let_Me_Love_U* website – but would she ever come out of hiding again?

Hello, BoxerGirl – if you fancy a bowl of milk, call me - BoxerBoy.

Villavito arrived, very slowly, easing his big white Mercedes through the meandering crowds until he stopped in front of the hotel, opposite a large red lorry that was delivering crates of Coca-Cola.

"Good morning, David!" he smiled. "Are we ready?"

Already, some optimist was honking a car horn.

"One minute," I said - closed down my laptop, stuffed my cell phone into my backpack and ran up the steps to the shop. "*Chelsea…!*"

"What you want?" She was in her doorway, waiting for me.

"Stick this in your safe?" I asked.

"You get Anni?"

"Not yet," I said, "but I'm sure she'll answer." I watched her squeeze my laptop into her safety box and close the drawer.

"We ready?" she asked.

"Are you coming with us?" I asked her.

Villavito was in the doorway, right behind me. "Of course Chelsea is coming!" he grinned. "This is my special treat…!" and he waited while she closed her office door and knelt down to snick the ground-level lock.

Ten minutes later, we were out of the city streets, had crossed the Pinklao Bridge and were heading into the country. I was in front with Raphael. Chelsea was in the back, stretched out and making merry with her cell phone. She had made herself responsible for my backpack and had it tucked under her knees. Bloody lucky Mr Backpack!

In between two calls, she leant forward and offered me a bottle of water. "You need," she said.

"Thanks," I smiled. Even though the Merc was air-conditioned, the icy-cold drink was welcome in that glaring sunlight.

"You have been this way?" Villavito asked me.

We were driving through plantations of banana trees and giant palms. Along the way, any number of roadside stalls were selling water melons, coconuts or bananas. "How many does he need to sell each day?" I asked.

"If he clears one hundred baht, he'll be OK," Villavito told me.

"Tough way to make a living."

"Up at daybreak, picks his crop – then sits by the road till night."

The perfect one-man business, I thought. *Making and selling from a deckchair by the highway.* "Where are we heading?" I asked.

"Towards Damrong," Villavito explained, then changed the subject. "But what about Anni?"

We passed a giant billboard for *Shrek 3*. "She's still alive," I said. Keep it simple. Villavito probably knew more than we did.

He eased the white Mercedes round an orange taxi. A sign on its rear window said: *I love farangs*. "How do you know?"

"We had a date," I said. "But the police got in the way."

He didn't seem surprised. "What went wrong?"

At least it was an easy story. "Some kid tried to nick my camera," I said. "So I smacked him."

"And you got arrested."

"As he hit the ground."

Villavito smiled. "Was it the Tourist Police?"

"Couldn't say," I said. "Uniforms, revolvers - like any other cops."

Villavito was quiet for a moment. "What happened?"

"They let me go," I said. How much did he know?

He slowed to let a bus to pull out in front of us. "A final warning?"

"Once more and I'll be off the turf for life." I glanced behind, but Chelsea was still busy with her cell phone. Better if only one of us was telling porkies.

"Any conditions?"

"Stop smacking people," I said.

"You can do that?"

"Unless provoked," I told him.

The *Siam Boxing Stadium* was a long low building, covered with flags and adverts, mainly for *Shell Rimula*. In the shade of a veranda, Villavito's customers jostled round fast-fry kitchens, the cola stalls and the lottery-displays, stocking up on food and drink or hunting for the magic ticket that would change their life forever.

"We park over here," Villavito told us. I should have guessed: he had a space reserved in this neat little alcove up in the stadium wall. At the end of the event, his car would *not* be baking hot.

I looked at Chelsea for an explanation.

"Mr Superman," she whispered. "He make big show."

"Let us not waste time," Villavito called, but before we could enter the Siam Boxing Stadium, we had to wait for him to check the boards of lottery tickets for his own lucky numbers.

Chelsea passed the time by making cell phone calls. I just stood around, taking a few pictures.

A few yards away, this pretty little girl was selling cans of Pepsi from an icebox. But as I snapped her, someone tapped my shoulder. He was rather large – and he wasn't smiling.

"Nice to meet you!" I said.

"I father – she daughter."

No problem, chief – I'd rather have a Singha. So I pointed at Chelsea. "She my girlfriend," I said.

He smiled and shook my hand quite vigorously. "My girl more beautiful than yours," he said.

Not the time to argue. "Absolutely right," I agreed. "But not a word to her - OK?" and I jerked a thumb in Chelsea's direction.

Daddy shook my hand again. "She here every week," he smiled.

It was better than an invitation to a massage parlour. Not every father has invited me to date his daughter. "See you again," I promised and hurried after Chelsea.

"Who he?" She was watching Raphael as he fingered his way through the racks of tickets for the winning number.

"He wants me to marry his daughter."

Chelsea laughed and jabbed my ribs with her elbow. "Poor girl!" she said. "Maybe she cost a lot to keep..."

By now, Villavito had made his choice, picked his tickets and paid the seller. From this point on, he only had to wait for the money. "Let us go," he called and showed us into the main arena.

Inside, the hall was lit by floodlights over the ring and decorated by even more adverts for *Shell Rimula*. The ring itself was a standard four-rope set-up with the active corners marked with red and blue logos for *Isuzu*. Along our side, there were tables and chairs for the judges and timekeepers.

On a narrow balcony over the main entrance, four TV cameras waited to cover the action. Then I heard the noise! It came from all around me, mostly from the darkness: high-pitched voices, calling, shouting and laughing.

Villavito led us up a small set of wooden steps and on to a platform. Here, two rows of padded armchairs were ready for the VIPs.

Then I realised just how important he was. As we made our way towards our seats, Villavito was surrounded by men in suits, men in training gear, attractive women – all wanting to speak with him, be introduced to him or just be photographed beside him. But to be fair, he didn't hog it all to himself.

"This is Mr Shannon," he would say. "My friend from London." He also brought Chelsea into the limelight. "And his very beautiful fiancée…!"

I'm not sure how Chelsea felt about being described as a fiancée, but she smiled graciously, shook hands where necessary and played her role as if this happened every day.

When the crowd of well-wishers had melted back into the darkness, Villavito invited us to sit and ordered coffee from someone in a yellow shirt.

As my eyes got used to the contrast between the darkness of the background and the glare for the ring, I began to focus on the crowd. Partly, I was looking for anyone in peacock blue. But as Alfie should have changed his shirt by now, there was little chance of finding him.

There were five or six rows of benches, raked towards the ceiling. As they began to fill, so the glare of the arc-lights bounced back from the whites, yellows, blues and reds of the shirts in the crowd. As the rows filled up, so the level of the noise increased.

"Only warming up!" said Villavito. "Wait till they start betting!"

To my right, the TV people had their commentary position. A grey-haired man in an expensive suit was telling his audience about the wonderful entertainment on the program.

"Six fights," Villavito told me. "World-wide audience!"

Judging by the excitement being generated by the TV presenter on my right, Raphael seemed to have a point.

"Big sport!" Villavito went on. "Very popular…" but stopped mid-sentence to speak to this tall, thin white guy who was wearing nicely-tailored light-brown slacks and a dark-green shirt.

"Who he?" Chelsea asked. She had given up on her cell phone. It was getting far too noisy for any in-depth girlie-girlie conversations.

"No idea," I said - but it didn't take long to get an answer.

"David," Villavito cut in. "Allow me to introduce Rudi Schiller – he is a South African."

A red light flashed across my brain. I stood up and shook his hand. "Good to meet you, Rudi," I said – then introduced Chelsea. "My fiancée," I said.

And by the way she smiled so sweetly, I guessed that Chelsea was willing to stick to the cover story that Villavito had invented.

Rudi smiled at Chelsea. "This is my Bella -" and stood back proudly to let us gaze in admiration at this gorgeous creature in a shining silver dress. She was tall, slim – and flaunted an imaginative cleavage.

"She will present the trophies," said Villavito.

Rudi and Bella took the two vacant seats on the other side of Villavito. When the coffee arrived, I took the chance to try to find out who he was. "Is Rudi involved in this event?" I asked.

By now, the first two boxers were in the ring and going through the *Wai Khru Ram Muay* - the pre-fight ritual where they prayed to their ancestors and offered respect to their opponents.

Villavito smiled. "No!" he said. "He's on my staff."

"Lucky Rudi," I smiled back.

"He's a trekker," said Villavito. "Next week, it's Yasu Thon."

Another warning flash, but I kept quiet. "Where's that?"

"Out east – towards Laos."

When the *Wai Khru Ram Muay* had been completed, the fighters returned to their corners and hung their *Mongkon* headbands on the post. A bell rang out, the boxers came together, bowed – and then began to circle each other. They wore boxing gloves and ankle bandages. One was wearing blue shorts – and the other was in red. Punches were thrown and kicks were aimed. Leather smacked on flesh and bones seemed to crack against each other.

"Must hurt to kick with bare feet," I said.

"Not if you get it right," said Rudi.

I tried to get a second look at Bella, but she had turned away from me and I couldn't see her face. She would have to wait until the interval.

As the boxers began to exchange more kicks and punches, so the noise from the crowd got louder and louder. People were shrieking and waving their arms as they tried to catch the eye of their bookie.

In front of our platform, a girl in a skin-tight vest was jumping up and down and yelling at the top of her voice.

"She's betting for my guests," Villavito told me. "Important people can't be seen to gamble, so she does it for them."

"For commission?"

"Maybe ten percent," he replied.

"Nice little earner," I said.

Then a bell rang out, the round came to an end and both boxers retired to their corners to be washed-down and encouraged by their trainers. As the boxers sat on their stools, so the crowd noise died - only to be replaced by the gentle, rhythmic chanting of a three-piece band from the benches on the left of our platform.

"Would you like another nice little earner?" Villavito asked me.

It was all so calm and matter-of-fact that I almost missed what he was on about. "You know me," I grinned. "Always on the look-out."

Raphael gave me a bit of a knowing smile. "That is good," he said. "We talk later - I may have something for you."

I let it ride and just sat back and watched the boxing. It was fast, furious – and extremely skilful.

"Having fun?" It was Rudi. He was standing behind me and leaning on the back of my chair.

"First time," said. "Fascinating."

"How long are you here for?" he asked.

"No specific plans," I said. "Depends on Chelsea."

Now the second break was over and the boxers were back in the middle of the ring. On the referee's command, the fight resumed. Both squared up, one man flashed a head-high kick – and the other hit the canvas like a bale of hay. And that was it – game over.

On impulse, I clicked a shot of the trainers and medics who were swarming around the fallen fighter. "Wowee…!" I smiled.

"That's how it goes," said Rudi. "All action in a Villavito fight!"

"Nice one, Raphael!" I said.

"He has promise," Villavito agreed. "He's earned his belt," and he moved away to help Bella into the ring for the presentation.

Seconds passed – the fallen fighter came back to this world and was helped to his feet. Both fighters hugged each other and stood together for the presentation. As the MC introduced the winner, so Bella slipped the belt around the young boy's waist - then he and Bella were hurried out of the ring to be interviewed beneath an enormous *Shell Rimula* banner for television.

"And she is…?" I asked Rudi.

"TV star," he smiled. "Presents a game show."

"Fair enough," I said – and took a picture of her as well.

Chelsea noticed, and was not happy about it. "Want you sleep with her?" she asked.

Jesus Wept! I don't want to *sleep* with her – or *screw* her - or *fuck* her. But will you ever believe me? "No, my little kitten," I began, "if I can't have you, I don't want anyone." As a remark, it should have got me off the hook. But it only dropped me even deeper in the shit.

16

There were five more contests, each in the same format – but with no more spectacular knock-outs. The one remaining memory came in Bout 6 – a junior contest – when the mother of a boxer climbed on to the ropes and yelled a stream of abuse at her pride and joy.

After that, it was a matter of handshakes, farewells and a slow amble through the crowd and back into the glaring sunshine. Thanks to Villavito's private parking arrangements, the big white Merc was delightfully cool.

"Where next?" I asked as we reached the car.

"Lunch for everyone?" Villavito asked

Chelsea answered for me. "Yes please," she said.

"First, we must visit the temple," Villavito told us.

I wanted to ask him *Why?* After all, I come from a background that believes in *Food First* and *God-bothering Later.* But who am I to judge? My agnostic backside won't leave a mark on anybody's pew.

"We will all ride together." It was more of a command than an invitation.

So, following the belief that the host is always right, I smiled at the prospect of another temple and settled in with Chelsea in the back of the Merc to make the most of it.

Rudi went in front with Villavito and Bella eased herself on the other side of Chelsea.

However, the *Wat Raiking* experience was quite enjoyable. Being one of the more in-fashion temples, it was crowded for a Saturday. There must have been hundreds - all milling around, lighting candles or praying to one or other of the Buddha images.

The temple was large and white and set on a marble plinth – *and* it had plenty of parking spaces. Sad to say, none were under cover.

In front of the temple, a green canvas awning covered the temple forecourt. Beneath it, stalls were selling little yellow candles, joss-sticks, lotus buds and smalls strips of gold leaf that answer prayers. Villavito bought enough for everyone.

"Now Chelsea can show us how to use them," he decided.

Chelsea played her part without fuss. First, she kicked off her sandals. "Now you," she said. She was beginning to enjoy herself.

After we had removed our shoes, she led us over to this small black metal frame that was already holding about thirty burning candles. She made a *wai,* then lit her candle from a nearby lantern and dripped its wax into the metal frame. When her pool of melted wax was big enough, she placed her candle in the frame – and made another *wai.* "Now you," she ordered.

Villavito, Rudi and Bella did as they were told – and I followed.

Then she held her joss-stick in the lantern flame until it started to glow – and kept it glowing by breathing gently on the red-hot tip. Once it was properly alight, she placed it in an earthenware pot of sand that was on a table in front of one of the Buddha images.

We all did the same.

From there, she moved to the Buddha image and placed her lotus bud at its feet. "Now you," she said again – and we did as we were told.

Last of all, she peeled her gold leaf strip from its protective tissue and carefully applied it to the Buddha's chest. "For love," she whispered as she smiled at me.

So I placed my gold leaf token right next to hers. "Let's hope it works," I whispered back.

No-one seemed concerned that three *farangs* were paying homage to Buddha. So long as we showed respect and behaved ourselves, they ignored us.

"You old smoothie!" said Rudi who'd been watching us.

"Her game – her rules," I replied, and took out my camera.

"You into photography?" he asked.

"Can be useful," I said.

"Do you publish?"

"Sometimes," I said. "I write for magazines," and snapped off half-a-dozen shots of candles, joss-sticks and Buddha images that were covered in little strips of golf leaf.

"Yasu Thon could be interesting for you," Rudi suggested.

"What's up there?"

"Farms – temples – adobe villages," he told me.

And diamonds? "When are you going?" I asked.

"Tuesday – maybe Wednesday."

I needed time to think – and my cell phone came to the rescue. It was Nixie. "Hi, kiddo," I said. (*It was none of Rudi's business, was it?*) "What's doing?"

"You find her yet?"

"Kind of you to ask," I said, giving nothing away. "Had an e-mail from my cousin only last night – sends you her love!"

But Nixie didn't get it. "Say hello from me," she answered and the line went dead.

"Bad news?" Rudi wanted to know.

"Not at all," I said. "My cousin is backpacking somewhere in the Philippines and hasn't checked-in for a week. My aunt's having kittens!" OK, it was a porkie – but if it kept him off my back, all well and good.

"But now you've found her?"

"So it would appear," I said. "Now tell me about Yasu."

He did, chapter and bloody verse. It went on and on and on, right the way round the arcade, in front of every Buddha figure and all the way along the *Table of the Million Pots* – where (once again) we were invited to spread our wealth to the four corners of Thailand.

"One hundred pots will buy you a virgin in Nirvana!" said Rudi.

"You made that up," I complained.

"Drop your dollars and prove me wrong!" and he sauntered along the table, scattering his coins at random.

Across the table from me was this cute little Chinese girl – so I nodded in her direction. "If it's true, I want that one," and I joined the South African in the virgin hunt.

"Then I want to one with the *Doraemon*," he replied and waved towards this gorgeous Thai girl who was wearing a blue and white T-shirt decorated with the well-known bug-eyed, sky-blue cartoon cat from Japan.

"She'll scratch in bed!" I warned him.

"Wonderful!" laughed Rudi and went on filling pots until he ran out of coins. Then he stopped and turned to face me. "Are you coming?"

"I'd like to," I said. "Let me clear it with Chelsea." What I really meant was *Let me run it by Sam*. But I couldn't make the call while Villavito was beside us.

"You boys having fun?" he asked.

"We are indeed," I said. We've just signed-up a couple of virgins for our first night in Paradise."

"Do as I ask and you can have all the virgins you want," Villavito smiled coldly. "Now let's find Chelsea and Bella."

We found them in the main temple, a long narrow building with a high roof and a magnificent altar decorated with the most amazing flowers. On top of the altar, a giant golden Buddha in an orange sash offered peace and goodwill. A dozen or so people were kneeling on the red carpet and saying prayers.

As usual, Chelsea was using her cell phone. Was this another cultural difference? Back home, they're barred on a golf course, but wee squirrel seemed to be OK with using hers on the *Holy Ground* of Thailand.

"Come here, darling!" she called. "Let us learn your fortune…"

Now I'm not one for lucky numbers, fortune cookies or horoscopes. Shit happens – and when it drops all over your shiny leather dancing shoes, there's nothing you can do about it. So why bother looking for doom-&-gloom predictions in the *Daily Mirror* every morning? However, when Chelsea calls, I tend to listen.

"Yes, my kitten?"

She was holding a wooden tube – like a pencil case. It was about eight inches tall and two in diameter, painted red with golden symbols and contained fifteen strips of bamboo.

"Kneel down," she said and gave me the tube. "Shake one out."

I shook the tube until I had teased one strip to the tumbling point – then let it fall. It had a number.

"Eleven!" Chelsea cried. "That's *very* lucky!"

I felt it might be.

"Come," she said and caught my arm to pull me up. "Now we find out what it means…" and she lead me over to a table where pre-printed sheets of prophesies were in neat little piles, all waiting to be read.

I picked up the sheet marked 11. It was in Thai. "Please?" I asked.

Chelsea studied it with great deliberation. "Is good," she said quietly. "You could be lucky…. "

"Go on," I smiled. "When's the wedding day?"

"You still not give me ring," she reminded me.

"Want it now?" and I reached into my travel bag.

"No," she said. "Later – this more serious."

"OK," I agreed, "what does it say?"

"That the girl you seek will find you." And she folded the sheet of paper and stuffed it into her handbag.

"I've told you – if I can't……" but she cut me short.

"Not me – it Anni!" Chelsea laughed back at me.

Before I could reason with her, my cell phone went off. "Yes?" I said in a near whisper. It just didn't seem right to be phoning so close to a giant golden Buddha, even one dressed in an *Orange* sash.

"David…" came a female voice.

"Anni?" I could hardly believe it.

But this time, Chelsea was too quick for me - and she snatched the phone clean out of my hand.

"ANNI!" she yelled – and then broke into to stream of rapid Thai. Eventually, she gave me back my phone. "We meet her tomorrow in Pattaya," she told me. "I rent a bus."

"Why do we need a bus?"

"Because Nolli come too – and she bring her children."

Now who could argue with that?

By now, we were out of the temple complex, had regained our footwear and were walking back to the big white Mercedes. "Where next?" I asked Villavito.

"I think we go for lunch," Raphael decided.

Why not? It was coming up to three o'clock – which made it far too many hours since breakfast at the Four Sons. "How about you?" I asked Chelsea.

"Where you take us?" she asked Villavito.

"Talad Klongsaun," he said.

"Recommended by the *Diner's Club*?" I asked.

"An excellent river-side buffet!" Villavito assured me.

Since the hurried conversation with her sister, Chelsea had hardly said a word to me. Instead, she'd been phoning round, booking buses and chatting to Nolli.

"Is that it?" I asked her. "All aboard for Pattaya?"

"If you paying, yes…!" she smiled.

"Anything you fancy, squirrel," I smiled back.

Once again, Bella eased her delicate little body in beside Chelsea – and Rudi rode shotgun up front with his boss.

Up till that moment, I hadn't realised that Villavito had been taking quite such an interest in our domestic chit-chat. "Who is going to Pattaya?" he wanted to know.

Too late now - the fox was in the chicken run. "We are," I said. "Ages ago, I promised that we'd take Nolli's kids to the seaside."

"How nice!" Villavito smiled. "How many has she got?"

"At the last count, six," I told him. "But I haven't seen her for a couple of days."

"What about Anni?" he asked.

"When she's ready, she will call me," I said – then wondered how many penalty-points I'd get for telling porkies in a temple forecourt…

Too late now. When my turn comes, I'd book myself in to the Pearly-Gate interview with a bus-load of lawyers. Otherwise, *Fat Chance*, as they say. But for now, it was enough to satisfy Villavito.

From *Wat Raiking*, Raphael drove us through a succession of villages - little more than single rows of small, square houses. Simple, yes - but each community had built its own beautifully-decorated temple.

The villages were quiet. Here and there, a man or woman had a makeshift stall, selling watermelons or coconuts. Now and then, we came across a family sitting in the shade of a veranda. Back home, there would have been a radio station for sport or one of the pop-music channels. Here, they seemed to prefer the silence. And don't forget the old black dog… lying dormant in a shady corner, sleeping through the heat of the afternoon.

"This will do," Villavito announced and swung the car off the road and into a busy car park. Here, we discovered where all the villagers had got to. There were hundreds of them – swarming all round the stalls.

"Let's hope they've had their lunch!" Rudi joked.

Chelsea turned whispered: "Always room for Mr Raphael!"

"Or everyone gets tossed in the river," I whispered back.

"Hope you are all hungry…" and Villavito parked between two large Toyota 4x4's.

The first few stalls were devoted to a rainbow of T-shirts, cheap-&-chunky watches and some gaudy little plastic Buddha images. "Go on," I said to Chelsea as she stopped to check the watches. "Enjoy yourself."

Not that she needed another watch, of course. She already had two that I knew of - one from Amsterdam and one from Patpong. But I had to call Lieutenant Sam.

I searched for his number and clicked the [Call] button. Sam's phone sang three bars of a cute little song – and then he answered.

"They want me to go to Yasu Thon," I said.

"When?"

"Soon," I said. "Tuesday or Wednesday….."

Sam paused for a second. "Be very, very careful," he warned me.

"Why – what's up?"

"Remember your Chinese boxer?"

"The lovely Kalli? - what about her?"

"She was attacked." he said.

Oh Jesus Christ All-bloody-mighty! "When? - where?"

"Last night - Klongsam ferry – *Yok Yor* side."

"Was she hurt?"

"Not badly," Sam explained. "Alfie was right behind her."

Nice one! "Buy him a beer from me," I said. "Was it a robbery?"

"Tried to steal her handbag."

Then it struck me. "Why was Alfie watching her?"

"She's a friend of Anni." Then: "What did Kalli tell you?"

"How to trace Anni..."

"There's your answer," Sam decided. "We'll keep her safe for a day or two – don't worry."

"Try not to," I said – but it didn't make sense. "Why pick on her?"

"If Villavito can find Anni by himself, he won't have to pay your finders-fee," Sam explained.

Bloody obvious. "No-one's really safe..."

"Not even you," Sam laughed. "So be very, very careful."

I closed the call and stuffed my phone into a pocket. Chelsea was still knee-deep in the watches. "That's enough," I told her. I didn't really mean to scold her - but Sam's news had rattled me. "I said you could *look* – not *buy*."

She didn't understand. How could she? So she dug me in the ribs again and carried on towards the stalls with the *fruit-&-veg*. For this, we had to walk on duckboards. Heavy rain up-country had caused the Chao Phraya to flood and the market area itself was under some eighteen inches of water. We – the customers – were fine. We were way above the high-tide level - but the market people were standing knee-deep in river water. Not that it seemed to bother them. They seemed to be enjoying themselves.

We admired the giant grapefruit and the stacks of egg-plants, pomegranates, green and yellow mangoes, the greenish oranges and the bright red rambutans. Nor could we stop ourselves from enjoying the luxuriant display of purple orchids. On the pastry stall, the custard tarts were out of this world!

"Come along," Villavito called back. He was admiring the filleted carp on the fish stall. "Or we could have these," he said and pointed to a bowl of prawns the size of sparrows. A jet of water was keeping them alive and fresh.

"How are they served?" I had to ask.

"Like this," our host explained – and pointed to a small barbecue where the prawns were being roasted – while-you-wait, as it were.

OK, I know the poor little prawn has to die at some point between the river and the dining room - but not like that!

Chelsea read my mind. Very softly, she squeezed my hand. "Darling - if you like, we have them raw?"

I counted to ten. "No," I said, "cooked is good."

When we reached the café area, this little Thai girl showed us to this aluminium table. She was wearing a pink T-shirt with a Disney logo and sawn-off jeans. Her hair was short, suggesting early teens?

(In some parts of Thailand – *according to Euro-tourist gossip, that is* - the length of a girl's hair can tell you if she's sexually active. If short, leave well alone – but once it has passed her shoulders, she's ready for action. But I've never dared to ask Chelsea about it…)

The dining area itself was on a pontoon, reaching out into the slow-moving river. From time to time, clumps of weed and the occasional coconut drifted along with the current. Across the river, there was this rather attractive bungalow. It had a mass of white and purple flowers cascading from its flat roof.

I rather fancied living there. "Any crocodiles?" I asked.

Chelsea was beside me. Rudi and Bella were sitting opposite and Raphael had assumed head-of-table, with his back to the water.

"No," said Rudi. "Far too noisy - crocs like peace and quiet."

I would try to remember that… The child in the pink T-shirt brought us bottles of ice-cold water and Raphael ordered Pepsis, river prawns, barbecued fish and enough rice to feed the Chinese army.

"Rudi tells me that you want to go to Yasu Thon."

Before I could confirm or deny it, Chelsea got in first. "You want to go with *her*?" she hissed, aiming her remark at Bella.

(*Thinking back, I firmly believe that if she'd bought that wretched watch, it never would have happened. But it did – and now the shit was well and truly in the fan.*)

"No," I said. "I want to go with *him*," and I nodded at Rudi.

"Why you want to go?" Chelsea demanded. She was blowing steam and ready to explode. "You want fuck him too?"

"My darling," I tried, "I want to research the adobe village – I think it would make a good article for *National Geographic*." All bullshit, of course – and a total waste of effort.

"I think you rather fuck with her than come to Pattaya for Anni!"

And for the rest of that day, the sound that filled my nightmare was a cover story being shattered into a million shards of broken glass. "So what's it to be?" I said, trying to laugh it off. "Dick or diamonds?" But the damage had been done. Now Villavito knew about Anni.

17

For the journey back to Om Noi, I rode in front with Raphael, while Rudi and Bella sat with Chelsea. When we reached the boxing stadium, they swapped back to their own car and left the three of us to make the most of a rather difficult return to Bangkok.

"Don't look at me," I said to Villavito. "I don't bug her brain."

"Does she understand how serious this is?"

"Women!" I asked him. "Do they understand *anything*?" But no matter how hard I tried to reduce the cock-up to a sexist joke, I knew that we were in it – up to the balls and sinking fast.

So when Villavito offered to: "Say no more about it," I could see that we were in *serious* trouble.

Back in Rambuttri – outside the hotel - I smiled a *Thank You for a Lovely Day* to Raphael and turned around to look for Chelsea. Too late. She was already in the back of a taxi.

Well, stuff you, I thought and sat at a patio table and ordered a Singha. For the first time in ten hours or more, I would be able to enjoy a moment of total peace and quiet, sipping beer while sitting at a roadside table, watching the ladies of the evening, touting for custom. Then my cell phone rang.

It was Viv. "I'm booked for tonight," she said. "KLM 0877 – arriving after lunch tomorrow."

"You want to be met?"

"No need – just give me a name."

In case she picked-up someone on the plane and wanted to make the most of it, I guess. "Four Sons Village," I said. "I'll text the address."

"Cool," came her reply. "See you tomorrow."

Now, feeling better, I skipped up the steps to the Reception window and made a booking for Ms Vivienne Parker.

"Five hundred baht," the receptionist smiled.

Cheap at half the price. I returned to my table and sent the Soi Rambuttri address as a text message. (*When I think back to the days of so many losing battles with overseas phone boxes, I give heartfelt thanks to the guy who came up with the mobile cell phone.*) Just as I was about to give it a thank you kiss, it chirped again.

This time, it was Chelsea. "I sorry," she said. "I *hate* him!"

I could hear the taxi's radio in the background. "Dare I ask who?"

"Him – crazy man."

"Would that be Mr Villavito?"

"No make joke! Not funny!"

My Singha arrived. "I don't like him, either," I said.

"What you doing?"

"Drinking beer."

"You want dinner?"

"Eventually," I said.

"I get you at seven."

Two hours later, I was sitting by the Chao Phraya, in the *Sala Thai* restaurant, eating steak and chips in the company of the most beautiful girl in all Thailand.

18

After we'd worked our way through the initial apologies, we eased our way into a very gentle evening. It was comfortably warm, the river was alive with illuminated boats – and the graceful movements of Temple Dancers in their flamboyant costumes had softened the aggression from the *Muay Thai* fighters.

"I so sorry," Chelsea had said again.

"Couldn't be helped," I said. We were trying to decide if Chelsea's outburst at Talad Klongsaun would make life difficult for Anni. "We'll just have to ride it out," I said.

"What he do?" Chelsea asked.

"Not a lot," I said. "He still wants his diamonds back."

"You think she have them?"

Good question, little kitten. "When we find her, you can ask her."

At 8am next morning, I was on the hotel patio, working my way through a crab omelette when Chelsea arrived in a taxi. Up till then, it had been quiet - just six of us on the patio for breakfast, easing ourselves into another day. Then Chelsea arrived.

"You no forget pay bus?" she yelled.

I took a final swig at my coffee. "No, little kitten, I have the cash."

"Then get on hurry!" and she waved her phone. "Nolli waiting!"

Good-bye crab omelette. "Is she coming here?"

"No," Chelsea yelled back. "We go find her."

Our 15-seater bus was parked some fifty yards along Soi Rambuttri, outside the Bella Bella House. Chelsea went inside and found our driver, sitting with his mates and drinking tea.

"We go now," she told him. And we did.

She sat beside me and gave me two bottles of water. "You not forget drink," she warned me.

It was a comfortable ride. The bus had three rows of seats. On instructions from Chelsea,

I sat in the first row and she came in beside me. Then we drove round a couple of streets or so and collected Nolli and her six children - although the two older girls were well past the age of being classed as children. Bottles of water were passed round, sweets and crisps were handed out and as the sun began to warm up the bus, I closed my eyes and let the journey unfold.

"You OK?" Chelsea whispered.

"Couldn't be better," and I took her hand, gave it a gentle squeeze, held it up and kissed it. And on this particular Sunday morning, it was not a yellow card offence. "May I give you the ring?" I tried.

We were up on the expressway, heading south. On our left, I could see this row of pastel-coloured houses. It looked peaceful, somewhere nice to live and keep a dog.

"You think it change my luck?" she smiled.

"Must be worth a try," and I scrabbled in my travel bag for the small square box that everyone (except Chelsea) had opened, looked at and admired. "With my love," I said and gave it to her.

She opened the box and gazed at the neat little diamond. "Is beautiful!" and offered her cheek for a kiss - then swung round sharply to show it to Nolli. "See – I said he get one!"

"Wow!" and as Nolli leaned over the seat to get a better view, so the two older girls pushed forward to join in the fun.

"Go on," I said. "Put it on." I was hoping this would be the ultimate concession of her love - but I was out of luck. With practiced ease, Chelsea slipped it onto the middle finger of her left hand – then held it up to let everyone admire it.

"Thank you!" she smiled and invited me to kiss her again.

"You got one for me?" Nolli grinned.

"And one for each of your beautiful daughters!" I laughed.

Once in Pattaya, the streets became a non-stop message board for shop signs, bar signs and building adverts. *Simon's Fish & Chips* was there – along with the *Vivian Restaurant* and the unforgettable *Shagger Bar*. In the *Jomtien Plaza*, there were *Shophouses for Sale* in *Excellent Condition* and *Ready to Use*. Always nice to know.

There were new buildings everywhere: commercial sites for businesses, condos for the workers. Last of all, we found the *Dongtang Beach*.

We turned a corner – and the kids went wild…! It was picture postcard stuff. The sea was blue, the sand was yellow and the beach was a rainbow of multi-coloured parasols. All we had to do was find a place to park the bus. Not my problem. That's why we hired a driver.

"They not been ever," Chelsea explained.

"Then we'll give 'em one to remember," I said.

Eventually, we stopped by a sign for the *Poat Servic* and everyone got out. According to the well-worn lettering:

1. Jet Sky per ½ hour 650 bath

2. Banana Boat per ½ hour 600 bath

3. Parasel Boat per 1 Around 5 0 bath

4. Speedboat to K lanisland 85hp 200 bath

5. Speed oat to Kopedisl nd 85hp 3500 bath

6. Speedboat to Kolanisland 200hp 000 bath

No doubt the ticket office would supply all the missing letters and numbers in exchange for hard cash. But as it was all in English, the kids paid no attention and just rushed down onto the sand. Within seconds, they had taken over a square of deckchairs round a picnic table, stripped down to their swim wear and were romping in the water.

Nolli touched my arm. "Thank you," she smiled.

"Good to see the kids enjoying themselves," I said.

Chelsea waved me into a deckchair and bought Pepsis for everyone from some kid on the beach. That was the signal. From then on, hardly a minute went by without some hawker offering food, drink, clothing, toys, sunglasses or lottery tickets. At less-frequent intervals, we were also offered tattoos, massages or birds in bamboo cages. But to be fair, no-one tried to sell us a time-share. One up to Pattaya.

Out of interest, I checked the way the parasols had been secured. As one who had never managed to get a parasol to stand without yards of washing line and a handful of tent pegs, I was amused to notice that the Pattaya method used a solid metal spike. All they'd done was drive it into the sand and bind it to the pole with a length of parcel string. All too simple, really. All I'd needed was a good old-fashioned earthing spike…..

On the fast-food front, Chelsea ordered rice and deep-fried baby crabs, Nolli went for the barbecued fish with noodle soup – and the kids seemed happy with anything that came there way. And when a vendor ran out of stock, he fired-up a primus stove and cooked another batch of rice, fish, prawns or whatever, right there on the beach.

Then Chelsea started playing with her cell phone. "Anni coming," she smiled when I looked at her.

"Does she know where to find us?"

"I tell her – by sign for boats."

"That should help," I said. Now that we all had inter-cell phone contact, it would be easy enough to find each other. Chelsea's phone was glued to her ear and mine was in my pocket, with my wallet. (*Better there than getting lifted.*) Why argue? Chelsea was happy, Nolli was happy, the kids were happy - and I was happy, lying there in a deckchair, underneath a Barcelona-coloured parasol – and enjoying the total peace and relaxation of being fanned by a gentle breeze from the water.

Then it all exploded like a hand grenade...

"She coming!" Chelsea squealed with joy and pointed along the beach. There she was: a Chelsea mirror-image in her *Laughin' Pussy* logo T-shirt.

I stood up to greet her – then two large Thais jumped out from the line of parked cars, raced over the beach and tried to grab her.

"*Mai-mai-mai!!!*" Anni screamed.

"NO!" cried Chelsea.

Even Nolli started running forward.

On instinct, I grabbed at the nearest earth spike and tipped a parasol over a neighbouring picnic, spilling food, drinks and *God-Know-What* in all directions. Now *they* were also squealing in fits of panic.

It isn't easy running on sand – but I reached the flailing scrum of Anni and her muggers in about ten strides. Then I swung the spike to smack the larger guy with a forehand side-swipe, right across the shoulders.

"*Ahh*!" and he collapsed like he'd been shot. To keep him there, I stabbed the earth spike into the back of his thigh.

Next, I grabbed Anni – pulled her towards me - and broke the smaller guy's grip. As she came free, the momentum pulled him off balance – and I hit him fair and square, right in the mouth. He started yelling, and coughing and spewing blood from lips, nose and a couple of broken teeth. For the moment, we were winning.

"RUN!" I yelled, grabbed Anni's arm and dragged her up to the road. "Don't be scared!" I shouted back as I dragged her across to the other side. "I'm Dave – just keep going – Chelsea's right behind us!"

Bless her little heart, she did – all the way up to a soft-drink stand where we could pause for breath and check if we were being followed. But there was no sign of anyone – not even Chelsea.

Back along the beach where we'd been sitting, there seemed to be a right old scuffle in progress. I could see Nolli trying to pacify our former neighbours. Then the kids came out of the sea to join in the fun. But after that, it all went quiet. Where had Chelsea got to?

No time no time to worry about that. "Quick," I said to Anni, "let's get you out of those clothes."

"What you mean?"

"Now they know you, they could try again," I told her.

"OK."

So we made our way towards the tents and bunting of a mini-market, some four hundred yards away. We were almost there - and then my cell phone rang.

"David…" It was Villavito. His voice was like ice.

"What do you want?" I asked.

"I am with Chelsea."

"Lucky you," I said. I needed thinking time.

"Would you like to see her again?"

"It was always my intention," I said.

"You will go to Yasu Thon for me?"

I played for time. "What about Anni?"

Villavito didn't even pause for breath. "Keep her safe," he said. "Visit Yasu - and give me Anni when you return."

"And if I don't?" I tried.

Villavito paused for a second or two. "I have been admiring the ring on Chelsea's finger." His voice was low, controlled and deliberate. "Would you like it back – complete with her hand?"

This was like poker – and all this bluffing was beginning to annoy me. "Go fuck yourself," I said. "You are *not* Don Corleone and this is *not* New York."

"That is why I like you, David – you have the British humour."

"Then try this for a laugh," I warned him. "Hurt her - and I'll blow your head off!"

By now, we had shuffled out of site behind a soft-drinks stall, away from the road and out of sight. We'd be safe for a little while longer.

"David…" Villavito replied. "I never took you for a hard man."

Anni tapped my arm and made a drinking motion with her hand. I pulled out a 100-baht note from my pocket and made a V-sign.

"Coke or water?" she whispered.

"Water, please," I smiled. Then back to Villavito. "No Anni – and no diamonds," I told him. "Not until I see the money."

"Is that why you worry so much?" he almost laughed. "You think I won't pay you?"

"Cash up front," I said. At least he'd stopped threatening Chelsea.

"Just hand them over, David," he said. "You cannot sell them."

"Wouldn't even try!" I laughed. "I'd rather drop them in the sea."

No response.

"But leave Chelsea alone and you might get lucky."

He paused again. "You wish to speak with her?"

"Go on."

Another pause - then Chelsea's voice: "Darling...? Is Anni OK?"

At that moment, Anni returned with the drinks. Mine had a straw – so I made good use of it. "She's fine," I answered Chelsea's question. "Sam's looking out for her," I whispered, more or less to keep her happy. Sometimes, truth is like a gold bracelet – best kept out of sight.

"Men no hurt her?"

"No," I said. "What about you?"

"He no hurt me," she said. "He want Anni diamonds."

"OK," I agreed. "Put the bastard back on."

"He want you," I heard her say.

"Be sensible, David..."

"So don't piss about," I said. "My game – my diamonds."

"So what is your plan?"

"I'll call you tonight," I said and closed the call. Then I turned to Anni. "Have you *really* got these bloody diamonds?" I asked her.

"Is for police," she said. "To buy me free."

"For the moment, *I* am the police," I said. "Where are they?"

"In Kanchanaburi," Anni smiled. "Where you no find them."

We'll see about that, little squirrel. So I took her arm and led her into a little clothing shop in the mini-market. Somehow, we had to get her safely on our bus and out of Pattaya.

Then I remembered Nolli – and that gave me an idea. From the clothing racks, I found this cute yellow pinafore dress with a sad-eyed puppy on its bib. White socks and sandals would be enough to hide a rejuvenated Anni.

"I *not* wear that!" Anni protested.

"You will today," I smiled. "But we'll change them as soon as we get to Bangkok, I promise."

While she was in behind the curtain, changing her clothes, I called Lieutenant Sam. "We're in Pattaya," I said. "I have Anni – Villavito may have taken Chelsea – and we're in *deep-shit* country."

"Can you get to Bangkok?" Sam asked. "Or do I order the SAS?"

"We'll get there," I said.

"About an hour from the city, there's a rest station – like a market. I will meet you there. Call me before you leave."

"Will do," I promised.

Anni came out from the changing area. She looked remarkably child-like. "Perfect," I said. "The broker's men will never recognise you."

"What broker's men?"

"Old pantomime joke," I explained.

Carefully, we made our way back to our picnic site by walking through the endless lines of parasols. From some fifty yards away, I could see Nolli through the crowd. And it looked as though she had rounded up all her children.

In among them, wrapped in a dark red towel - Chelsea! When she saw us coming, she broke into a beaming smile, jumped up and started running along the beach towards us.

I got my shot in first. "Here's your missing daughter," I said loudly to Nolli. "Found her chatting-up a couple of lads at a bar up the road – now where's the bus?"

"Is waiting," said Chelsea and she threw her arms around my neck and kissed me. "Thank you save my Anni," she said. "But why she dress like baby?"

"So Villavito's men won't know her," I explained.

"Then we go?"

"Like rats up a drainpipe," I smiled.

"No understand you," Chelsea replied – but instead of arguing, she just got on with herding Norri's kids back on to the bus.

19

As our bus eased its way out of Pattaya, Anni crawled into the back with the two older girls and tried to hide her shame at being dressed as a ten-year old.

Somewhere between Pattaya and Chonburi, Chelsea leaned over and with Anni's help, told Nolli what had happened. I could hear them whispering away for over half an hour. And when Anni reached the part where the big boy got spiked, Nolli gave a gasp and looked at me with wide-open eyes.

My other problem was to tell the driver where to stop. But as I had even less success with him, I decided to watch the road, read the signs and look for a place with eats, drinks and toilets within 60kms of Bangkok.

As it happened, our driver had the same idea. It was like a service station but without fuel pumps. The toilets were immaculate and the shops were interesting. One sold nothing but dried fish, while another sold bottles of wood chippings.

"Make good whisky," Anni explained. "Fill with water."

"Want one?" I asked her. She seemed to be an expert.

"I get one for our mam," said Chelsea. "You have money?"

Don't I always?

Back on the sidewalk, I looked up and down the parking bays for Lieutenant Sam – but he saw me first.

"Villavito tried to get rough?" he began.

As we made our way along the sidewalk, I told Sam what had happened. "He threatened Chelsea – but I hung on to Anni," I said. He didn't ask me where I'd hidden Anni, Perhaps he already knew.

"Weren't they partners?"

He meant Chelsea and Villavito. "In bed or in business?"

"You tell me," Sam replied. "She's your woman!"

"Couldn't say," I said. "Never asked her."

"Perhaps you should."

"Is it part of the scam?"

"Not impossible," Sam decided. "She's no good as a hostage."

"Not even as leverage?"

"No," Sam decided. "Out here with you, she can report back."

"Hadn't seen it like that," I confessed.

"What about Anni - will you hand her over?"

"Not to him – and not to you, either," I said. "First, I need to get my hands on those diamonds."

While we were talking, Sam and I strolled casually along the line to the Coffee Shop. We checked the menu board.

"Cappuccino for me," I said. "And you?"

"Espresso."

While we drank the coffee, Sam asked about Yasu Thon. "When are you going?" he asked.

"It will come up soon enough," I said. "How do you feel about it?"

Sam didn't need much time to think. "It will be dangerous," he told me. "No courier has ever gone twice."

"Do they pay them off?"

"Yes - with concrete boots," Sam smiled. "But I have something that may help you swim," he went on and gave me this neat little shoulder bag, skilfully woven with royal-blue threads.

"A new style man-bag?" I asked.

"Holds more than your after-shave," Sam laughed.

The bag was heavy - and when I felt inside, my fingers closed around the wooden butt of an automatic pistol.

Sam read my face. "A 9mm Colt with two spare magazines – eight in each," he added. "You have used a handgun?"

"A 9mm Browning," I said.

"Any special tricks?"

"Aim for the balls to blow the head off," I told him.

"Sounds about right," Sam grinned. "But no witnesses – OK?"

"No witnesses, OK," I agreed and stuffed the Chelsea-blue shoulder bag into my backpack.

Then Anni walked in. "We look for you," she said. "Bus ready."

"One of Nolli's kids," I told Sam. "Isn't she a sweetheart?"

"So like her sister," Sam agreed.

"Sisters," I corrected him.

"Forgive me," and he gave Anni a smile of apology.

"Take good care of her," and he tapped my arm. "And call me."

"Will do," I promised.

It was close on 8pm before the bus dropped us at the Four Sons hotel in Soi Rambuttri. As I dragged my weary body up the steps to get my room key – there was Viv, all scrubbed and shiny, waiting for me on the hotel patio.

"How did you know?" I asked.

"Dolly up in the Reception told me where you'd gone," she said. "And I guessed you'd be home for bedtime."

"Mother's orders," I said.

Our Viv was still the same spiky-haired, bouncy-busted blonde. Tonight, she was wearing a silky pink vest. As usual, she wore no make-up – except for this amazing vermillion lipstick.

"And this is Chelsea?"

"It is – meet Viv," I said. "She's a mate from London."

"Why she here?" Chelsea asked.

"To keep you safe from the evil Villavito," I told her.

"She want sleep with you?"

Viv just laughed. "Not until you find a cure for global warming!" Then she took a long hard look at Anni's yellow pinafore with the puppy motif. "Who's the kid in the panto cossie?" she wanted to know.

"This is Anni," I said. "She's in hiding."

"From a pissed-off audience?"

I took a 1000-baht note from my wallet and gave it to Viv. "She's done *Snow White* - could you help her find something more suitable?"

"What for? – *Peter Pan* or *Sleeping Beauty*?"

"*Ali Barber and the Forty Thieves*," I said.

"She'd make a lovely *Puss in Boots*!" Viv laughed. "But first - what the *fuck* is going on?"

Once we'd ordered drinks all round, I gave it to her, chapter-&-verse, starting with Chelsea's birthday party at the RiverSide, Anni's disappearance, Nixie and her little helpers, Thai boxing - and ending with the *Punch-up at the OK Pattaya Corral*.

"And now, I have to negotiate with the Big Bad Wolf," I finished.

"Deal me in and I'll pay for the beer," Viv offered.

"Watch and learn, sweetheart," and I called-up Villavito's number.

Anni sat there, wide-eyed and listening. While she was still in disguise, she would be OK.

Two rings: then Villavito answered. "David - are we talking?"

"It's your agenda," I offered.

I could hear whispering. Then Villavito spoke. "Are you ready to hand them over?"

Why will people *never* listen? OK, Raphael – let's play hard ball. "Not yet," I said. "For a start, you owe me forty thousand dollars." Paused for a second, and then went on: "and if you want me to go to Yasu Thon, you can round it up to a full 50k."

Viv looked up in horror. "Are you serious?" she mouthed.

"Deadly," I whispered back.

"David, I will only pay you when I have the girl and the diamonds," he said. "Yasu is another matter altogether."

"Raphael," I said. "I'm only in it for the money."

Villavito actually laughed. "Let me come and talk to you," he said, "man-to-man, face-to-face."

At the thought of a one-to-one session with the *Al Pacino* of the Philippines, I skipped my hand into my backpack, wrapped my fingers round the wooden butt of the Colt and let my thumb play with the safety catch. "You're on," and I checked my watch: it was 20.35, give or take a minute. "Four Sons - 21.30 - you, me and a bottle of *Black Label*."

"Looking forward to it," he said. "My regards to Chelsea."

Cheeky bastard! Maybe Sam was right. There was nothing to be gained by holding on to her – but if Villavito let her stay with me, she could be his poisoned apple.

"I will see you there," Villavito agreed and closed the call.

"What now?" Viv asked.

"Upstairs," I said.

"Only if you promise a night to remember," Viv laughed.

"In your dreams!" I shot back. I took Chelsea's hand and lead my little party up to the second floor, into my room and out onto the balcony. From there, we could look down OK, but the glare of the streetlights made it hard for anyone to look up.

We leaned over the balcony together and picked out a table on the patio. "If I call and leave it open," I said, holding my cell phone, "you'll hear whatever we talk about."

"Sounds good," Viv agreed.

"Use the camera," and I set it to the *No-Flash* position. "And this," and gave her my *Philips* voice recorder.

"Do what we can," Viv promised – and played with the buttons to see how everything worked.

Anni had made herself at home on a folding wooden chair. "It take long?" she asked. "I want new clothes."

Just like her sister. "All in good time," I told her.

"You want my diamonds?"

"Yes," I said. At least she was following the storyline. "But only to keep you and your sister out of jail."

"You give Mr Raphael?" Chelsea was not at all pleased. She was standing with her back to the balcony, just watching me and Viv, waiting for the glance that would betray our secret love affair. Fat chance!

"Not if I can help it," I smiled. "Why are they in Kanchanaburi?"

"My friend – she keep them safe," Anni told us.

"Can you call her – tell her we're coming?" I asked Anni.

"Sure," Anni agreed. "*No problemo.*"

Someone had been watching too much satellite TV, but I ignored the comment. "We'll go tomorrow," and I looked at Viv. "OK?"

Viv nodded. "Good idea," she agreed. "We can have a bit of catch-up on the way."

It was then that Anni asked the question that no-one else had thought about. "Where I sleep tonight?"

"With Chelsea, of course," I said.

"But that leave you an' her," Chelsea objected.

"We have to sleep somewhere" I said. "And you've got Anni."

"You want sleep or fuck-fuck?" Chelsea wanted to know.

"Sleep," I said. "We're far too tired for a fuck-fuck."

"Speak for yourself!" Viv grinned.

Chelsea thought about it very carefully. Her culture wouldn't let her sleep with me. She didn't want her sister to share with Viv - and a *me-and-Anni* pairing was a total no-no. "I sleep with Anni," she finally said to Viv. "You sleep where you want."

"Don't worry, sweetheart!" Viv said to Chelsea. "I'd rather let Satan shag me with an icicle!" Then she turned to Anni. "Let's get you out of those stupid clothes," and all three of them skipped down the stairs in fits of laughter.

Villavito arrived on the very dot of half-past nine. It was a lesson in precision to watch him walk along Soi Rambuttri. He had parked the big white Merc against the wall of the Victory Temple, near Soi Chana Songkram, where the taxis like to sit and wait for meandering tourists.

Villavito wasn't meandering. He knew what he had to do – where he had to be – and at what time.

As I watched his deliberate progress through the strolling tourists, I noticed he was being followed by an oversized Thai who seem to be suffering from a limp. My fault. I should have *really* stuck it to him.

Up above and out of sight, Viv, Chelsea and Anni were watching from the balcony, ready with the camera and the voice recorder. As Villavito approached, I clicked the [Send] button on my phone and left it on the table for everyone to see. Seconds later, I was pleased to hear an answering chirp-chirp-chirp from somewhere in the night above my head.

"Good evening, David - you are well?"

As ever, annoyingly polite. "Enjoying the evening, thank you, Raphael - won't you join me?"

"Too kind, Mr Shannon," and he came on to the hotel patio, up to my table and pulled out the chair opposite mine. As he had wished, we were now face-to-face.

"Would you like a drink?"

"Allow me, David." He clapped his hands and Mr Limp-Along handed a bottle of *Black Label* whisky to one of the waiters.

Without hesitation, the waiter placed the bottle in an ice bucket, picked up two whisky glasses and brought them over to our table. He set a glass in front of each of us, placed the ice bucket on the next-door table – and poured a generous measure into each tumbler.

I picked mine up and raised it as a toast. "Your health!" I said. (*Forgive me, Lord – more lies!*)

"To a successful venture!" Villavito replied.

"*Slange*!" and I drained my measure and tapped the empty glass on the table as a challenge for him to follow me.

Instead, he sipped like a virgin. "You know why I am here?" he asked, fingering his glass like a family heirloom.

"Yasu Thom," I said. "What the deal?"

By now, the waiter had refilled my glass. But I've been caught that way before. Once is impressive; twice is stupid. So I left the whisky alone until we'd reached an agreement.

"It's not difficult," Villavito told me. "You go with Rudi – meet my contact – and come back with my birthday present."

"Which is worth how much – on a real market?" I added.

"About a million dollars, David."

I was surprised that he openly mentioned a value. But it was a quiet evening and the other half-dozen drinkers on the patio were only interested in the television. "And you trust me?"

Villavito paused to take another sip of his whisky. "What could possibly go wrong?" he asked. "You'll be watched all the way."

That's true, I thought. "And if I do, you'll leave Chelsea alone?"

"Are you offering guarantees?"

If she was a part of his team, he had all the guarantees he needed. "I'm only doing this for money," I reminded the Philippino. "What better guarantee could you want?"

Villavito ignored my comment. "You have recovered my other diamonds?" he asked me.

"Possibly," I told him.

"Anni…?" and he looked around the hotel patio, hoping to see her.

"Safe," I smiled. "Very safe."

"You will let me have her?"

"Not until you give me fifty-thousand dollars," I said.

Villavito took another sip of his whisky. "On delivery," he promised, and offered me his hand.

"Agreed," I said.

Then Chelsea appeared. She slipped her arm around my waist and kissed my cheek. "Darling, can I have a Pepsi, please?"

"You may keep the *Black Label*," Villavito smiled.

"Too kind," - but the shit was getting deeper by the minute.

20

For the moment, Anni was safe. She shared a room with Chelsea. Viv reckoned that whatever my darling kitten had arranged with Villavito, she wouldn't risk harming her sister. Not with us two watching – and not before we'd recovered Anni's diamonds.

Yes, me and Viv *had* shared a room – but not in that way. (*I may get horny from time to time – but I don't carry icicles.*) Instead, we did it turn and turn about: two hours watching and two hours cat-napping, with the door wide open. We had to look after Anni. She was the key to the whole business.

"Did you record the conversation?" I asked at one point.

"Clear as a bell," she said – and played it back to me.

"Pictures?"

"Got him cold," Viv promised.

I'd told her about my deal with Lieutenant Sam and his promise to keep the girls out of the *Bangkok Hilton*. But only if I delivered Villavito.

"Then all you have to do is hand him over," she smiled.

"Leave it with me," I yawned. It was my turn on the bed.

At seven, we all met up for breakfast on the patio.

"What's the plan?" Viv wanted to know.

By now, I was into my third black coffee. "Kanchanaburi?"

"Who's going?" Viv asked.

"You, me and Anni," I said.

"And me, darling," Chelsea chipped in.

Wait until you're asked, my sweetheart. "Want to?" I asked her.

"She my sister – I look out for her."

I just bet you will! "OK, travel lady," I smiled. "What's the best way to get there?"

"We hire bus?"

"Why don't we join a tour?" I suggested. "So we blend in."

"What you mean, darling?" Chelsea asked.

"If we join a tour, we'll be a part of the crowd…" I said.

"… and make us harder to follow," Viv explained.

Chelsea didn't get it. "Who want follow?"

"Best not ask." I checked the hotel patio – half-a-dozen tourists, no-one taking any interest. Then back to Chelsea: "Can you book us a ride to the River Kwai?"

"Same bus as yesterday," she said.

"It'll do for me," I said.

About an hour later, we were on the same little bus that had taken us to Pattaya – and brought back one more girl. But today, we were sharing with two French girls, a bearded Viking from Norway and two Israelis who would only speak in German.

It was warm, snug, peaceful and comfortable - and I drifted off with Chelsea neatly folded in beside me. Viv and Anni were somewhere at the back, swapping chit-chat over a copy of a contact magazine from a pick-up bar in Amsterdam.

Next thing I knew, I had Chelsea yelling in my ear: "Wake up now!" she ordered. "We here."

Yes, Kanchanaburi - right by the gateway to a very large cemetery. Flat, black headstones were laid in long straight lines. Each memorial tablet has its own little bush or flowering shrub. Dozens of visitors - mainly European - were walking around it, taking their time, showing respect.

"You know?" Chelsea asked me.

"War graves?" What else could they have been?

"Kanchanaburi," said Chelsea. "For soldiers at River Kwai."

Viv just stared. "*Jesus – fuck!*" she said. "Did you know?"

"Not until we got off the bus," I said.

Nearby, a poster advertised the:

New Death Railway Museum

Which promised these visitor attractions:

Coffee Shop

Nice View

Air Conditioned

With:

Free Coffee or Tea for all Admissions to the Museum.

116

Nearby, a wooden shack – *The River Kwai Mansion Hotel* - had rooms for 300 baht a night. The squaddies would have liked that - especially the *hot water* and it being *clean* and *safe*. How times change….

"Where first?" I said to Anni. "Where do we find your friend?"

Too late! Across the road, in the shade of the *River Kwai Mansion Hotel*, a line of stalls were selling hand-made ear-rings, bracelets, bangles and necklaces - intricate designs, amazing colours: totally irresistible. And at modest prices.

"Give us a minute," Viv called back. "These are brilliant!" and she dived into the crowd around the stalls.

"I know better!" Chelsea squealed and dragged them away, down the street, past the *Death Railway Museum and Research Centre* to the *Art Gallery and War Museum*.

Of course, Chelsea was right. Back at the Mansion Hotel, the bits and pieces were made from everyday material – and cost pennies. Here, in a shop opposite the *Boon-Heng Wave Radio Station* (operating on 93.25Mhz), they used real gold. I looked in horror: rings, bracelets, pendants, watches, lockets – and all at real-gold prices. It didn't take long.

"Darling…?"

When I hear that tone in her voice, self-preservation tries to hide the wallet in the deepest corner of my backpack. "Yes, kitten?"

"Darling… can I?" She was pointing at this bracelet.

"How much?"

"Oh… darling…!" and she gave me her special doe-eyed look that *always* gives me a ram-rod erection.

I looked at the boy who was running the shop. "How much?"

"Ten thousand baht!" he smiled.

From experience, I've learned the quickest way to clear the hard-on problem is to use a Visa card. It's just like ice-cold water. "I'll give you eight," I said.

"Is good," he agreed and we completed the transaction.

Chelsea was dancing with joy – a gold bracelet, just for the asking. "See – see!" and she showed it to Anni and Viv.

"Very nice," Viv smiled.

Anni just looked away.

"I love you, darling!" and Chelsea offered me her cheek to kiss.

Thailand Honey….. "Now can we find the friend?" I asked.

"I call her soon," Anni promised.

Across from the gold shop, this rusty old railway engine waited to be photographed. It had been used on the railway to haul ammunition from Singapore to the army in Burma. It was framed by the flags of thirty nations. To be fair, I took its picture. No-one else was interested.

"Darling, you want drink?" Chelsea asked.

"I want to find your sister's friend." But I should have known better. We were now on Thai time. Nobody needed to hurry.

"You need water," Chelsea insisted. It was her cure for everything, including my sexual frustration.

As always, there was a café. It had benches, but no parasols. "This will do," and I made a space for me and Chelsea between two British boys and a couple of Swedish blondes. Viv and Anni stood in front of us and sipped cans of icy Coca-Cola.

"Here," said Chelsea and gave me a bottle. It was deliciously cold and very welcome in that scorching heat. For a moment, I thought back to the lads on the railway line and wondered who'd brought them any kind of water.

One of the Brits was staring at Chelsea. "She your bird?"

"What if she is?"

He'd been drinking and the heat was affecting his hormones. "If she bums you over, can I 'ave a go?" and he sniggered like a schoolboy with a *Playboy* under the blankets.

Chelsea heard and caught my arm. She guessed what was about to happen. "Not here," she begged me.

I squeezed her hand: my short-arm jab was under control. Then back to the boy: "When you're old enough," I promised him.

"Piss off!" But his mate was already on his feet and dragging his buddy out of harm's way.

Chelsea smiled. "You good boy," she said and kissed my cheek.

One of these days, this cheek-kissing will go on the agenda - and I will ask permission to go for lips. But until then, a kiss on the cheek is better than getting 'bummed-out'.

"Can we see the bridge from here?" Viv asked.

Our café was on the side of a pedestrian precinct with shops on both sides and the River Kwai at the far end. "You can go," she told us. "Me and Anni not like it."

So Viv and I strolled along towards the river. The bearded Norwegian and the French girls followed along behind us. At the end of the precinct, we stood in a line and gazed over the balcony rail at the muddy waters of the River Kwai – and then along to the infamous bridge that was just about a hundred yards away.

"Will she be OK?" Viv asked.

I looked around for anyone who could have been an *Alfie* – but no-one seemed to be watching any of us. No matter. Why would anyone hassle Anni *before* she had recovered her stones? Anyone could see that we were making progress. That would keep her safe for now. Once she'd got them back, we could start worrying again. "Until she surrenders the diamonds, yes," I said.

"Fucked if I would," said Viv.

It made good sense. "Fucked if I would, either!" I agreed.

We stood and gazed at the bridge, trying to imagine what it had been like. But it wasn't easy.

"Bloody buildings!" Viv complained.

She was right. The bright blue roof and numerous pontoons of the *River Kwae Restaurant* drained all the emotion and feeling that we might have felt for this bridge and its history and buried it deep in a giant pot of boiled rice.

"Come on," I said. "Let's make a plan."

"Like what?"

"Keep an open mind – and see what happens."

For inspiration, we wandered back through one of the clothing arcades. Dresses of every colour and for every age were hanging on the wire grille that acted as a wall – blues, greens, every shade of yellow, rainbow patterns... and fleecy things with large pink spots that could have been a child's pyjamas (that is, if Thais wear pyjamas).

Next, we came across a display of shopping bags, handbags and travel bags. After that: imitation swords, rifles, books of the war, pictures of the war – and *The Bridge on the River Kwai* on DVD.

I looked at Viv. "Any bright ideas?"

"Not yet," she replied.

"Nor me," I said. But the jewellery display caught my attention and I picked up a string of small glass beads. About the size of marrowfat peas and cut with facets, diamond style. "These might help."

"As what?" Viv asked.

"Something for Raphael."

Viv read my mind and saw the opportunity of a double scam. "You'll *never* get away with it!" But there was a hopeful smile on her face.

"It's only a *Just-In-Case*," I said.

"What do we need?"

"Let's go find a jiffy bag," I suggested.

"To switch with Anni?"

"Not a word to madam," I finished.

By now, we were back to the little café. Chelsea and Anni were chatting away to the bearded Norwegian. I went over, put my arm on her shoulder and said for everyone to hear: "We're off to find a 7-11 – Viv needs aspirin."

"Is OK, darling!" Chelsea smiled. "We got half-hour."

"Won't be long," I promised – then turned back to answer Viv's question. "Just a simple package," I said. "Stuffed with little glass beads."

"Do you know what Anni's package looks like?"

"No – but nor do Mr Villavito's little helpers."

We walked on past the Mansion Hotel, up to the main road, turned left and zig-zagged our way through the other tourists, trusting our luck. Somewhere along here, we'd find what we needed.

"Has Anni told you anything at all?"

"No," I said.

"And do you expect her to?"

"No," I had to concede. "She'll keep them well hidden – they're her only chance of getting out in one piece."

As those diamonds were my only chance of escape as well, I needed something to wave at Villavito's people when we ran out of luck.

It didn't take long. We found the kind of general shop that sold us what we needed: a small jiffy bag, a roll of sellotape and two ballpoint pens - one blue, one black – (and don't forget the aspirins).

Outside in the street, I broke the string on the beads, poured about thirty of them into the jiffy bag, sealed it with a cross of sellotape – and then got Viv to sign *Villavito* while I added *J Henry Wilberforce*.

"Not perfect," I said, stuffing it into my bag. "But it will do."

Chelsea and Anni were sitting in the little café. I bought bottles of water for everyone and squeezed in between them.

"You get aspirin?" and Chelsea looked up at Viv.

"Sure did." And Viv covered our asses by waving the pack.

"Has Anni found her friend?" I asked.

"Not yet – she work in Tiger Temple."

"Halle-*fuckin'*-llujah!" I laughed. "How do we get there?"

"By bus," Chelsea replied.

21

Ten minutes later, we were back outside the cemetery and standing next to our bus. We were one body short. The French girls were there, Harald the Viking was there and the two Israelis were talking together just a little way along the road. Anni was still with us – and Viv was taking her aspirins, washing them down with ice-cold water from a plastic bottle. We just needed a driver – and Chelsea was on her cell phone, trying to find him.

Then my own phone rang. It was Villavito. "You have something to tell me, David?" he asked.

"Depends what you want to hear."

"Humour me," he offered. "Tell me about my diamonds."

"We're on our way to get them now," I said.

"So I believe." He sounded far too certain.

I looked up and down the street, but couldn't see anyone who could have been watching us. Nor could I see anyone who looked like an *Alfie*, either. "Is it the guy in the green shirt?" I asked Raphael.

"Don't be silly, David," Villavito replied. "I don't have time."

"Her game – her rules," I said. "I'm on the case."

"Deal with it *NOW!*" Villavito hissed.

"You'd have more luck beating shit out of a jelly," I said.

"Is that another stupid English joke?"

"Could well be," I said. "Anyway, what's the panic?"

"I need you in Yasu."

This was not the time to argue. "When?"

"Rudi is travelling tomorrow," said Villavito. "He is looking forward to enjoying your company."

"How is he getting there?"

"By bus, of course," Villavito told me.

No chauffeur-driven limousine? No big white Mercedes? Was this a cost-cutting exercise?

Would we have to submit receipts with our expenses? "From where?" I asked.

"Bangkok, of course."

"Which bus station?"

"How should I know?" Villavito laughed. "Ask your favourite little travel clerk!"

"Might just do that," I agreed. "Now give me Rudi's number." Always best to have back-up, especially on this trip where nothing had come even close to following a plan.

"Listen carefully," Villavito agreed, and gave it to me.

By now, Chelsea had found the driver and was encouraging her passengers to get back on the bus. "You come – *now*!" she insisted.

Once I'd got Rudi's cell phone details safely stored, I wished Villavito a cheery farewell and hauled myself into my seat and waited to be taken to the tigers.

From Kanchanaburi, it's some 35 kilometres to the Tiger Temple and it takes about an hour. When I opened my eyes, we were in the parking lot of the *Wild Animal Rescue Centre*.

"Is this it?" I asked Chelsea.

"Yes – this Tiger Temple," she said and we all followed her into the tea room. It had a TV set, a Pepsi machine and tables made from rough-cut planks, sliced from the tree-trunk like thick-cut ham. Pots of soup and pans of rice were warming on a stove. "You want eat?"

"Not now," I said. "First, I want Anni to find her diamonds."

"She call her friend," Chelsea promised. "She come soon."

"OK," I said. "Let's go look at the tigers."

At first, the tigers were as hard to find as Anni's diamonds. We paid our admission fee, bought T-shirts with *Tiger Temple Thailand* (front and back) for 300 baht. We had the choice of white, grey or black.

"Why?" I asked.

"'Cos tigers no like red or orange," Chelsea explained.

Fair enough. "Why 300 baht?"

"Help feed tigers," and she opened the leaflet that came with the ticket. "One hundred baht - each day - feed tiger," and she waved the *Contribution Form* in my face. "You want buy one?"

"Maybe later," I smiled. "What colour shirt do you want?"

"Black," she decided.

"Your call," and I handed over the money.

Once last job: we were required to sign the waiver that absolved the temple from any *close encounters of the tiger kind*. Then, like Allan Quartermain-and-Party, we all squeezed through the narrow opening in the wall and bravely went in search of our own *King Solomon's Mine*.

Inside, we found ourselves walking on a path of broken stones on a paddock of sun-baked earth. Pigs of all sizes were scurrying in and out of the legs of cattle grazing round the trees and shrubs. If there *were* any tigers, they were well-fed tigers: good news for the domestic beasties.

"I no like," said Chelsea.

It was time to be the big brave soldier. So I put my arm round her shoulder. "I'll protect you," I promised.

She shook me off. "No in temple – no allowed!"

I added *'No Hugging'* to all the other rules of cultural dis-engagement that apply to all *farangs* who visit Thailand on short-stay holidays. "OK!" I laughed. "I'll go and hug a tiger – they quite like it."

About two hundred yards along the path, we came to a sign nailed to a tree. In English and Thai, it said:

→ *Tiger Canyon*

→ *Tiger Cages*

Chelsea read it very carefully. "I not go," she said.

By now, the rest of our group was up the path, ahead of us and my little kitten was all for going back to the safety of the Pepsi zone. I caught her arm. "It's perfectly safe," I said. "You're a friend of the tigers."

"How I be that?" she wanted to know.

"When you signed the form," I told her. "And they *never* hurt their friends, especially the beautiful ones!"

She was still unsure - then broke into a beaming smile. "You lie!" she laughed. "You make it up – tell me stories..."

"OK," I said, taking her hand. "Let me prove it."

"How you do that?"

"If we both get back alive, it must be true."

It made no sense at all to Chelsea, but with a shrug of her shoulders, she let me to lead her up the garden path to the Tiger Canyon.

"You guys OK?" Viv called back.

"Any sign of anybody's friend?" I replied.

"Not yet!" Viv laughed.

At which point, the bearded Norwegian chipped in to the conversation. "Let us hope you find her soon," he said in perfect English. "Mr Villavito is beginning to get worried," and he held up his mobile phone to underline what he meant.

It was now or never. "You can tell your master that we have what he's looking for," and I dipped into my backpack and pulled out the fake package. "Listen..." and I shook the envelope to let him hear the beads rattling around inside it.

The Viking looked totally surprised - while Chelsea was about to throw up.

"Later, kitten," I hissed and slipped the package back into my bag.

The Viking tried to stop me. "You show me, first?"

"Fat chance, Olaf," I said. "Sealed – Raffa's eyes only."

He started punching numbers. "I call him?" he offered.

I snatched the phone out of his hand. "My job," I said. "One more word and I'll feed you to the fuckin' tigers," and tossed his cell phone at one of the pigs – who began to eat it.

My genuine offer to save the temple the cost of a pig-snack was a bit too much for our bearded buddy. "He not like you talk at me this way!"

"Who gives a rat's-arse?" I said. "Raphael is not the only diamond hunter in town..."

About fifty yards away, this inoffensive little guy was sitting on a bench under a tree and sipping water from a plastic bottle. "See that man?"

"What about him?" the Norwegian asked.

"Thai police," I said, very quietly. "Should I call him over?"

Eric Bloodaxe thought about it for a moment. "And what would you tell him?" he asked.

"That we were asking about a honeymoon in Norway," and I put my arm round Chelsea for a proper lover's hug. You know, across the back, under the arm, hand-on-tit, like we used to chance it in the cinema. God Bless the little darling, she never even flinched...

By now, Viv was back with us. She must have seen me waving the package under the Norwegian's nose. "All OK?"

"Absolutely," I said. "We were just admiring the magnificent acacia trees."

"And which might they be?" Viv asked.

"Fucked if I know!" and we carried on walking up the path to where a crowd in every colour of shirt imaginable (except red or orange) - were milling around a couple of monks in their saffron robes.

Then Chelsea tugged my arm. "Not understand," she said. "When Anni give you packet?"

Oh dear God - time for another round of porkies. "She didn't," I said, then fished the jiffy-bag back out of the travel bag – clean side up - and shook it so that she could hear the rattle. "These are a handful of glass beads I'm sending to my sister," I told her. "She makes costume jewellery and she asked for some samples."

"Why you tell him lies?"

I was beginning to wonder that myself. In the long run, truth is always easier. So much less to remember. "He was trying to threaten us," I told her. "I told him to piss-off."

"If he tell Mr Raphael, you get Anni in trouble."

I put my hands on her shoulders, turned her round to face me and looked into her gorgeous dark-brown eyes. "Anni's not in any trouble, I promise you," I told her. "Trust me?"

Chelsea thought it over for fully half a minute. Then she smiled and kissed my cheek. "If I trust you, will you love me?" she asked.

Only if I can trust *you*, my little squirrel... "No problem there, sweet lips!" Holding hands, we carried on towards the tigers.

Up ahead, we just walked into this open space... and there they were. Six, seven – maybe eight tiger cubs: none any bigger than your average pet dog. Each was on a lead and being handled by a young girl in a yellow shirt.

"Tigers don't mind yellow?" I had to ask.

"So they know who feed them," Chelsea told me.

We were in a crowd of thirty or so, just standing, amazed and watching, getting excited, kneeling down, photographing and stroking these beautiful little creatures.

In the middle of this area – in the shade of this enormous tree - there was a wooded sleeping platform in front of a cage. A large blue notice was nailed to the tree:

Veterinary Hospital Project

Start   *: 27 Jan 08*

Complete   *: 11 Apr 08*

Two monks were sitting in the shade and playing with a tiger cub. It was just like any domestic kitten. It rolled over, hung on to an arm and nibbled at fingers and thumbs and was happily purring away to itself from sheer pleasure. It was easy to imagine the cubs in the cage and the monks sleeping out in the open air to keep up the bonding process.

I paused for a moment to watch this young girl who was feeding her own little cub. Her yellow shirt had a majestic tiger printed right across her back - with *SAIFA Lightening* written underneath it.

"The sponsor?" I asked Chelsea – but the leaflet couldn't help us.

The girl was using a plastic bottle fitted with tiger-proof teat. And the little guy was standing upright, hanging on to her arms and drinking away, eyes half-closed and with same amount of joy on his face that I get from a well-poured pint of Guinness.

After a moment or two, I became aware that the crowd had gone into a general hush and had started to move back, as if making space.

I looked through the crowd and saw two young monks in saffron robes who were leading two much larger tigers into the clearing. These were adults. These were serious pussies!

"Aren't they magnificent"" Viv squealed. She was in her element – snapping away from every possible angle.

Chelsea hugged my arm. "You stay close – not leave me."

"Never in a million years!" This was a dream come true. We should come here every day... As far as I'm concerned, Chelsea-hugs are what this life is all about. The more I get, the happier I'll be.

One of the tiger-monks was waving to us. "You come – you see!"

"That's for me!" cried Viv – and she was in there, stroking white-tipped ears and patting muscular shoulders.

"Happy girl?" I called to Viv.

"Thank God for tigers!" she yelled as she pushed and elbowed her way through the crowd of visitors to take more pictures.

Anni was in the middle of the clearing, talking to one of the yellow-shirted girls. With luck, this could be the long-lost friend.

"Could that be her?" I asked.

"Me not know – she have lot of friends."

My hopes shot sky-high when I noticed Anni and the girl slipping off together in the direction of a walled area on a small hill just about a hundred yards from where we were standing.

"What's up there?"

Chelsea skimmed through the leaflet to find the answer. "Called *Tiger Falls*," she told me. "Special home for grown-up tigers."

Sounded interesting. "May I go?"

"I wait here," and she settled on a bench in the shade of a tree, opened her cell phone and checked her messages.

"If you need me, bell me," and I waved good-bye with my phone.

Half a second later, Viv was beside me. "OK to tag along?"

"Please do," I said. Just in time. The Spy from Norway was only a few paces behind. On impulse, I took his picture.

Viv noticed. "Fancy him?" she asked.

"No," I said. "His bum's too small."

"I think he fancies you."

"Just my bleedin' luck!" and I pointed to Anni and her friend who were leaning into the enclosure to look at three fully-grown tigers. "He wants to get his paws on her carats."

"That makes two of us," Viv smiled back.

It was only girlie chat between kids. No-one was handing over diamonds. "Come on," I said to Viv, "let's take a look at the scenery," and set off towards this temple building that we could see through the trees. I wanted to call Lieutenant Sam – but there were too many people around *Tiger Falls* to tell him the whole story.

The temple building was ten feet off the ground on square stilts of red brick. An A-shaped roof of green tiles protected the actual temple – which was small and square and built of wood. Inside this, they kept their magnificent Buddha.

A flight of twelve wide steps of reddish marble lead the way to the temple - and on the fourth step, a bright green notice reminded visitors to:

Please take off your shoes

In front, a stone icon decorated with snakes. Just as I was about to take out my phone and make the call, a sweet little voice piped up with even more information.

"This *Wat Pa Luangta Bua Yannassampanno*," Chelsea told us, quoting for her leaflet. "Home of Golden Jubilee Buddha Image."

"Is that right?" I smiled.

"King pay for gold himself," Chelsea went on.

"Some man," I said to Viv.

Chelsea had noticed my cell phone "And why you make phone call?" she wanted to know.

"I was about to call you," I lied. "I wanted you to see this."

"And we wanted you to tell us what it all meant," Viv added.

Sometimes, you can overcook the story. Chelsea was not entirely convinced. "No more to tell," she said and took my hand. "We go back find bus?"

"Is it time to go already?" I asked her.

She checked her watch – and as it was the Amsterdam watch, this must have counted as a special occasion. "Driver meet girlfriend in Four Sons at eight tonight," she explained. "If he late, she find new man."

It was coming up to four o'clock. "Then we'd better not keep her waiting." I smiled. But when I tried another lover's hug, her arm snapped faster than a mousetrap.

"Make monk unhappy," she explained. Game over...

22

We rounded up our party: Chelsea, Anni, Viv, the two sexy French girls, the elderly Israelis and the dodgy Norwegian, and set off for Bangkok. And no, we never even came close to recovering Anni's packet of diamonds.

"What happened to the friend?" I asked Chelsea.

"Her mother sick," came the answer. "She leave early."

No point in going any further. Although Chelsea had never told me a lie, her version of the truth could be imaginative. "So we still don't have the diamonds?"

Chelsea shrugged her shoulders. "Maybe tomorrow," she smiled.

As I said – why go any further? Asking Chelsea questions was like pushing ferrets into a rabbit warren: every time you tried, you only chased more bunnies into the undergrowth.

I did manage to send a short text message to Lieutenant Sam: *On our way back to BKK – being watched – unsafe to collect package.*

Within fifteen minutes, Sam had replied: *Will meet you for a beer at Four Sons hotel – and may I talk to Anni?*

Not an easy one to answer. "Mr Sam?" I asked Chelsea.

"Who he?"

"The policemen who arrested us in Patpong....."

Chelsea looked uncertain. "What about him?" she asked.

"He would like to talk to us," and I showed her the text.

"Why he want Anni?" She turned to her sister and gave her a reassuring smile.

"To see that she's OK," I explained. "He's looking after us." Not entirely true, but Chelsea could only handle easy words. Keep it simple, keep her in the loop.

"Wait – I ask her." And they chatted away together, heads together as if they were discussing a new boyfriend. Then: "She want Viv to stay."

Maybe they were closer than I realised. "Sounds OK to me," I said and sent a *She agrees* message to Sam.

An hour later, we were back in Soi Rambuttri, edging our way through the wandering tourists until we reached the corner by Four Sons.

"You give him two hundred baht," Chelsea told me.

Why argue? I gave her cash to tip our driver.

"Anyone for a beer?" I asked.

"Not now," said Chelsea. "I must look to office," and she scampered up the steps to see if she had missed anything during the day. Anni went with her.

"Don't fret, big boy," Viv grinned. "No man drinks alone when I'm around," and she ordered two large bottles of Singha. Then back to me: "How's she doing with her visa application?"

"Couldn't say," I confessed. "She has all the paperwork – and she keeps it in a large green folder in her desk."

"Is that all she's done?"

"If we ever stop dashing about, she'll give it to her lawyer."

"Does she have to?"

"It may cost," I said, "but it's the only way."

"Sharpening the pencil?"

"Or greasing the gears...." and we sipped our beers in semi-silence until Lieutenant Sam came striding along Rambuttri and joined us at our patio table.

"Good evening, David," he smiled.

I made the introductions. "Sam, meet Viv." I said.

"Cheers, mate!" Viv grinned and ran her fingers through the bleach-blonde spiky hair. "I'm a British lesbo."

"I would never have guessed," Sam replied and then called "Heineken!" to the nearest waiter. Tonight, Sam was in casual dress – with a bright red polo shirt, light grey slacks and a pair of sand-coloured trainers.

First job: deal with the Norwegian. On my camera, I clicked [Display] until it showed the pictures from the Tiger Temple. "Know him?" I asked. "One of Villavito's people."

Sam looked closely. "Not familiar," he said. "But Raphael uses so many little helpers – what did he do?"

"Followed us around Kanchanaburi and reported back," I said.

"You should be used to that by now!" Sam laughed.

"We can deal with Chelsea," I said, "but the observer could be anyone," and I waved an arm across the eight or nine other drinkers or diners on the hotel patio, "we have to watch all pockets."

"But we can't be *sure* she's doing it," Viv chipped in.

"Better to be sure she isn't," Sam replied.

Which was fair comment. "And if she is?"

"We'd have to take her out of the game," was Sam's opinion.

"Sounds a bit drastic," I said.

"Mr David Shannon," Sam began, "bloody English gentleman. Do you think that Villavito is offering a game of golf?"

"He only wants me to fetch his diamonds," I said. "Where's the problem? "

"And Dave's being well paid," Viv offered.

"Once you step on that bus, you're a pawn in his game," Sam warned me. "Why do you think I gave you the gun?"

"You never said...!" Viv broke in.

Sam held up both hands to stop her talking. "David – why exactly are you doing this?"

Good point. I had to think. Yes, $50,000 tax-free dollars had been a good incentive. But there *were* other considerations. "To keep Anni out of trouble," I whispered. "And to keep Chelsea out of jail."

"Noble gestures," Sam agreed. "But when I said that no-one gets to courier twice, were you listening?"

"I was," I said. "You mentioned *concrete boots*."

"And did it register?"

"Of course it did," I said. "But I'll be OK – I've got leverage."

Four tables away, a party of Brits were swilling beer and getting boisterous. One of the serving girls had been invited to *Dip yer tits in this, my darlin'!* – but it seemed good-humoured and the girl ignored it.

"And what *is* your leverage?" Sam asked.

"First, he needs his delivery," I said. "Next, he wants Anni – and third, he wants to recover Anni's little package."

Sam stopped for a couple of seconds to sip his Heineken. "Why *are* you doing this?" he asked. "You could pack your bags and fly home tonight – no-one would blame you."

"Good idea," said Viv. "I'll take you to the airport."

"Wait on, sex-pot," I said. "I'm doing this for Chelsea." And I didn't even have to think. It just came out, like a confession.

Sam just laughed. "Then it must be love!" he said. "Men do many crazy things for women."

"Is that from experience?" I smiled back.

"But what about the reasons?" Viv asked.

My turn to spend some thinking time at the Singha bottle. "If it all works out," I said, "we can save the girl, recover the diamonds – and nail the villain."

"*James Bond* lives on!" Viv laughed.

"But I can't drive an Aston Martin," I replied.

"Then learn to ride a fuckin' elephant," Viv hit back.

Sam was still in business mode. "Has he told you anything about the consignment?"

"It's supposed to be worth a million dollars, give or take," I said.

"To the Chinese or to Villavito...?"

"He didn't say."

"Then what?"

"I'm to travel on a bus with Rudi."

"Rudi?"

"A South African," I said.

"Ah – Rudi Schiller - key member of the *Trekkers*," Sam told me. "And after you have taken delivery?"

"We haven't got that far," I said. "But if I'm a courier, I'll have to bring them back to Bangkok."

"Absolutely," Sam agreed.

"On his own?" Viv asked.

"Yes, dear lady," Sam explained. "This is a one-man show."

"Pull out NOW!" said Viv, standing up to make her point. "It's far too dangerous – let me run you to the airport."

"What would I say to Chelsea?"

"When she gets her visa, you can fly her to London," said Viv.

The drinking party was now into its repertoire of football songs... with *"You'll Never Walk Alone..."* at full volume.

"It's his dragon," Sam was grinning, "and he has to fight to save the adorable Chelsea."

"What *is* he saving her from?" Viv asked.

"The *Bangkok Hilton*," I said. "If we get Villavito, she walks."

"Is that right?" Viv asked Sam.

"And her sister," Sam confirmed.

"Are they worth the bother?" Viv fired back.

"Ask David," Sam replied. "It's his life."

"That's what scares me," said Viv. "And you don't seem to care."

Sam took her hand and smiled. "You have to trust me, Miss Viv," he said. "I really do care."

"Wish I could believe you," she said, sitting down again.

"David does – and that will have to do," Sam replied. "Now could you run up to the shop and ask Chelsea and Anni to join us, please?"

"OK, Sam," Viv agreed and went up the steps to the shop.

Sam nudged me. "Cheer up," he said. "I have an agent in Yasu."

"That's comforting."

"Sulita will contact you – but do not mention her to *anyone*."

"Not even...?

"Not to Chelsea – not to Anni – or to Ms Pinko," Sam warned me. "You may be expendable, Mr Shannon – but Sulita is not."

Lieutenant Sam was being serious. Just as well I had the handgun. I was going to need it. "How will I find her?"

"In Yasu, stop at the green ATM," he said. "Let her come to you."

Seconds later, Viv was back with Chelsea and Anni.

"Before we go on," Sam opened, "can we order dinner?"

Good idea – unless it was *Last Supper* time, of course. But either way, shit happens. So let's enjoy. I thumbed my way through the pages of Thai and European dishes. "Prawns," I said. "And an omelette."

"Sounds good to me," said Viv.

"Me and Anni want *Pad Thai*," said Chelsea.

"Sounds perfect." Sam gave our orders to a waiter.

By now, the Brits were into serious drinking. Bottles of Singha were being ordered, guzzled and then re-ordered as fast as the waitresses could keep them coming.

Fair enough. That's why they were here – and why the hotel made them welcome. But when they started banging bottles on the table and singing: *"Get yer tits out, sweetie – can't yer see I want to fuck yer!"* at one of the terrified hotel girls in broad Geordie, Chelsea decided she had heard enough.

She got up, walked over to their table, pointed at the leader and made a zipping motion across her mouth. "*You - be quiet!*" she said firmly — and stood there, hands on hips, 5'3" of total authority.

"Sorry, love," came the apology.

"*Now you sorry her too,*" and she pointed to the frightened girl.

"Just havin' fun," said the boy. "No offence, miss."

"*You drink – not sing!*" and Chelsea came back to our table.

We all just gazed at Chelsea in total admiration. "Well done, our kid!" I grinned.

Sam said nothing. Instead, he took another drink of his Heineken and turned to Anni. "How many times did Villavito run the diamond scam?" he asked, first in English, then in Thai.

"Many times," said Anni. "Fifteen - maybe twenty."

"Did he ever sell genuine diamonds?"

"Not in hotel," Anni replied. "Always bad ones."

"And he only brings bad ones from Laos...?"

"He only make me switch bad ones," Anni told him.

"You have the real diamonds?"

"Yes," said Anni. "Keep them safe."

"Good girl," Sam smiled. "You'll be OK."

"Now excuse me, please?" Anni asked. "I go toilet," and slipped away from our table, circled away from the drinkers and hopped up the steps to the hotel's *Ladies*.

As I followed Anni's progress, I noticed a serving girl in a low-cut dress and very short skirt. She was now in charge of the Brits – and looked capable of dealing with them. Her low-cut dress was easy on the eye...

By now, Sam had turned his attention to Chelsea. "How many couriers did you supply?"

"I not know – maybe ten – maybe more."

"And afterwards – what happened to them?"

"All go Laos or Cambodia," Chelsea told us. "Mr Raphael make me buy tickets for the bus."

While Sam was interrogating Chelsea, I was following the low-cut top around the drinking table. And then: "Where's Anni got to?" She was off the radar, nowhere to be seen at all.

My cell phone rang.

It was Villavito; once again, with perfect timing. "Do not fear for Miss Anni," he said. "She is perfectly safe."

133

I flicked my cell phone on to *speaker* so that everyone could hear what he had to say. "Come on, Raphael – what are you playing at?"

"Just reminding you..." He was enjoying himself.

"Leave her alone!" Chelsea screamed. *"She just a kid!"*

"Why are you messing about?" I yelled at Villavito.

"I want the real diamonds," said Villavito. "No more tricks – my *Trekker* network is far too important!"

"Is all your fault!" Chelsea yelled, now punching away at my head and shoulders. *"I tell you Anni get in trouble!"*

"Easy, kitten," I tried. "She'll be OK..." But it didn't help

"You too smart – now he kill my sister!"

"No he won't," I said. "Not until he gets his bloody diamonds!" Then I had this awful thought: *how did he know about the beads?* Who knew? Not that many people – and I was sitting next to one of them. Quick-thinking time... "If it all comes right in Yasu, is that the end of it?"

"We will have a little party," Villavito laughed. "Just you – me – and the *Laughin' Pussy*..." and that was it. Cards dealt: let's play poker.

23

After Villavito cut the cell phone line, we had a full five seconds of stunned silence... Nobody said a word. Nobody moved – and nobody seemed able to breathe. Then every colour of bell-oil hit the air-conditioner. The noise from our table turned the next-door football party into a prayer meeting at a Methodist chapel.

Chelsea was the first one back to life. "*I find her!*" she yelled – and she was all for dashing up the hotel steps and tearing the place apart - but Sam grabbed her arm and held her back.

"*What the fuck's he on about?*" cried Viv.

"*No more tricks?*" Sam was glaring at me. "*What does he mean?*"

"*It him!*" Chelsea screamed – and started swinging her fists at my head and shoulders again. "*He try trick Mr Raphael.*"

"*It's fuck-all to do with Dave,*" Viv yelled back. "*It's Villavito.*"

"I do not understand you." Sam was calm. "Please explain..." and he just sat there, hands outstretched, Buddha style. If he was expecting world peace and universal good behaviour, he was right out of luck!

"*Hey you wanker!*" yelled one of the lads at the drinking table. "*Fuckin' shut it – right?*" and earned a chorus of laughter from his mates.

"*Aye,*" said another voice. "*Show her where to zip it!*"

"*Chelsea – shut it – NOW!*" I tried.

There was no need. She was all punched out and flopped herself across the table, buried her head in her arms and started crying. "*You promise care for Anni...*" but her words were drowned in a flood of tears.

"*Let me dick it to 'er!*" came a third suggestion.

I tried to put my arm about her shoulders - but she shrugged me away. "*You promise me...*" she sobbed. "*You promise me...*"

"*Come on, darling' suck on this!*" came someone else.

Sam got up and went over to the football table. To get their attention, he flashed his Bangkok police badge. "One more word from ANYONE," he warned them, "and you'll spend the night in jail – OK?"

"Sorry, guv," the first apologised. "Is she OK?"

135

"If you all keep quiet, she will soon get better," Sam told them.

"Sure thing, chief," came the final word.

Now Sam was back on our planet. "Now explain these *tricks*."

"OK," said Viv. "You or me?"

"It was my idea," I said. "I'll do it."

I was about to pull the Kanchanaburi package out of my travel bag and explain it to Sam when little squirrel Anni came skipping down the hotel steps on her way back to our table.

We all just stared at her in disbelief.

"Why so sad?" Anni laughed. "All you miss me?"

Chelsea jumped up and threw her arms round Anni's neck – but now, she was laughing so much that she could hardly speak. "You OK?" was the best she could manage.

Anni couldn't understand it. "I only go toilet," she said.

"It's fine," I smiled. "We had a call – thought you'd been taken."

"Who take me?" she asked, sitting down and drinking her beer.

"It was a threat from Villavito," Sam told Anni. "He is saying he can do it anytime he wants – just like on the beach," he said to Chelsea.

"I not seen Mr Raphael," said Anni, confused by the love and attention from her sister.

"You were lucky," I said. "He's not that all that far away."

"Probably up in the Gods," said Viv, pointing up to the balconies.

"OK," I said, "we'll just have to be more careful," and I looked at Viv. "Could you handle being a Mother Hen?" I asked her.

"For Anni?"

"Anybody else you fancy?

"Not right now!" Viv laughed.

"You'll do it?

"She'll be safe with me," Viv promised. "But Chelsea...?"

"Forget Chelsea," Sam broke in. "Tell me about these *tricks*..."

"Yes," said Viv with an air of resignation. "Time to come clean."

I reached into my travel bag and pulled out the packet that we had put together in Kanchanaburi and dropped it on the table in front of Sam. "It was just an idea," I said.

"What's in it?" Sam demanded.

"Glass beads..."

"To scam Villavito?" Sam asked.

"No," I said. "Just to buy time from his heavy squad."

"Who knew about it?" Sam asked.

Good question. "Me and Viv, of course," I said.

"Well don't look over here!" Viv laughed.

"You're clean enough," I said.

"And you scrub-up pretty well yourself," came her answer.

"Up yours, darling." I remembered our exchange with Eric the Viking out in tiger country. I had flashed the package in his face – and yes, I had mentioned *beads* to Chelsea. That would have to keep for later. Some things were best kept in a Chelsea-free zone.

"It could have been the Norseman," I said.

"Why do you say that?" Sam asked me.

"Pearls before swine," said Viv, catching on.

"Or diamonds before the pussy cats," I offered.

"You English!" and Sam looked totally lost.

"I know it's a Wild Life charity - but diamonds on a tiger-walk?" I said. "He could have guessed I was bluffing."

"I see what you mean." From the tone of his voice, Sam didn't sound convinced.

"What happens now?" Viv asked.

White-Queen's-Knight to Yasu, I guess." OK, so it was Chelsea's mess, but someone had to clean it up. It was time to work out a battle plan. First job, get Chelsea involved. "Will you help me deal with Mr Villavito? I asked her.

"How we do that?" she wanted to know.

"We'll go and find him," I told her.

"OK, 007," Viv broke in. "You know where he's hiding?"

"The answer's in Yasu," I said.

"Would he risk being seen up there?" Viv asked.

"If he wants to deal with Anni out of town, yes," I said.

"But Anni stay here," said Chelsea.

"Too true," I said. "She's not going anywhere near Yasu."

"So what's your plan?" Sam asked me.

I opened my backpack and pulled out Anni's old T-shirt. After we'd changed her clothing at Pattaya, I'd stuffed her cast-offs into my bag. "There you are," I said. "He wants to see a *Laughin' Pussy* – so we won't disappoint him."

"I no understand," said Chelsea.

"Nor me," said Viv.

"I'm listening." At least Sam was trying.

"It's easy enough," I said. "Until he gets his paws on the goodies, he can't blow the final whistle."

"David's right," Sam agreed. "He wants his diamonds – and the longer we keep him away from Anni, the safer she'll be."

"This keep Anni safe?" Chelsea spread the T-shirt on the table.

"Yes, little kitten," I said. "Anni will be safe with Viv."

"Promise?" Chelsea needed loads of reassurance.

"Promise," Viv smiled.

"Promise," and I took her hand and kissed it.

"Then what?" Viv wanted to know.

"We shoot all bad guys, grab the bling, make our escape - and we all live happily ever after!" and I put my arm round Chelsea's shoulder and gave her what I hope would be a let's-get-sexy hug.

"No shooting in public, David!" Sam laughed.

"What you mean?" Chelsea asked.

"Like in cowboy films," I said. "*Yasu ain't big enough*.... and then I blow him away in a cloud of gun smoke."

"Then what?" Chelsea wanted to know.

"I go back to the saloon, kiss the girl and have a whisky."

"You no kiss me in saloon," said Chelsea. "Not allowed."

Enough of the foreplay. I looked into her eyes. "Villavito won't get the chance to hurt Anni," I said. "You and I are going to fix him."

Sam chipped in with a word of support. "We can do it," he promised Chelsea. "But if we had your sister's diamonds....."

Anni shook her head. "I no got them."

"Yes," I said, "We spent all day looking for them."

"My friend – she sick," Anni went on.

"Can we find a work-around?" Viv asked me.

"Either way, it's going to be a problem," I said and turned to Viv. "It's back to the pantomime again," I smiled. "Could we really sell him a bag of magic beans?"

"Let me think about it," Sam offered.

After that, there was little more to say or do. We got stuck into our meals, knocked back a few more beers and then decided to call it a night. By now, the football party had retired to some massage parlour to explore Thai culture and the patio was deserted.

Sam came to the bar with me to settle the bill. "Who else knew about the beads?" he asked.

"Chelsea," I told him. He had to know sometime.

"You still want to take her with you?"

"Someone has to wear the *Laughin' Pussy* shirt," I said.

"Just watch your back, that's all," Sam warned me – then changed the subject. "And what are your plans for tomorrow?"

"Mo-Chit bus station for 10am," I said. "Link up with Rudi Schiller - and that could be a problem."

"Why?" Sam wanted to know. He was reading the bill and doing arithmetic on his fingers.

"Because he met Chelsea at Om Noi on Saturday," I said. "And unless he got pissed on Sunday, he's bound to remember her."

"He won't accept her as the sister?"

"He might – but it's risky," I said. "She had a bit of a barney with his girlfriend."

"Well done, Chelsea!" Sam laughed. "Then I'll arrest him."

"On what charge?"

"Suspected diamond trafficking," Sam answered.

"How long can you hold him?"

"Until you are safely out of the country," Sam promised.

"That should help."

"Look out for Sulita."

"Thank you Sam - see you in a day or so," and we shook hands.

Viv and Chelsea were just sitting at the table, saying nothing. "OK, ladies," I said brightly, "your place or mine?"

Chelsea gave me her doe-eyed look. "What you mean?"

As a form of defence, her *what you mean* approach was more effective than a bullet-proof chastity belt. "For TV," I said. "My room has three movie channels."

"I not sleep with you till Anni safe," she said. No room for any level of negotiation.

I was out-of-bounds – and it served me right for trying to cut a corner. I should have known. But it was almost progress of the *getting closer* kind. "You have a deal," I said, making the most of what was on offer, "and it all starts tomorrow when we catch the bus for Yasu."

"It's your ass," said Viv. "What would you like me to do?"

"Find a way of getting Anni out of Thailand," I said. "And see if you can persuade her to find those diamonds!"

"Sexist sod!" Viv laughed. "I always get the easy jobs!"

24

"You want me wear this always?"

We were in the Mo-Chit bus terminal, sitting by their Coffee Shop and working our way through a packet of dried squid that Chelsea had decided was the only way to kick-start her day.

"Until they've all seen it, yes," I told her.

The *Laughin' Pussy* shirt was causing bother. Overnight, it had been washed and ironed in the laundry room of the Four Sons Hotel. Not officially, of course – but Chelsea could always call on someone for a favour. I had no reason to complain: my kit had also been through that laundry.

"Why you want them see it?"

Once again, I explained that the shirt was Anni's trademark – and when they saw me walking down the street with a gorgeous girl in a *Laughin' Pussy* shirt, everyone would think that Anni was in town.

In general, I'm pretty good at keeping my temper, but her non-stop wittering about this bloody T-shirt was beginning to eat into my sanity. It wasn't her fault, of course. How could it be? We never blame the ones we love. And that's the basic weakness in our species.

Last night had been a bit of a trial. It was OK for Chelsea and Anni. As before, they just bunked down in their own little burrow. But the pressures of the tourist season had forced me to share with Viv again. And as she's a totally-committed member of the lesbo-sisterhood, the double bed was clearly marked as *No-Man's Land* in every sense of the expression.

This left me with an uncomfortable chair and the Australian TV channel. So far, so good. But from 9pm until 6am next morning, there were only two programs...

The first was devoted to the *History of Lokomotiv Moscow* - an absolute *must* for anyone even remotely interested in Russian football.

On its own, it was watchable. But the main feature was an Agatha Christie story set in a Devon hotel during a blizzard. To stretch our disbelief, the script coughed up half a dozen murder victims – and the indestructible Miss Marple.

Although I tried to cat-nap, the programs were recycled into an endless of game of football in waist-high snowdrifts where the dead came back to life and lynched Miss Marple from a crossbar.

After that, the strongest, blackest coffee was my only defence against Chelsea's constant harping over the *Laughin' Pussy* T-shirt.

"When they see it, can I take it off?"

For the journey, she had drawn her silky black hair into a swishing ponytail and looked simply beautiful. Even so, it couldn't save her. "For all I care," I said, "you can swap shirts with Villavito!"

But she wasn't put out by my flash of bad temper. "Darling, you not happy?"

That was the easy bit. But when she turned up the volume on those gorgeous dark brown eyes, I could hardly stop myself from falling at her feet and begging her forgiveness. "Just need more coffee," I said.

"Miss Viv not let you sleep?"

"No," I said.

"No let you sleep in bed?"

"No," I said.

"What you do?"

"Watched a lot of television."

"Poor darling!" Chelsea smiled. "OK, now you sleep with me."

"In bed?"

"No," she laughed. "On bus!"

It was coming up to half-past nine. The terminus was crowded: buses arrived, people got off and scurried away. Taxis pulled up, people got out and found their buses. Steady in/out traffic, all day long.

"Here – try..." and she handed me a strip of dried squid.

It was long, thin and brittle – and tasted salty. "Too kind," I said.

"You like?"

Difficult to say, it was a new experience. "With chips, perhaps – and a squirt of tomato ketchup?"

"When you live with me, I feed you every day!" It was just about the longest sentence I had ever heard her speak and by far, the best offer she had ever made to me.

"Got yourself a deal!" I smiled back.

On one side of Mo-Chit, they had the bus bays. On the other, a spacious drop-off/pick-up zone for taxis on the other traffic. In between, they had a concourse with seats, shops, toilets and a ticket office for the fare-paying customers.

Within ten minutes of getting there, we had visited the coffee stall, any number of food outlets – both hot and cold – and the majority of the cold-drink sellers.

"Just look and see," Chelsea explained.

"And then?"

"You give me hundred baht."

"What for, little kitten?"

"Water for journey."

"Good idea..." She also bought a stack of biscuits, cakes and a couple of packets of *Tattinn*, a crispy kind of snack that I've only ever found in Thailand - and is irresistible.

"You like?"

"Too true," I smiled back.

"Not eat all now – long journey."

"Yes, my love," I promised.

We were travelling light. I had a holdall and my backpack. Chelsea had her own holdall and her beauty box, which held her comb, lipstick, compact and enough food to feed an army in the Afghan mountains.

We'd been walking up and down, checking each and every stall for a second time. At last, we found two fold-up seats together.

"Sit here," she said and held out her hand. "Five hundred baht."

"What for now?"

"Tickets for bus – or you want walk?"

"No," I said, giving her a note, "as you look so sexy, we can ride."

"You say that 'cos I look like Anni." But she wasn't complaining.

I took her hand and kissed it. "Remember, I said it to Chelsea!"

Then I saw him. He was head and shoulders above anyone else – and dressed in khaki shorts and a T-shirt with a *Lion King* motif on the front and wearing a white *Greg Norman* golfing hat. It was Rudi, our South African contact. From the look on his face, he was in the mood to horse-whip someone.

"Remember, you are Anni," I reminded her.

She made a face and tugged at the T-shirt. "Lucky me," she said.

"Rudi!" I called. "Great to see you!"

"You early," he grunted. There was no apology for being late.

"Anni's good with taxis," I said, then looked around for his girl friend. "No Bella?" I asked.

"Shit, no!" Rudi replied. "She's a five-star cow – and she won't sleep in a hay barn!"

"Unreasonable," I smiled. "What's in store for us?"

"You'll be OK," he said. Then looked at Chelsea, moved in close - and whispered. "Is this our thieving little tart?"

We were lucky. Chelsea couldn't keep up with his South African accent. "That's right," I said. "Chelsea's sister."

"Was that the cute little cunt you brought to Om Noi?"

"The very same," I said.

"They all look black to me!" Rudi laughed. "Just hope you fucked her shaggin' arse off!"

Chelsea gave me a sideways look. Some words are common to all languages.... and *fucked* is one of them. She understood that bit well enough. I took her hand and squeezed it.

"Game, set and match!" I said to Rudi.

"Teach her to rattle at her betters!"

"She won't do it again, that's for sure."

"Nor will this one," and he stared at down at Chelsea.

I was about to ask him what he meant when my cell phone buzzed for an incoming text. "Excuse me," I said. "It might be mother."

"Go ahead," said Rudi. "I'll go buy a ticket."

It was Sam. *Keep him sweet – will take him in Khorat.*

I sent a short answer. *Be quick – she's going to kill him!*

I saw him first Sam replied.

I let her read Sam's messages. "I no like your friend," she said.

"He's none too keen on Anni, either," I told her.

By the time Rudi returned, the bus for Khorat was beginning to load. We stuffed our holdalls into the luggage bay and scrambled aboard. It was already three-quarters full.

"You – sit here," said Chelsea and claimed a double seat on the near-side of the bus, about three rows from the back. She took the window seat – which left me sitting by the aisle. As luck would have it, Rudi was my nearest neighbour. I was lucky - he offered a get-out.

"Mind if I sleep?" he asked me.

"Not at all," I smiled back. "It's a great idea." I snuggled up to Chelsea.

"I *hate* that man," she whispered.

"It'll be OK," I said and gripped her arm. "We're safe on the bus."

There was no response. Pissed-off? Yes she was – in spades! "What's wrong?" I asked her.

"I *hate* that man," she said - but this time, so that everyone could hear her. Then she screwed away from me and stared out of the window.

As an everyday bus, it was OK in the comfort department. It had dark-blue curtains all the way round to keep the sunshine out. Up front, a TV set was there for movies. Right now, the treat-of-the-day on show was *Mission Impossible* – which seemed appropriate.

Rudi shuffled in his seat. "Is the little cunt unhappy?"

We passed a bus stop where some twenty or so young girls were standing around a heap of bags and holdalls and chattering away to each other. If only Chelsea could have joined them...

"Someone's ruffled her feathers," I said.

"That'll be the easy bit," said Rudi. "All set for Yasu?"

Well no – I wasn't – but this seemed to be a good time to begin. "What will happen?" I asked.

"We change at Khorat," said Rudi, "then go on to Yasu."

"How long?"

"If we're there by midnight, thank your God," said Rudi.

It was going to be a long, hard day. "Piss-breaks?" I asked.

"Not a problem," Rudi laughed. "We all gotta go sometime."

I hoped he meant our toilet stops. "And in Yasu?" I went on, "what happens there?"

"We'll be met," he told me.

"Where?"

Our bus slowed down in the traffic and came to a stop beside a posse of motorcycle taxis. Six blue bikes were parked on the pavement – and four weary-looking drivers were sitting in plastic chairs in the shade of a giant red parasol.

"A small place - the *Yod Na Khon* Hotel - you'll hate it!"

"Why?" I couldn't stop myself from asking.

"It doesn't have a bar," Rudi smiled.

"So long as there's a 7-11, we'll manage!" I laughed. "Who's on the reception committee?"

"Goes by the name of Van Rijder," Rudi explained.

"Dutch?"

"No," said Rudi. "He's a Boer - like me, from Durban."

"What he doing this far off the savannah?" I asked.

"Missionary work," said Rudi. "If you drop the goodies into his collection plate, he might let you take the little scrubber up to your room..." and he looked at Chelsea. She had worked herself into the window and her face was hidden by the curtain.

"And if I don't?"

"I'll take her up to mine!" and he screwed his face into a snigger.

"Suit yourself, good buddy," I replied. "Plenty more around."

Chelsea shifted in her seat. She was not asleep – just listening.

"You OK, kitten?"

"He touch me once - I kill him." Although she said it very quietly, I could tell from her voice that she meant it.

"Get in line," I smiled. "I get first shot."

A little hand unwrapped itself from the folds of her clothing and settled into mine. "Thank you, darling."

Then Rudi leaned across and whispered: "An' I don't care which little sister you got – just don' fuck with Van Rijder – OK?"

"Wouldn't dream of it!" I laughed - then offered up a silent prayer. "*Jesus... get me to the church on time - and I'll be good forever...*" and hoped that Sam would know where to find us.

25

The road to Khorat was a different kind of countryside. OK, there were the usual palm trees, banana groves and melon fields on either side of the road – but this route ran along a line of rocky hills.

From time to time, we passed a temple, a shrine or two – and then this workshop with concrete animals on display: elephants, lions, antelopes and giraffes, all painted and ready for sale.

After that, we came to the military installation – a camouflaged guard house with a handful of soldiers, sitting in the shade, playing chess or reading newspapers. In a nearby field, an armoured car – emerald green and two-tone grey – sat waiting for action.

Roadside stalls of bamboo and grass sold soup and rice and ice-cold drinks. Others sold melons, coconuts or bananas. One sold lucky charms and pendants. Always useful on a road in Thailand.

"Here – you have drink," and Chelsea dug a bottle of water out of her beauty box. "Have biscuit..." and she gave me the packet.

It was one of those wonderful crumbly biscuits with the squashed-fly currents and the taste of golden syrup. "Thanks, love," I said.

"Want more?"

"You bet," I smiled - anything to take my mind off Mr Van Rijder.

Sunflowers, rubber plantations, rows of houses with bright blue roofing tiles - it just went on and on and on... Sara Buri... Kaeng Khoi... At last, the driver pulled in for a pit stop.

"Thank you, God!" said Rudi, standing up and stretching his legs.

"You go first," said Chelsea. "I watch bag."

It seemed like an ideal opportunity to catch up with the folks back home. I found a stall in the Gents and sent a text message to Viv:

Dave sent: *All OK? Heading for Khorat. How's our little friend?*

Viv replied: *She's fine – I'm fine – and we have an idea.*

Dave sent: *Glad to hear it - still afloat.*

Viv replied: *Hang on to your oars.*

When I came out, Rudi was hanging around the piss-bowl area, probably hoping I'd be making phone calls. "Nice to stand up," he smiled.

"Far to go?"

"Two hours – maybe three," he said.

"Why didn't we fly?" I asked. "It only takes an hour."

"Airlines keep records," he said. "Take our names."

That made sense. "Can I choose my own route back?" I asked.

"Ask Van Rijder," Rudi told me. "Depends if he likes you."

Dear God, was this a crazy reality show? If you win the vote, you get to choose your own way home. "Will do," I said and made my way back to the bus.

When I got there, Chelsea was already on the passenger concourse, standing by a barrow with *Pepsi-Pepsi-Pepsi* on its front. It had barbecued sausage and deep-fried fish cakes. "You want?" she asked me.

"Looks inviting," I agreed.

"One hundred baht," she said and held out her hand. Once she had the money, she set about the ordering process, speaking rapidly in Thai and pointing at this, that and everything else.

Finally, she told me to sit on a hard-bum plastic seat in the passenger zone of this roadside halt - and there, she served me with a hot lunch, then gave me a can of ice-cold Pepsi for afters. At times, she could be totally adorable.

"I now go wash hands," she said.

"OK, lass," I said. Now I could text Sam

Pit-stop two hours from Khorat I sent him.

A minute later, he replied: *Ready and waiting*.

So are we I said. Then I noticed Rudi watching. "It's my mother," I said, holding up my phone. "She worries if I don't come home at night."

"Get her a cat," Rudi suggested.

More trees, more temples, the occasional river, a water buffalo knee-deep in muddy water. At intervals, the bus would stop: passengers got off; others got on.

By four o'clock, the heat began to fade. By six, it would be dark. It had been a long, hard slog and we still had God-knows-how-many-hours to go. If anyone had offered a bed for the night, I would have taken it.

"I hungry," Chelsea complained. She had finished the biscuits and was almost out of water.

"Can't be much longer," I tried.

And then the trees got thinner, farms became more frequent. Grazing animals appeared – and we were treated to rows of brick-built houses with glass windows and tiled roofs.

"We will stop here for about an hour," Rudi told me as we got nearer to Khorat.

"Same bus for Yasu?"

"No," he said. "New bus – new tickets."

"More comfortable seats?"

"You English," he laughed. "Always wanting miracles!"

True enough – but not in that way, sunshine. Two minutes later, we were in the town: real streets with shops and houses, pavement stalls and busy-busy motorbikes.

"That's us," said Rudi. The bus had pulled into this enormous terminal and he was on his feet, ready to go.

As I stood up to follow, my cell phone buzzed me a text: *Get him into the café.*

"Come on, kitten," I said to Chelsea. "Let's go get a coffee."

"No want coffee," she yawned, hardly moving. "Just want sleep." She was curled up in a ball and looked so comfortable. It seemed unfair to disturb her.

"Later, little kitten," I said. "First, we have to changes buses."

We dragged ourselves off the bus and found that our bags had been unloaded and lined-up by the benches in the passenger zone. Just like at Mo-Chit, there were food and drink stalls, all ready and were waiting for us. But this place had one extra feature – a fully-functional restaurant.

"You get coffee – I sit with bags," she offered. "Bring me water."

"You, got it, sweetheart," – and then I saw them - three policemen in their khaki uniforms. They were at the far end of the concourse and walking slowly towards us. Not that Rudi was difficult to spot. The big white *Greg Norman* was a dead give-away.

"Who would they been looking for?" Rudi asked.

"Who cares?" I grinned. "Let's go find the coffee pot."

For a moment, I thought he was about to argue, but he shrugged his shoulders and followed me into the café.

As my eyes adjusted to the gloom, I saw the plastic tables with the little round stools, a row of soft-drink counters. After that, the hotplates and carousels of cutlery.

Then: "You are Rudi Schiller?"

We both turned round to find ourselves face-to-face with the policemen. One had a hand resting on the butt of his Smith & Wesson.

"I am," said Rudi and carefully pulled his passport from his trouser pocket. "How can I help you?"

"You come with us," said the larger policeman.

"Why?" I asked, pushing forward.

"You – sit down!" said the other. The gun was out of its holster.

Rudi raised both hands. "Is OK, David – keep out of the way."

"This isn't right!" I protested.

"It's Thailand," said Rudi. "We are *farangs*."

"Want me to come with you?" I asked.

"No way!" said Rudi. He sounded far too casual, like he'd been expecting it. Maybe it happened at regular intervals. "You go on - Raphael will sort this out. I'll meet you there tomorrow."

The second man jabbed Rudi with the barrel of his revolver. *"No more chat – you come now,"* and they snapped a set of handcuffs on the South African's wrists and pulled him away.

"Want me to phone anyone?" I called.

"No need," Rudi smiled back. "He'll hear about it soon enough."

I waited until the pick-up party had left the restaurant, then hurried back to Chelsea. "It's all OK," I told her. "He's been lifted."

"He what?"

"Arrested," I explained. "Sam's men have got him."

"So we safe?" and her face lit up like a sunbeam.

"For the moment, yes," I said. "Let's go inside and celebrate."

"What about bags?"

"Take them," I said.

"What about his?"

I had to think on that one. "We'll take it with us," I decided. Although I didn't like the man, I didn't have the heart to leave his holdall on the sidewalk of a bus terminus, somewhere in the middle of Thailand. "Let's hope he isn't carrying a bomb!" I laughed.

"He not," said Chelsea. "I look already."

So we lugged our bags inside, picked a table near the *Pad Thai* hot plate and I let Chelsea order for us both. Although the café wasn't crowded, there were enough travellers around to stop us feeling lonely.

The staff wore yellow shirts. One was sweeping the floor while another was clearing the used crockery and washing down the tables.

"Why me here?" Chelsea asked me.

We'd been served, found the carousel and collected enough cutlery and straws to see us through the evening and were making the most of the Khorat version of my little kitten's favourite meal.

"To catch Mr Villavito," I said. "Mr Sam doesn't like him."

"Why not?"

"Because he's a criminal," I said.

"Why me here?"

Fair question. "Because you helped him," I said. "You sent all those backpacker *farangs* to smuggle the diamonds."

Chelsea paused for a moment to eat a spoonful of her meal. "We only do what he tell us," she said.

"That," I said, "is between you and Anni and Mr Sam."

"What you mean?"

We were back into pantomime.... *If she knew a little of the little I knew..... then she'd know a little....* "At the end of all this, someone's going to jail," I told her. "And if we can nail Villavito, it might not be you."

"Why me go to jail?"

"Because you were a naughty little kitten," I said.

"I no understand," she said, sucking her water through a red straw.

We were back to stuffing ferrets into rabbit warrens. "Well," I said, "if we *don't* get Villavito, you'll have five long and miserable years in the *Bangkok Hilton* to work it out."

26

If I thought that threatening Chelsea with a spell in prison would focus her mind, then I would have to try harder.

"If we want catch Mr Raphael, why we go Yasu?"

Once again, a fair question: start from the top and work down through the layers. "Remember those diamonds that Anni had to switch?"

"In RiverSide?" Chelsea nodded.

"Well," I told her, "they come from Yasu."

"How you know?"

"Sam told me," I said.

"What we do?"

"We pick up a shipment and give them to Villavito," I said.

"Then what happen?"

Very good. Not one *I no understand* in almost a minute. "Sam can arrest him as a criminal," I finished.

Chelsea took another shot of her water. "You think it work?" she asked. "You keep me out of prison?"

"Let's hope so," I smiled. "Now, do you want to phone Villavito and let him know?"

She didn't even blink. "Not now," she grinned. "Battery flat!"

"Bad luck!" I laughed. "Let's go shopping."

By now, it was dark. In Thailand, it doesn't take that long to go from day to night. Some stalls had rigged-up strings of electric lighting. Others just made do with candle-powered paper lanterns.

"What you like?"

"Something sweet," I told her.

"No!" she laughed. "Not good!" and went for healthy – like fish and rice. "One hundred baht!" and she held out her hand.

Last of all, we found the ticket desk, a card table with a cash box and several rolls of tickets. "Yasu Thon," I said, help up two fingers and gave the boy a thousand-baht note.

He laughed, tore off two tickets, gave me a handful of notes and coins, pointed to a bay and said something in Thai.

"It that bus," Chelsea translated. "It nearly ready."

"Then let's go to Yasu," I said.

If a long-distance bus is hard by day, it's even harder by night. There's nothing to look at, except the odd village or a candle-lantern by the side of the road.

I started by sending a text message to Viv. *All OK?* I asked her. *Here all in order – Rudi arrested in Khorat.*

Two minutes later, I received an answer from Head Office. *Nice one, squirrel – Anni fine - Os & Xs.*

I showed it to Chelsea.

"That good," she said and snuggled-up beside me. For a moment, I thought she was going to close her eyes and go to sleep. No chance! There was more. "Why you think me trick you to Mr Raphael?" she asked.

Best get it over and done with. "Someone told Villavito about the beads," I said.

"You think it me?"

"Only three of us knew," I said.

"How you know?" Now her eyes were wide open.

"Viv and I made up the package," I told her. "And I told you in the tiger garden after we'd met the Norwegian."

"Why you think it me?"

Our bus rumbled off Route 2 and into one of the little villages. It cruised between rows of unlit flat-roofed houses until it reached the village store which was lit-up like a fairground. Here, it stopped. Two passengers got off and scurried away into the darkness. Then the door swished shut, there was a hiss of air from the brakes and we were back on our way again.

Why did I think it was Chelsea? "Because they tell me you were his girl friend," I said.

Now she really was awake. *"That lie!"* she hissed. "I only ever work for him," and she shifted her body away from me and folded her arms in a gesture of defiance.

"I heard you were lovers," I said.

Now she was spitting fire. *"That is awful lie!"* she protested, glaring into my face. *"I never even let him hold my hand."*

"So who would invent that kind of a story?"

"People jealous," Chelsea replied.

"Of what?"

"You and me," she continued.

"Flattering," I smiled. "But it doesn't sound right."

"You *farang*," said Chelsea. "People jealous you my boyfriend."

By now, we were back on Route 2 and beginning to pick up speed. If we'd had a map, I could have followed our progress.

"Other girls jealous I get visa," Chelsea went on. "Lot of girls get *farang*, but no-one help with visa. Only you." She took my hand and kissed it.

"Seems unfair," I said.

"They jealous," Chelsea whispered. "Tell you many lies..." and before I knew what was happening, she had placed my hand on the top of her thigh.

"Later, kitten," I removed my hand, slipped it round her shoulder, under her arm and let it settle on her breast.

Chelsea turned her face towards me, asking for a kiss. We had reached the point of no-resistance. I had lost the battle. Right or wrong – whatever the truth in her story or the lies that had created her smokescreen, I was now firmly back in her spell. After all, it's bloody difficult to cross-examine a girl when you can feel her nipple growing harder, stroke by gentle stroke. We huddled into each other and tried to sleep for the remaining four or five hours of the ride to Yasu Thon.

Two hours went by – then three. Then four: "I want bed," came a little voice from somewhere in the fold of my shirt.

By now, we were the last two people on the bus. One by one, the others had waited for the bus to stop and then made the break to freedom under the cover of the jet-black darkness. Eventually, it had to be our turn. "Here," I tried, "drink the last of the water."

"No water – just bed." She sounded dead to the world.

"Sounds like a good idea," I said quietly and wrapped my arm around her again.

Another hour, and then we passed a roadside stall. Always a good sign. Then a house – and a farm building – and then ahead... streetlights!

"Come on, kitten," I said. "We could be nearly there." I checked my watch: it was getting close to 11pm – provided we were still in Thailand, of course.

The lights shone down on empty streets and it seemed that every building had a heavy-duty steel grille. It was an urban *Marie Celeste*. If this was Yasu, where were all the people?

154

"This it?" Chelsea was looking out on a wasteland of houses, shops, parked cars and the occasional bank.

"Doesn't look too hopeful," I said.

Then the driver gave us a shout.

"Where we go?"Chelsea asked me.

"It's a hotel called *Yod Na Khon*," I said – and she passed that information on to the driver.

At this point, our bus became a taxi and began to cruise the empty streets in search of the *Shangri-La* that (God willing) would service a couple of bus-weary travellers. And if there was any mercy left in this world, we might be spared a late-night session with the diamond-smuggling Van Rijder.

"Ya-ya!" yelled our driver and he slowed the bus.

It was not a Hilton. It was not a Holiday Inn. It wasn't even a RiverSide. It was a tunnel between two buildings that ended in a car park. On one side, a little guy in jeans and grimy T-shirt was asleep on a wooden bench. On the other, a doorway opened into a Reception area.

As we got off, this tall thin girl stepped out of the shadows. She was dressed in a red silk sari and her shining black hair was piled high in the traditional style. "You are Mr Shannon?" Then she clocked the *Laughin' Pussy* T-shirt. "And you are the famous Miss Anni?"

"That's us," I said before Chelsea could drop us in it.

"You are most welcome to Yasu!" she smiled. "I am Yasmin."

"Nice to meet you, Yasmin," and I gave a *wai*. "Call me Dave."

Yasmin returned my greeting and with a graceful movement of her arm, invited us to enter the hotel. I had my backpack round my shoulders and our holdalls in my left hand.

"Moment, please!" Yasmin called for a porter to take the holdalls.

Once inside, it was less intimidating. The Reception desk was on the right with a key rack, pigeon holes for messages, a TV set and a Chinese-style shrine. Ahead, a flight of stairs lead up to the bedrooms.

Yasmin handed me a key. "Room 201," she smiled.

"You OK with this?" I whispered to Chelsea.

"It have bed?"

"I guess," I replied.

"Then OK." She took the key and started up the stairway.

It was OK. Twin beds, a set of drawers with a TV set, one extra chair, a bathroom with all the necessaries and a small refrigerator. It also had a massive wardrobe and a chest-of-drawers.

"That should do us very nicely," I said. Anything to shut the door and get some rest.

Sadly, Yasmin hadn't finished with us. "You change now," she smiled, "Mr Van Rijder will see you at the *Old Western Ranch*."

"What's that?" I had to ask her.

"Country-&-Western," she said. "Mr Van Rijder's place."

Chelsea looked at me with horror. "I need bed," she complained.

"It's been a long day," I said. "Could we see him tomorrow?"

Yasmin bowed her head. "So sorry – no – has to be now."

I looked at Chelsea. From her expression, she was ready to burst into tears. "I'm the guy you need," I said. "Can she stay here?"

Yasmin thought about it for a moment and then decided to compromise. "That we can do," she agreed.

"Thank you, darling," Chelsea smiled. "Please lock me in."

I turned back to Yasmin. "Five minutes?" and I removed my shirt.

"I wait in Reception," Yasmin smiled.

When she had left us, I took Chelsea's hand. "Nothing will happen before morning," I promised her. "But would you like this?" and I showed her the 9mm Colt that Sam had given me.

Her eyes went wide with shock. *"Where you get that?"*

"From Mr Sam," I said.

"How it work?"

So I gave her a quick one-two on the safety catch and how to point it the target. "Then squeeze this," I said – and gave it to her.

On impulse, she pulled me close and kissed my cheek. "I keep it under pillow!" she laughed. "Now lock me in and promise not you fuck Miss Yasmin!"

There were times when her English was a bit too good. "Fat chance!" I grinned. "You come first – always have done – always will do."

In the bathroom, I stripped off and ran the shower. The water was cold. Never mind. There are days when anything is better than the grimy afters of a twelve-hour bus ride. *Cold* would have to do.

By the time I had finished, Chelsea was asleep. From the pile of clothing on the floor, I guessed she was naked. Just my luck! But I had things to do, places to go. So I put on a clean set of everything, hid the pack of beads and the two spare clips of ammunition in my bag of dirty laundry, left the bedside lights on, picked up my backpack, kissed my kitten lightly on the cheek and locked her into Room 201.

Yasmin was waiting in Reception. "Miss Anni OK?"

"She will sleep till morning," I told her.

"Then we go?"

"Just one thing," I asked. "Could you find me an ATM?"

"You need money?"

Stupid question! "Don't leave home without it," I smiled.

"We can find one easily enough," Yasmin promised.

27

A large navy-blue 4x4 Mitsubishi truck was waiting in the hotel driveway. Yasmin opened door and waved me into the bench seat behind the driver.

"Don't forget the ATM," I reminded her.

About a minute later, we pulled up under the bright green logo of the Kasikhon Bank. To one side of the forecourt, the ATM that Sam had mentioned.

"Is this OK for you?" Yasmin asked.

"Ideal," I said and climbed out of the truck. As I inserted my AmEx card, this kid came out of the night. She was short and very neatly put together, had long blonde hair and was dressed in a yellow shirt and jeans.

"Hi, buddy!" she called in the kind of American accent that you only hear on TV. "Can you work these foreign things?"

Good question. Back home, they're *Customer Friendly*. Out here, where all the instructions are written in Thai, it's a bit like playing *Scrabble* in a blindfold.

Yasmin was over by the Mitsubishi, watching every move.

"Plug-&-play," I said. "Want to watch me screw it up?"

"Hey! – a fuckin' Brit – that's brilliant!"

"Yes," I agreed. "And you?"

"Cambodia," my new friend admitted. "My dad spent time with the Peace Corps – I'm Sulita," and she offered me her hand.

Not quite what I was expecting. "Lovely to meet you, Sulita," I said. "Dave Shannon."

"You too, Dave," Sulita smiled. "Where you headin'?"

"My friend Yasmin..." and I pointed back to the truck, "...is taking me to an all-night bar for a Country-&-Western session."

"Sounds great! My daddy came from Tennessee!"

"Is that right?"

"Waylon Jennings – Big Jimmy Flatfoot... Muddy Waters..."

"Old Man River?"

"One of the greatest!" Sulita was ecstatic...

I looked at Yasmin. "Can she tag along?" I asked. "Us white guys have to stick together."

"Go on," Sulita pleaded. "I've been here over a week – and Dave's the first guy who knows what I'm talking about."

Yasmin didn't look happy. Maybe she'd heard of *Old Man River*.

"I won't steal your date, I promise!" Sulita grinned.

"We can't leave you on the street," Yasmin decided.

"Thanks," I said. "Let's get some cash." Once I'd pushed the buttons and answered the questions, the Kasikhon gave me 5000 baht. "Let's go," I said and climbed back into the 4x4.

Fifteen minutes later, we had found the *Old Western Ranch* – a wooden pavilion in the middle of nowhere. We parked, crossed a patio, pushed open a pair of saloon doors and entered the *Grand Old Oprey*, Thailand style.

It was a small stage with a giant poster of the *Democracy Monument* as a backdrop. Two guitars and a keyboard were stoking *Ring of Fire* to full volume.

We followed Yasmin through the maze of tables. In a corner furthest from the stage, a man in a tartan shirt stood up, flung out his arms and hugged me. "Very nice to see you, David!"

"Mr Van Rijder?" He was tall, grey-haired and lean - most likely, in his sixties. And his accent was heavily South African.

"Cornelius," he offered. "And what happened to Rudi?"

"Someone didn't like him," I smiled.

"He should be nicer to people," Cornelius replied. "We tell him, do we not, my dear?"

Yasmin smiled at her boss. "Indeed we do, Mr Van Rijder."

"But he never learns." Then Cornelius took my backpack. "Just a formality, David," and he reached inside to search it. "Three questions," he began.

"What would you like to know?"

"First – where are they?" He meant Anni's missing diamonds.

"Safe," I said.

"Second – where's the *Laughin' Pussy*?"

"In bed – asleep," I said. "Worn out."

"Third – who's the heifer in the yellow shirt?"

"Cornelius," I said, "meet Sulita, an American who's lost in a world that won't speak English."

"Is that a problem?" Van Rijder wanted to know.

"Yes, if you want to use an ATM," I said.

Van Rijder laughed, then looked her up and down. "My dear," he offered, "you are welcome to join us."

"You're a lovely man!" Sulita smiled and made a point of sitting next to him.

This left me with Yasmin. "Drinks all round?" I asked her.

"Mr Van Rijder doesn't drink," she said. "He likes to listen."

"Bully for him," I said. "I've been on a bus since dawn."

"I don't suppose he will mind." And Yasmin called for a waiter.

Sulita and I enjoyed a couple of beers and shared a fairly substantial bowl of chicken and rice, with freshly-baked rolls. Later, I would make up a couple for Chelsea.

While we made short work of the meal, the musicians crashed their way through the basic C&W repertoire of Don Williams and Tammy Wynette – with a little Dusty Springfield for good measure.

As the night wore on, Van Rijder worked his way around the table until he was beside me, leaving Sulita with Yasmin for company. "You are satisfied with your hotel?" he asked.

"Will be when I get there," I said. "It's been a long hard day."

"Indeed it has," Cornelius agreed.

"What about tomorrow?"

"Breakfast at ten," he said. "Yasmin will collect you."

"We'll be ready," I promised.

"Then I will wish you a comfortable night," he said. "Yasmin will take you home."

"And Sulita?"

"Of course."

"Been good meeting you," I said and shook his hand.

Back at the hotel, Sulita flung her arms around my neck. "Jeez – I'm glad we used the same bank tonight!" she was laughing. "Here's my number if you need me." She pushed a piece of paper into my hand and gave me a smacking kiss, right on the button. Then she just vanished into the night.

Yasmin walked me to the hotel door. "What do you know about her?" she asked, meaning Sulita.

"As much as you do," I said.

"Don't get too close," Yasmin warned me. "You're a busy man."

"I couldn't cheat on Chelsea," I smiled back, pushed my way past her and went inside. And although I tip-toed up the stairs and opened the door as quietly as possible, Chelsea was sitting up in bed, gun in hand – just in case.

Somehow, it didn't look right. "Don't shoot me yet," I told her. "I've brought you a chicken sandwich."

28

Once in a while, God deals a hand so good you feel afraid to play it. And that's how I felt on that Wednesday morning when I awoke to find myself three feet away from a naked Chelsea.

I just gazed at her. She looked so calm and peaceful – and so very beautiful. I could throw back my blanket, cross the gap between our beds and slide in beside her. She was there for the taking. All I had to do was thank the Lord, play the cards and go for glory.

A test of character? Then she opened her eyes and smiled at me. "Thank you for supper," she said. "Give me nice long sleep," and she sat up, yawned and stretched her arms. Just to taunt me even further, she turned to flaunt her breasts. She knew! Too bloody true, she knew.

"Ready for breakfast?" I asked her.

"You only think of food?"

And there was me, with a five-card flush that ended with a Jack of Clubs. "Not all the time," I said – and crossed the Rubicon to climb in beside her.

From this point on, there was no going back. We were now *an item*. We might never see Thursday. So let's go to hell with a fucking good bang!

We did – then both exploded in a rainbow of simultaneous passion. Suddenly, it came into focus. I was here because I loved her, needed her and wanted to protect her. "What now?" I whispered in the lovely little ear.

She threw back the cover and eased her gorgeous body out of bed. "I go have shower," she laughed, picked up her holdall and skipped into the bathroom.

"If the water's warm, I'll join you." But it wasn't – so I didn't.

Once washed, we dressed in style - me in yellow, Chelsea in the *Laughin' Pussy* shirt - and went downstairs, hand-in-hand, to find Yasmin waiting in Reception.

Her long black hair was tied back into a pony-tail and she was dressed in orange silk. "You sleep well?" she smiled.

I looked at Chelsea; Chelsea looked at me. Was it obvious? "Thank you, yes," I said. "Great beds!"

Yasmin shook her head in disbelief. "Whatever will Chelsea say?"

I offered her my phone. "Want to drop me in it?"

"She can wait," said Yasmin. "First, we go to Mr Van Rijder."

He wasn't hard to find. Yasmin's large black Mitsubishi was out in the car park at the back of *Yod Na Khon* – and from there, we eased our way through the tunnel and into a wide and busy Main Street.

There, we found people! This was Yasu: enthusiastic and ready for action. Instead of grilles, we now had shops. On both sides of the street, two-stroke motorcycles were parked in long straight rows. But the bicycle beat everything. They were there in swarms, like butterflies, fluttering gracefully along the street.

Above the shops, adverts for *Isuzu* and *Yamaha* and *Pedigree Chum* were easy to read. Everything else was in Thai and although Yasmin was veering the 4x4 through the traffic like a slalom skier, I was able to identify a pharmacy, an optician and a shop selling digital cameras.

Seconds later, we were forced to stop by a sports shop where three young girls out front were sharing a joke. I smiled at the one in the green shirt and snapped her picture.

"I think she fancy you," Chelsea smiled.

"If you let me out, I'll ask her," I said.

"It safe," Chelsea replied. "She lady-boy."

"Can't win 'em all," and I kissed her cheek.

Two stops later, we had reached the cross-roads and Yasmin was revving the engine, almost demanding a gap in the traffic.

"Mr Van Rijder will be furious!" she was complaining.

"You can't do tits about the traffic," I said.

"Mr Rijder is not a patient man," Yasmin replied. "He will not be happy if we are late."

"This is Thailand time," I said. "What difference will it make?"

"Mr Van Rijder is a South African..."

"Where all the trains run on time." On my left, I saw this collection of orange buckets, all lined-up on the pavement. "Hey - a Buddhist shop!" I said to Chelsea. "What can I buy you?"

It was an amazing sight. Ritualistic garlands hung from the ceiling and wafted in the morning breeze. The dozen plastic buckets were filled with household cleaning products and wrapped in cling-film. Behind the buckets, a line of brand new Buddha images, wrapped in plastic covers.

"Nothing," said Chelsea.

"She's right," Yasmin agreed. "You cannot buy a Buddha image."

"I've got one at home," I pointed out.

"Not bought," Chelsea corrected me. "Only rented."

"I'm not allowed to own one?" I still had my camera ready and as we eased around the corner, I clicked a couple of shots of the shop.

"You are not allowed to photograph the Buddha's face!" Yasmin yelled at me. She was quite upset. "In Thailand, not permitted."

Nor is prostitution, I thought. "So what are the buckets for?"

"Gifts to monks," Chelsea explained.

"Am I allowed to buy one of those?"

"No," she said, "you make donation."

You're having me on, I thought.

A girl in a bright blue dress was minding the shop. As we pulled away, she smiled and waved to me.

"And you not buy her, either," Chelsea warned me.

Seconds later, we were stopped again. This time, by a man and a woman pushing a barrow of flowers across the road. "Now those, I can buy!" I laughed and before Yasmin could stop me, I was out of the truck and helping to push the barrow. When we reached the other side, the woman smiled and nodded her thanks.

"No problem," I said and picked a bunch of purple orchids from the display. "May I?" and I gave the woman a 20-baht note.

Again, she smiled and nodded.

"Here you are, kitten," and I passed the flowers to Chelsea through the open door of the truck. "With my love!"

By now, Yasmin was on her way to a nervous breakdown. "Can we get on?" she snapped.

"Faint heart never won fair lady," I replied and gave Chelsea a delicate kiss on her cheek.

Now it was Yasmin's turn to score a point. "Mr Van Rijder is paying you a lot of money," she reminded me. "You should remember why you are here."

Good line, sweetheart – which she had delivered while zipping round an orange bus and in between two *Sam Lor Pun* riders who were racing each other on their bicycle rickshaws. Michael Schumacher could not have done it better.

Impressive, yes – but I couldn't let her get away with it. Why waste an opportunity? "Fifty-thousand dollars buys a lot of orchids," I smiled. "Surely I can buy a minute for a beautiful girl?" and I gave Chelsea another kiss. However, before we could upgrade our bickering to the level of the personal insult, Yasmin swung the 4x4 off the road and onto the forecourt of the chosen restaurant.

It was built on a wooden frame with a bright red corrugated roof and open on all four sides. The dining area had two lines of small, square tables, each being covered by a pink table cloth. Aluminium chairs were padded with brown plastic backs and semi-acceptable cushions.

At the far end of this room, a sign above the karaoke system promised *Sabuy - Folk any Style*. A *Chang* beer machine was by the door - and the flags-of-all-nations fluttered in the morning breeze.

Cornelius Van Rijder was sitting at a table, waiting for us. Today, he was wearing a red cravat and a red-check sarong. In front of him, two cups of black coffee and a plate of sliced tomatoes.

"Good morning David!" he smiled as we entered. "And good morning to you, Miss Anni."

He didn't say anything to Yasmin. Perhaps the other coffee was hers from an earlier visit.

"Good morning, Cornelius," I thanked him.

"You sleep well?" In the relative silence of the restaurant, his South African accent seemed even thicker.

"Thank you, yes – we did," I replied.

"You have had your breakfast?"

"No," said Chelsea. Never one to stand on ceremony, she pulled out the chair across from the South African and sat down.

"What would you like?" and as Cornelius waved an arm, a waitress in a clean white apron came up to the table.

"Coffee – egg on toast," I said, now sitting in beside Chelsea. "And for you?" I asked her.

"Mango juice," she decided.

"Good choice," Cornelius agreed and told the waitress.

Yasmin took the chair beside her boss. "What are our plans for today?" she asked him. She seemed anxious to keep the agenda on track.

Cornelius speared a piece of tomato with his fork and dunked it in his coffee. "As we have a little time at our disposal," he told her, "I'm going to show our guests around our beautiful town."

All fixed-up and settled.

Moments later, our coffee and mango juice arrived, followed by my egg-on-toast. Or rather, egg-IN-toast – as my breakfast had been translated into a sandwich.

"You OK with that?" Cornelius asked.

"What the hell!" I grinned. "There's an egg – and toast – that's close enough," and I picked it up with both hands.

After breakfast, our first *visitor attraction* was a play park, dominated by a life-sized model of a T-Rex. It had been built in an upright pose, head back, mouth wide open and flashing its flesh-ripping teeth.

"Dinosaurs have been found in Thailand," Cornelius explained.

"Just the skeletons, I hope," I said.

"I would imagine so," Van Rijder replied without humour.

Then Yasmin decided to get *up-close and social* with a long-dead reptile and sat on one of its paws to be photographed. "I want to send it to my mother!"

It was easy to imagine the picture I would have liked to send her mother, but the T-Rex wouldn't co-operate. Every creature has its limits.

There was a pond fringed by coconut palms, many bearing fruit. As a kid in the East End, the only coconuts I'd ever seen had been used for making donkey-trotting sound effects in the school's nativity play. Now here they were, growing wild, up a tree – and ready for harvesting.

"Over here!" Cornelius had found a soft-drink cart. Bags of crispy snacks were hanging along one side and a large green parasol made an ideal sun-shade. "Who wants ice cream?"

"I'd rather collect the diamonds," I whispered to Chelsea.

"Me too," she agreed. "Not like being Anni."

"Yes, it's hard to remember who you're supposed to be." Then I noticed the girl who was in charge of the cart. She was tall, slim and had the blackest hair, skilfully cut in a fringe around her face - and wearing faded jeans and a bright pink shirt. She looked just a little bit familiar. And then the penny dropped.

Jesus Christ – Sulita!

Chelsea noticed my surprise. "You know her?"

I was about to tell her – but then remembered Sam's warning. "Never seen her before in my life," I lied. "She reminds me of a girl who used to work in Tesco," I said.

"Was she your friend?"

"Not really," I said, "but once, she let me nibble her Hob-Nobs."

"It was good?"

"No," I told her, "I really wanted hot-buttered crumpet."

Before Chelsea could produce another *what-you-mean*, Cornelius was offering us a Walls *Cornetto* each, complete with rainbow sprinkles and chocolate syrup dribbling in sticky rivers down the cone. "There you are, Anni!" he smiled, handing them over.

"Say thank you to the nice man," I said.

"Thank you, Mr Van Rijder," Chelsea nodded.

"Most welcome, my dear," the South African replied.

While we licked and slurped at our ice creams, he guided us towards the banks of the Chee, the river that flows through Yasu Thon. A new-looking bridge crossed a weir and half-a-dozen men were leaning over the parapet to fish in muddy waters.

"What are they hoping for?" I had to ask.

"Anything eatable," Van Rijder told me.

Beyond the weir, the river opened onto a flood plain. Here, reeds and water lilies grew in abundance - and some five or six little broken fishing boats had found a final resting place.

Now Van Rijder was beside me "A useful facility," I heard him say. "So close to the city – but virtually deserted."

"Nice for the water rats," I said.

Van Rijder ignored my comment. "Last year," he continued, "the police removed the bits of this body that the crabs didn't want."

Was there a point to this? "Is that right?"

"They reckoned it had been there for all of a year."

"Did they identify it?"

"No," Van Rijder sniffed. "Not even from his backpack."

"No ideas at all?" *When will I learn to keep it firmly SHUT...?*

"He may have been a courier," Van Rijder muttered. "From time to time, they have been known to go missing..."

Messages come in all shapes and sizes – and here was one, waiting for an answer. I could see it all too clearly. This wetland was the perfect place to dump a body. God-willing, it would not be mine. "Wonderful setting for an *Agatha Christie*," I replied with a grin. "It would occupy the *Little Grey Cells* for the rest of the week."

"You have seen enough?" Van Rijder wasn't here for levity.

No point in making any more smart remarks. "Shall we move on?"

"I have something else to show you..." and he started walking back towards to 4x4.

"When do I collect the merchandise?" I asked him.

"All in good time," Van Rijder replied.

From the play park, Yasmin drove along a tree-lined highway that ran as straight as any Roman Road. We passed temples, shops and road-side stalls that sold fruit and soup-&-bread lunches.

Then Yasmin slowed the truck and turned into a dusty, bumpy, country dirt-track that eased its way through tiny farms where cows or pigs or horses was doing their best to snack from the side of the road. By peering into the bamboo groves, it was possible to see the lean-to shack that served the farmer and his family as a home. They were the *other half* of the Thailand equation.

As we humped and bumped our way along this heavily overgrown lane, so the groves, trees and bushes began to thicken. Eventually, we stopped at this large wooden gate that looked like the entrance to *Jurassic Park*. A notice in Thai had been spelt in large red letters.

"It say *Keep Out*," Chelsea told me.

Yasmin hammered the horn a couple of times and the gate was opened by a Thai in a dark-grey jump-suit.

"So why are we going in?" I asked her.

"Ask him – his gate," Chelsea whispered back.

Cornelius heard her. "To let you admire my little hobby," he explained with a touch of conceit in his voice.

Once through the second gate, the jungle opened out to show a large pond covered by water plants and orange poppies. Here and there, outbuildings were partly hidden in the greenery. "Adobe," Cornelius explained. "We make them out of mud."

"Like in Mexico?"

"Exactly!" and he climbed out of the Mitsubishi.

"Cheap to build," I said – and then without thinking, I asked: "Are you growing heroin?" *Oh shit! How wrong could anyone possibly be?*

"No," Van Rijder smiled. "Crocodiles..." and he waved across the lake towards a couple of dark brown logs that were floating on the surface. He threw a stone at the nearest one.

As the pebble skipped neatly across the pond, the log turned into a crocodile and showed annoyance by thrashing its tail, rolling over and disappearing below the surface.

"Why?" I had to ask.

"For their meat!" Van Rijder replied. "It has a delicate taste, is low in fat and high in protein."

"It all sounds very healthy," I said.

"Wait till they sell it in your local Tesco!"

It sounded all too simple. "How do you harvest them?"

"With great difficulty!" Van Rijder laughed. "Its brain is very well protected and difficult to hit with a bullet or a captive bolt."

I could well imagine. "Is there any other way?"

"Yes indeed," said Van Rijder. "You can always hack its head off with an axe."

Some job description! "How many are there?" I was keeping a watchful eye on the fifty meters of open ground between us and the pond.

"Not the easiest creatures to count," Van Rijder smiled. "We have some fifty adults and over two hundred babies in the rearing pens."

"That's a lot," I said. "How do you feed them?" Not the brightest question. At that moment, the wetland over by the *River Chee* was the better option.

"We throw them a carcass from time to time," said Van Rijder.

"Horse or cow?" I asked.

"Depends what we have available," Van Rijder smiled.

"How often?" Was it by the hour, the day, month or year?

"They let us know when they're getting hungry." As if to prove his point, a ripple over by the water's edge produced a large brown snout and a set of smiling jaws. Then there were two – and three – and a fourth began to haul its lumbering body out of the water.

"Time to go?" I asked.

"Yes," Van Rijder agreed." Let us go and find some diamonds."

29

According to the legend on the nearby notice board, *That Kong Kao Noi* – or the *Shrine of Kong Kao Noi* – is a neat example of a brick-built *chedi*. It stands on a square plinth, is superimposed by a lotus pedestal with a torus moulding - and dates back to the 24th Century (B.E.). And if the legend is telling the truth, it is not unlike the *Phra That So Kotaboon* structure in Laos. (But you'll have to trust me on that one.)

Yes, it's amazing what you can learn if you bother to read the published information. Mind you, it doesn't always help. On a neighbouring notice issued by the Tourism Authority of Thailand, the *Useful Phone Number* is written in Thai – which is great for them, but doesn't help those of us who've travelled all the way from Kentish Town.

However, *mai pen rai*, as they say in this part of the world. But when I made a point of telling Chelsea, she just asked me: "Why you want to phone them?"

Good question – and I didn't have an answer.

Nearby, a square domed building housed a Buddha. It wore a saffron sash and sat in dignified splendour behind an altar decorated with icons, gifts and flowery tokens. Regardless of Yasmin's fears, I stood in the entrance to the shrine and took a couple of pictures.

"The Lord Buddha will not mind," Chelsea smiled.

From the crocodile farm, it had taken us just on half an hour to reach this temple. Once we'd found our way out of the jungle, the main road back to town had whipped us into the car park at *That Kong Kao Noi* in a matter of minutes. There had been a shower of rain. It should have been refreshing, but it turned the Mitsubishi into a sauna.

"I sick," Chelsea had complained.

"Can I kiss it better?" I asked her.

She turned me down. "Is not so bad," she said, rejecting my offer of a gentle massage.

However, Van Rijder put her mind at rest. "Nearly there," he assured her. Minutes later, we pulled off the road and into the dirt track that took us into an acre of open ground that served as a parking area for the temple.

"Get me water, darling?" Chelsea asked.

"Of course, little kitten," I promised – and looked around. Along one side of the car park, stalls were offering bits and pieces, bric-a-brac and other knick-knacks for sale. At first, it was hard to decide if it was a market or a shopping place for tourists.

There was a stall with Colas, Fantas, 7-Ups and any amount of bottled water. It was in the safe hands of this little old lady in a green sari.

"Four, please," I asked her, pointing at the bottles of water that were cooling in a bucket of ice.

"Hundred baht..." She had a squeaky, high-pitched voice, a wrinkled face and not enough teeth.

On a nearby stall, I noticed sets of large round trays – with a choice of canvas or wicker bases, like a gardener's riddle. "What are they for?" I wanted to know.

"Sticky rice," Yasmin explained.

"Which is?"

"Used on the Great Wall of China!" she laughed. "Very filling!"

"Can you eat it?"

"Oh yes," she said. "Tonight, you must try it."

After the warnings down by the river and the visit to the crocodiles, the idea of an evening meal was encouraging. "What's it like?"

"Sticky!" Cornelius laughed. "You have not heard the story?"

"Of what?" I asked. Chelsea was strolling along the line of stalls, looking at the hats. At that moment, she was trying on a *Roy Rogers* made of white straw with a cute red hatband. Shortly, she would be asking for the *honey* to pay for it.

"This boy was working in a field," Cornelius began, "and his mother came out to bring his lunch."

"That's what mothers do," I said.

"But when the kid opened his lunchbox, all he found was this great big lump of sticky rice."

"No cheese?"

By now, we had crossed the parking area and were approaching the first of the souvenir stalls. Further along, Chelsea was still field-testing the white cowboy hat.

"So the kid got mad," Cornelius went on. "*What's the use of all this crap?* he starts yelling."

"That's no way to treat your mother," I said.

"Too damned true!" Cornelius laughed. "And then he smacked her one – right across the face – with his shovel."

"Poor woman!" I said. "What happened?"

"Killed her – stone dead – right there in the field!" and he flung his arms into the air to emphasise the enormity of the crime.

As a performer, Cornelius had a feeling for the dramatic and could easily have toured the world as an *Othello*. "Then the kid sat down and tried to eat his lunch."

"Callous little sod," I said.

"That's not all," Cornelius went on. "No matter how much he stuffed in his miserable mouth, he just couldn't finish his lunch."

"So what's the point of the story?"

"Don't complain about a meal until you've tried to eat it, I guess," Cornelius finished.

I stopped walking and looked at him. Was this another warning to finish the job, deliver the goods and keep everyone happy? "Did you make that up?" I asked our leader.

"Not at all," Van Rijder smiled. "It happened right here in Yasu."

"Really?"

"Not so far away from where you're standing," he said. "There's a temple with a *chedi* in a pond that marks the spot."

"All for a handful of rice..." I said quietly.

"It's the way of the world," said Van Rijder and moved off to look at some hand-carved souvenirs at a nearby stall.

If it *was* a warning, then a bit more *Yes Sir / No Sir* might be worth a try. I followed on – but kept a few steps behind him. Watch and wait; see what happens.

Two stalls away, a young Thai girl was looking at some hand-woven bags that were stretched on a washing line across the front of the stall. She was dressed in three-quarter length jeans and a sky-blue shirt. Her long hair cascaded down her back in a sensual black waterfall. For some reason, she looked familiar. I had to make sure.

I walked up beside her. "They look OK," I said.

"Very good for carrying diamonds," Sulita replied.

"Nice to see you again," I said. "I think it's getting close."

Sulita chose a dark blue shoulder bag with black edging. "I'll tell Mr Sam," she said. "Text me when you get them," and she paid for her bag with a handful of change and wandered off.

Then it was Chelsea's turn. "Who she?"

"I asked about these bags," I said. "Might get one for my sister."

Chelsea wasn't interested in shopping bags. "You like my hat?" she asked.

OK, so it made her look like an American tourist on a golfing holiday - but if it made her happy, did it really matter? "How much?" I wanted to know.

"One-fifty baht," came her answer.

As it was too hot to argue, I gave her the *honey*.

"Thank you, darling!" and she skipped away to pay for the hat.

I turned back to see the other goodies on the stall. They had the usual little elephants and Buddha figures and some rainbow-coloured parrots made out of paper.

Smaller paper birds were in tiny wicker cages. Others were sitting on perches that you could hang in an open window. When there was a breeze, these little guys would flutter their pretty little paper wings.

It was hard to get a proper look at anything. This old woman in black just wouldn't stop showing me all these different items, like flutes and bongos and pan-pipes, all made out of bamboo.

Then she insisted on showing me these gold-coloured cushions. They were round, about 6" across and made of satin. To finish them off, they'd been quilted into something like giant pin cushions.

"You take! – you take!" she kept insisting

Van Rijder was beside me. "Which do you fancy?"

"I'd take them all if I could," I said.

"What's stopping you?"

"They won't fit into a holdall."

"The cushions would," he said.

"What would I do with them?"

"Take them to Mr Villavito," was the answer.

So this is what it was about. We were in a temple gift park, buying pretty little cushions stuffed with *God-Knows-What*. And Van Rijder hadn't touched anything. It was almost an under-achievement.

I took the cushions and squeezed them. They made a rustling sound, like pebbles in a bag of sand. "Is this what I'm here for?" I asked.

"Give her one hundred baht," Van Rijder told me.

"Why?"

"Because you're a tourist buying souvenirs," my host explained with infinite patience.

"OK," I agreed and paid the old woman. "Is that it?"

"Not quite," Van Rijder replied. "I would still like to see that packet that Miss Anni has stolen from my dear friend, Raphael."

"Back home, we'd say *alleged to have stolen*," I reminded Cornelius. "So far, they're only *missing*."

"Are they still *missing?*"

"For the moment, yes," I said.

"When will they be found?"

We were walking back towards the Mitsubishi. Yasmin and Chelsea were already there, sipping on bottles of water. I hoped she'd bought one for me.

"When I'm absolutely sure that Anni and her sister are safe," I said. "That was my deal with Raphael – and I see no reason to change it."

"Are you sure?"

Well no, it was my deal with Sam - but I had to say something. "I'm working for Raphael," I said. "No changes without his say-so."

"If he asks me to check them?"

For the moment, the *Yes/No* plan went on hold. "Cornelius," I said, "a lot of people would like to check them."

"Is that so?"

"And a lot more people would like to save me the bother of looking after them," I said.

Van Rijder was not happy. "Am I one of them?"

"I hope not," and I gave him a reassuring smile. "But I owe it to Raphael to take good care of his property – OK?"

Although he was burning up, he went along with my argument. "I will call him tonight," he promised.

"Do that," I said. "And ask him to have my fifty-K all packed up and ready to go."

After that, the ride back to Yasu was a non-speaking affair. Even Chelsea sensed there was thunder in the air – and for once, she kept it firmly shut. Yes, I still had the packet of glass beads at the bottom of my backpack, but I couldn't see how to use them.

Fifteen minutes later, we were parked at the back of the *Yod Na Khon*. "What happens now?" I asked Van Rijder.

"It is far too late for you to catch a bus tonight," he decided.

"We're staying one more night?"

"You will catch the bus tomorrow."

"Is that OK with you?" I asked Chelsea.

She nodded. "If we have proper dinner, yes."

Van Rijder laughed. "Don't fret yourself, Miss Anni," he smiled. "Yasmin has selected a magnificent restaurant for this evening."

"What time?" I asked.

"Yasmin will pick you up at eight."

I checked my watch. It was only a couple of minutes after four. "That's great!" I grinned to Chelsea. "We can have a nice cold bath and relax for a couple of hours."

She didn't look too unhappy at the idea. "If we get some beers as well," she agreed.

Up in our room, I plugged in our cell phones to give them a re-charge. Then having swilled a couple of cans of Singha, we stretched out on our respective beds and tried to rest. But when you're in possession of about one million dollars in smuggled diamonds, it's not that easy to close your eyes. At that moment, I was happy to be carrying Sam's 9mm Colt.

My one comforting thought? No-one would be likely to steal that amount of ice from Raphael Villavito. In the middle of that thought, I must have dropped off – because when Chelsea knelt on the bed to wake me, it was getting close to eight o'clock.

"Take shower – wear clean shirt," she ordered.

She has already showered - and in that brilliant vermillion T-shirt, she looked totally irresistible. So I wrapped my arms around her slender little body and pulled in close. I could almost taste her perfume. "Kiss me first," I grinned.

"What come second?" she smiled back.

"I'll take a shower and change my shirt," I promised.

"That all?"

"For the moment, yes," I said. "We have a date for dinner."

When we went down to Reception, we found Yasmin waiting for us. "Mr Van Rijder will meet us there," she promised.

Yasmin's choice of restaurant was in walking distance. In Yasu, most things are. Once you reach the crossroads, you have four choices – north, south, east or west. Just about everything lies within minutes of the Buddha shop.

I wasn't bothered. If our date with Yasmin gave him a chance to search our room, he would be wasting his time. Anything of value was in the backpack that was safely slung over my left shoulder. "Did he speak to Mr Villavito?" I asked her.

"He may have done," she said. "I can't be sure."

"Don't fret," I said. "I'll ask him later."

Chelsea just walked beside me, holding my hand. To me, that was a gesture of trust and it made me think more about her and less about myself. Somehow, I would get her out of this mess. But there were far too many *if's* in *somehow*.

Our diner was an open-fronted shop with tables down each side. Halfway up on the right, there was a charcoal stove – and on the left, a marble-topped counter displayed the menu for the evening.

The idea was to look, decide - and explain it to the cook, in Thai. Fortunately, I had Chelsea. Otherwise, I could have gone hungry.

She chose fish, prawns, chicken, salad and enough rice for both of us. Water came as standard – then chose a bottle of Chinese wine.

"Is it red or white?" I asked her.

"Red, of course," she snapped. "White is for old women."

"Good choice," I agreed, now firmly back in my box.

Yasmin went for the chicken. "I will also order for Mr Van Rijder," she said. "He likes his meat rare."

Just like his crocodiles. "You know best," I said.

From that point on, we didn't talk about anything important. Yasmin asked about London - and had I been to *Planet Hollywood*?

When Van Rijder arrived, he made short work of a side of pork, washed it down with several litres of *Chang* – and then passed on Villavito's wishes for a safe journey back to Bangkok.

"That was kind of him," I said.

"I spoke to him earlier," Cornelius admitted. "So long as you give him *all* the diamonds," - and he stressed the ALL in capital speech – "he will keep to his agreement."

"He'll have the money counted and waiting?"

"You can trust him, yes," Van Rijder smiled.

To be honest, I felt safer with a crocodile – but if we could save our ace till last, we might still walk away with all our limbs intact. For reassurance, I put my hand in the backpack and stroked the comforting butt of the pistol.

Van Rijder noticed. "Something you need?" he asked me.

"Aspirin," I said. "I'm getting a headache."

Back at the hotel, we wished Yasmin a fond "*Goodnight*" and made out way up to our room. After our pre-breakfast moment of glory, there seemed no point in pretending any more.

"Your bed or mine?" I said to Chelsea.

"What it matter?" Chelsea smiled. "You still get *me-me*!"

"Nice one, squirrel!" I said and snuggled in beside her.

30

It was coming up to seven when I woke. First job of the morning: an ice-cold shower. Don't get me wrong, I'm not a health-freak - but the plumbing was a problem. It was either *cold* or *nothing*, so I went for *cold*.

When I returned to the room, Chelsea was sitting up in bed and calling someone on her mobile. "Thank you, darling!" she smiled as I threw my towel across the bed. "Phone now working."

"Oh shit!" I swore to myself.

"What wrong?" Chelsea asked. "Just calling my friend."

"It's not you, kitten," I told her. "It's the phones."

"What you mean?"

"They've been off all night." I said.

"It matter?"

"Only if someone like Sam has been trying to reach us."

"Why him want us?"

Good question. Cornelius seemed happy enough. Raphael had agreed to my proposal. Rudi was in jail, and if Sulita had wanted us, she could have knocked on the door. "No-one special," I said. But I had forgotten about Viv.

As I switched my cell phone ON, it rang. I flicked the *listen-to-me* button – and just said: "Dave..."

"*Viv,*" came the short reply. "*Where the fuck have you been?*"

"What's up?"

"Been trying to ring you all night – what are you doing?"

"Sod all," I said. "Left it on *charge*, that's all."

"*Well aren't you just the fuckin' dipstick!*" she yelled at me.

"How come?"

"You had a visitor."

"Dare I ask?" but my pulse rate had already hit three figures.

"A South African – Rudi something..."

Jesus Christ! Who sprung him? "What did he want?"

"Asked if Anni was OK."

"And you said...?"

"That she was safe in Bangkok - then I realised," Viv added.

Bollocks! "Did you call Sam?"

"Don't have his number."

"It's OK – I'll do it," I said. Rudi was on his way, but not for a social call. He was coming after Anni's diamonds.

"Anything I can do?" Viv asked me.

"Work on the escape plan," I told her. "See if you can persuade Anni to find her sodding nest-egg."

"Are we having a panic attack?"

"Too fuckin' true!" I said. "We may be travelling sooner than expected." I had no idea of where or how – but we were in it, right up to the jewel-box.

"Love 'n kisses!" Viv promised as she closed the call.

By now, Chelsea had sensed that we were in trouble. "What wrong?" she asked.

"Remember Rudi?"

"Man in silly hat?"

You've got a nerve! I thought, remembering the *Roy Rogers*. "Right on, my love," I said. "Well, some bastard has let him out of jail."

"Is that bad?"

"It isn't good," I told her. "He's on his way."

"To see us?"

"Don't worry," I smiled. "It'll take him a while to find us." To get us up and running, I cleared my backpack, just leaving the essentials – passports, Colt, spare magazine, pack of glass beads. Everything else could go in the holdalls.

"We have chance?" Chelsea asked.

"Oh yes," I said. "He doesn't know about the pistol."

Chelsea smiled at me. "What else?"

"He doesn't know about Sulita, either," and I called her number on my cell phone.

"Who Sulita?"

"Right now," I said as her number rang out, "she's the best friend we've got."

Sulita answered within three rings. "You guys OK?" she asked.

"No," I said, "we're not."

"Tell me..."

"Rudi Schiller is out of jail and on his way."

"Are you sure?" Sulita asked.

I needed coffee - but the *Yod Na Khon* hotel didn't do room service. "Where else will he go?" I asked her.

"Does he know where to find you?"

"Van Rijder or the wicked witch will tell him," I guessed.

Sulita thought for a moment. "Let's go *worst case*," she suggested. "If he's driving up, he won't be far away."

"Very comforting," I said.

"Don't worry – I'll be there in ten minutes."

"We'll wait here," I promised.

Which I should have done - but the need for coffee was burning my brain. I picked up my wallet and tossed the backpack into the wardrobe. For the moment, it was better out of sight. "In search of coffee," I told Chelsea. "You want anything?"

"Get me a coke?" she asked.

"Will do," I promised, then unlocked the door and swung it open like a sheriff entering a Wild West saloon. Big mistake - I never even saw it coming.

S-M-A-C-K!!! He caught me right on the side of my face and I went down. All I could see through a blood-filled eye was a pair of cowboy boots in light-tan leather and a pair of embroidered denim trousers. It was easy to guess who was wearing them.

"Fuck you!" I managed to say.

"Fuck you back," Rudi Schiller replied and placed a well-aimed boot into my ribs.

Then Chelsea screamed – and I passed out.

"*Wake up, David! Come on - wake up!*" Sulita was dabbing my face with a handful of ice-cubes wrapped in a towel. God knows what he'd used, but it hadn't been your basic knuckle sandwich. I've tasted one or two in my time and I know the difference. This one had been filled with something heavy.

"Chelsea?"

"She's gone," Sulita was wearing a black flak-jacket that had *Thai Police* in two languages across the back. "He's probably taken her."

"Bastard," I said. "Are you sure?"

"As can be," Sulita replied. "She's left her cell phone behind."

Good point – but my head was on fire and needed a bucket of ice-cold water. "I'll buy that," I said.

"Why did you open the door?"

"I was going for coffee," I said. "Miss Muppet needed coke."

"And all you got was a kick in the head," my carer laughed. "Can you stand up?"

"Just about," and with a little help, I staggered over to the bed. "When I find him, I'll kill him." Then remembered my backpack. I pushed my aching body one more time, stood up, opened the wardrobe door. It was still there - and still intact.

"Sam's gun?" Sulita asked.

"Damned right," I said, suddenly alive. "First, I need caffeine."

Sulita knew this coffee shop. She walked me up to the junction, turned left and then along for about another hundred meters. It was right across the road from another sportswear shop. Here, the girls were dressed in orange shirts.

Our coffee shop was run by the tall, slim girl with shoulder-length black hair. She was wearing a salmon-pink shirt with a *Sports Club* motif in silver letters.

On the wall behind her counter, a *Yoga Girl* poster and an orange flag for the *Ms Sports Club*. "Wait here," my carer told me. "I'll get something for your head."

"Like an axe?" I asked – but then remembered the crocodiles.

While Sulita went in search of pain-relief, our *Sports Club* friend served our coffee. She'd made it glass cups and saucers – and the cream on top had been swirled into a flower-petal pattern. We also had chocolate sprinkles. It looked sensational - and tasted even better.

Two good slugs of the medicine and Sulita was back. "Try these," and she gave me a packet covered in Chinese writing. "They'll put you right in seconds," she smiled.

"Are the legal?"

"Only in Yasu," Sulita whispered.

I tried them – and they did. Within five minutes, the rainbow of pain dissolved into a clear blue sky and I became a living, breathing, pain-free, organism again. "Amazing!" I said. "I'll take some home."

"Better not," she warned me. "You'll end up in the *Hilton*!"

Fair point - time to move on. "What can we do about Chelsea?"

"I'll call Mr Sam," came Sulita's answer.

Which she did – and she spent several minutes in a deep and animated conversation. After she had brought him up to date, she held up the phone. "You want to talk to Mr Sam?" she asked me.

"Yes," I said and took it. "Sam," I began, "how did he get out?"

"Villavito has very influential friends," Sam reminded me. "The lawyers had freed Mr Schiller before he was back in Bangkok."

It had to be something like that. "And now he's got Chelsea."

"It's OK, David - I've given Sulita everything she needs."

"Such as?"

"A Jeep and phone-tracing resources."

"What about Alfie?"

"He's watching Viv and Anni," Sam reminded me. "But I'll find you another pair of hands - I'll tell Jimmi to call Sulita."

"Who's Jimmi?" I asked Sulita.

"One of the garden gnomes," she told me. "He was the guy on the bench outside the hotel."

Back to Sam. "Looking forward to meeting him," I said – then reviewed our problem. "Any idea where Rudi could be?" I asked.

"No," Sam admitted. "But as you have Anni's diamonds, he'll come to you."

Good thinking - but with a flaw: he didn't have Anni – and I didn't have her diamonds. "Got you, Sam," I said. "Leave it with us," and handed back the cell phone. "What's the plan?" I asked her.

"Complicated," she said.

We had the Jeep – and we had technical *resources*. If we could get Rudi to answer his cell phone, the backroom team could triangulate the signals and locate him to within five hundred meters.

"It's not precise," Sulita explained. "But it'll give us a clue."

Dead right, my love, it's way-off being precise - but it would get the game off the ground. "What other resources do we have?" I asked. A regiment of border guards would have been useful.

"You have me," Sulita smiled. "What more could you want?"

"Jimmi?" I suggested.

"Let's hope he's in the area," Sulita agreed.

If he wasn't, she could always smile the South African into submission. "Shall we start?" I had Rudi's number on my contact list. If he was after the diamonds, how could he resist me?

"I'll ready the monitoring team," and she called her office.

"Wish me luck," I grinned and selected Rudi's number from my *Contacts* list. Bless his little dollar-loving heart, he answered me!

"What you want?" Over the digital line, he sounded even more of a bullying South African.

"Is that him?" Sulita asked.

I nodded, she told her *resources* – and they began tracking.

"Why are you calling me?" Rudi was asking.

No point in wasting time. I gave it to him straight. "I'll swap the girl for the diamonds."

"For that load of shit? - don't make me laugh!"

"Not the crap from China," I said. "The stones that Anni stole from Villavito."

A second's pause – then: "Fuck off, David - you don't have them."

I reached into my backpack, found the dummy package, then held it by the phone and gave it a shake. To my relief, the glass beads rattled nicely. "There are other interested parties, Rudi..." I said.

"But I have your Chelsea."

OK – he'd managed to work it out by himself. What a smart little soldier. "Let me speak to her," I asked.

"Hey you - fuck-bunny! Tell him how big my dick is!"

I heard Chelsea's voice. She sounded frightened. "Please help me, darling," was all she was allowed to say.

"It's OK," I said softly. "You'll be out of there by lunchtime."

That was it. Call over. Now it was Rudi again. "In your dreams!" he laughed. "I may want to keep her... she owes me a fuck."

I looked at Sulita and mouthed: "Any joy?"

Sulita shook her head and signalled me to keep him talking for as long as possible.

"Come on, Rudi," I said. "You know she's Villavito's girl."

"So what's she doing with you?"

"He sent her along to keep me on track," I tried.

"Well fuck him with a red-hot poker!" Rudi sneered. "He owes me one – I'll take it from her."

"Forget the balls," Sulita whispered. "Aim for the wallet."

So I followed her advice and went for the *slutfest* side of his nature. "Take the diamonds," I said. "Think of all the dripping pussy you could fuck with half-a-million dollars!"

For fully five seconds, he said nothing. For some people, thinking takes a lot of time. "Come on, Rudi – yes or no?"

"Give me time to try her out…" and he laughed at his own crude sense of humour. "Call you back on one hour."

"What's the matter – does it take that long to get a hard on?"

"She should be so lucky!" and he shut me down.

Sulita had picked up most of it. She put her hand on my arm. "Don't worry," she told me, "he may be a sexist bastard – but he's a *whites-only* sexist bastard."

"Does that make a difference?"

"He won't go *black*," she predicted. "He's only winding you up."

"Hope you're right," I said. "It's not her fault."

"Not entirely true," Sulita reminded me.

Yes, Chelsea had a criminal past. "That's why we're here," I said.

"Dead right," Sulita agreed. "Let's go wave the diamonds!"

"Difficult," I said.

"Why?" Sulita wanted to know.

"Because I haven't got them."

Sulita laughed. "Then shoot straight - and shoot often!" she said.

31

Until the techno-kiddies in Police HQ had drawn the bearings on a local map, there was nothing we could do. That annoyed me. I wanted to charge in and save Chelsea.

"Easy, hero!" Sulita smiled. "Don't play his game."

"I want to get her out of there," I said.

"St George and his lance to the rescue!" my resource laughed.

"Sod the lance," I said. "I'll rip his head off!"

"Of course you will." Her phone went *chirpy-chirpy* and we both came back to Planet Earth. We were focussed again. She spoke for ten or fifteen seconds – then pulled a large-scale map from her flak-jacket and spread it across the table. While she talked, she ran her finger over the open country to the south of Yasu Thon.

"What or where?" I asked.

Her finger circled an empty space with one significant feature: a pond surrounded by greenery. "I don't know this part at all," she murmured.

"I've been there," I said. "It's full of crocodiles."

Sulita laughed. "Mother warned me there'd be days like this!" then she re-folded her map and put it away. "We'll call it Plan A," she decided. "First, I'll tell Jimmi – then we'll find that Jeep."

Sulita's Jeep had been parked behind the *Yod Na Khon* Hotel. It was black with heavy-duty tyres, a canvas roof, a magnificent radio aerial and a pair of those intimidating red/blue flashing police lights. It also carried a solid set of rally bars.

"Nice," I said. "Should do the job."

"We've cleared your room," she said. "It's all in the back."

I looked and saw our holdalls. "What about the bill?"

"Paid," Sulita told me. "Once we go, you won't be coming back."

"No complaints," I told her. Then my cell phone rang.

"Is it Rudi?" Sulita asked. She was ready to call her office.

I checked the display. "Van Rijder," I said. In all the excitement, I'd forgotten about our bus ride back to Bangkok.

"Better answer it. We don't want him looking for us."

Now that was a sensible suggestion. *Keep the crows in the cornfield* as they say in Kansas. *Once they get to your barn, it's deep-shit all over.* "Cornelius!" I said brightly, "how kind of you to call – we were just on our way."

"Let us have breakfast," he offered. "I have a present for you."

"Too kind," I said. "But the taxi's waiting."

"Ask your driver to bring you here. I want to say goodbye."

"If I can make him understand me," I said and closed the line. "Time to go," I told Sulita.

In fifteen seconds, we were on our way. Out of the car park, through the massed ranks of assorted bicycles, up to the Buddha shop, a sharp right turn at the junction and out into the country. Could she drive? Too bloody true - and she was fun to ride with!

"Tell me about this reservation for reptiles?"

There were times when Sulita's choice of language made me wonder about the daddy-in-the-Peace-Corps story. She didn't speak like your average Thai. No doubt, she's been to a university – but not to a university in Thailand. "It's down a long country lane," I said. "Has large wooden gates and seems to be surrounded by a chain-link fence."

"What about the crocs?"

"Van Rijder reckons about fifty big ones."

"Gets better and better!" Sulita laughed. "Can he control them?"

"Not sure that he needs to," I told her. "They just seem to float about in the pond."

By now, we had burned-up the easy-rider part of the highway and were about to dive into the overgrown plantations.

"Hang on to your hat!" Sulita yelled. "This cat's a bouncer!"

She was right. I'm not saying that the Mitsubishi was a softer ride, a smoother ride or ever a better ride. But in the defence of the bouncing *resource*, when we came down this part of Thailand yesterday, the Mitsubishi wasn't being driven by Sulita.

"If you want to be sick, lean out the door," she yelled.

Some parts of the ride I recognised – like the tiny shop with all the Coca-Cola adverts and the lean-to shack with the family's washing draped over the bushes. But most, I didn't. Either we were using a different route or we were bombing along at such a rate that everything merged into a mirage of green. Any livestock we met just got out of the way - and the two-stroke motorcycles dived for cover as Sulita cleared the way with a burst of her red/blue lamps.

"And if they don't, we've still got the cow-catcher!" Sulita shouted as this rider and his pillion went for safety behind a couple of coconut palms.

We came to a junction. Two farm tracks had come across each other, mingled for a moment and then rambled off in separate directions.

"Where are we now?" Sulita muttered - then stopped the Jeep and pulled out her map. She ran her finger along our lane until she reached the crossing. "Have we passed any other junctions?" she asked me.

"Not noticed any," I said.

"Nor me," she agreed - then moved her finger to the area around the pond and tapped the faint black line that seemed to represent the only way IN or even OUT. "Left it is," she decided. And we were off again – but this time, more slowly. "So he doesn't hear us coming."

For the next ten minutes, we kept on grinding out a steady, bumpy progress down this long, green tunnel that twisted and turned inside a never-ending forest of bamboo.

"Keep the faith, David," she smiled. "If we miss the gate, we'll find the pond."

"Is that Plan B?"

"Of course," she laughed as she eased us over a succession of pot holes. "As Mr Sam's appointed deputy, I can play this any way I want."

"So long as you let me splatter the bad guys," I said, "I'm easy."

"Glory, glory, Hallelujah!" Sulita laughed.

Then we saw the large wooden gate with the *Keep Out* sign in bright red Thai letters.

"We have a choice," I said. "Leave it here and go on foot...."

".... or open the gate and drive in," Sulita finished.

"But if we do that," I said, "we'll need to leave the gate open for a quick escape."

Sulita thought about it. "And leave the crocs to help themselves from the village supermarket?"

Not the best idea. "Then we'll hide the Jeep in the bamboo."

We backed into this narrow path to someone's chicken-run. "Hey – mind that bike!" I told my driver. Someone had abandoned a neat little 125cc Yamaha right where we were trying to park.

"Show me," and Sulita scrambled across to look out of my window. "Hey! - that's Jimmi's!" she laughed.

"Here we go," I said. The *Magnificent Three!*"

"Follow me!" and Sulita leaped out of the Jeep, ready for anything. "Now let's kick ass," and she pulled on a dark blue baseball cap that had *Police* across the peak in large gold letters.

First, we had a gate to open. I slung my backpack over my shoulder and followed her.

"Last time, this was opened by some guy in a jump suit," I said.

"Not any more," Sulita replied – and pointed to a bleeding mess of a human body lying in a nearby ditch.

"*Jesus Christ!*" I said. "What happened?"

Sulita removed her cap. "Dave," she said, "meet Jimmi."

As we stood and looked down, the idea of splattering the bad guys didn't seem quite so funny. "Poor little sod," I said. "We owe him one."

"Get back in the saddle, sunshine," Sulita ordered. "Now we know for sure that he's armed."

And dangerous; Jimmi had been shot at least four times. "Is he...?"

She didn't need to check his pulse. "Very," she said quietly.

To one side of the main gate, there was a stable door, held shut by a simple latch. "What do you reckon?" Sulita asked me.

"He won't shoot anyone *until* he has the diamonds," I reasoned. We eased up the latch and opened the gate.

Inside, we found a chain-link gate that opened sideways on runners. It was held by heavy-duty anchor bars and a padlock.

"Who's got the key?" Sulita asked.

I looked around, hoping that the last guy to use it might have left it hanging on the wire. "Can I blow it away?" I asked. It was something I'd always wanted to do.

"No you may not!" and Sulita looked horrified. "You'll frighten the crocodiles!" Instead, she unzipped a pocket in her flak-jacket and found a tiny Allen key. "Watch and learn," she said as she eased it into the padlock. With a flick of her wrist, the lock sprung free and we were able to open the sliding gate.

"Police training?" I asked.

"Penn State education," she confessed.

"Prison or university?"

"Fifth grade," she replied.

The pond was dead ahead and the mud-coloured buildings were on our right. "Start with Head Office," I said and started walking towards the largest of them.

"If we meet a crocodile, what's your plan?" Sulita asked me.

"When you see me running, try to keep up."

Our target was an adobe hut with a corrugated roof. An open door was shaded by a bush with orange flowers. With twenty yards to go, a figure in a cowboy hat stepped into the sunlight. It was Rudi – and he was holding a shiny .45 Smith & Wesson. I decided to stop.

"You should have phoned me first," he called out.

"We were in the area," I said. "Thought we'd look you up."

"Fuckin' great," Rudi growled. "Who's the cunt in fancy dress?"

"My sister – she's on holiday – asked if she could see the farm."

"Would she like to help me feed them?" Rudi asked.

"Only with your dead body," I replied.

"Just remember who's been screwing your girl," he called back.

From the corner of my eye, I'd notice that Sulita had moved to an angle of some 45^0 to my right. If he tried to shoot at either of us, he would risk being nailed by the other.

"Bring her out and let me see her," I said.

"Come here," he called and he waved his gun to hurry her along. "Fuckin' move it!"

As she stepped into the daylight, I could tell that she'd been crying. "Has he hurt you?" I called.

"No," she called back. She sounded weak.

"Are we ready to trade?" I said.

At that moment, I was conscious of another vehicle driving slowly along the bumpy little lane. Its engine was revving more than was really necessary. Someone else was in a hurry.

"Let me see what you have," Rudi offered.

I help up both hands to let him see I wasn't carrying a weapon. "OK to come forward?" I asked him.

"Piss me off and she gets it," Rudi warned us.

All this time, Sulita was standing to my right. "It's OK," she said. "I'm watching."

Slowly, step-by-step, I moved towards the adobe hut – and as I walked forward, so Sulita came slowly forward as well.

"Hold it!" Rudi ordered. "Close enough."

We were about ten yards apart. From a standing start, I estimated it would take two seconds to reach him. I tried to decide if he could set himself, aim and fire in that time.

"I am taking off my backpack," and I let it side off my shoulder and rest on the ground. All the time, the other vehicle was getting nearer.

"Go easy, man," Rudi warned me.

"I am reaching into my backpack," and I let my hand rummage around until it settled on the package. I tried to ease the flap away. It had to be open – and the beads had to spill on the ground in front of him.

"Get a fuckin' move on!" Rudi was getting impatient.

"Sorry – can I use both hands? It's full of washing..."

"Use your dick for all I care!" he laughed.

I felt the flap give way. "Got 'em," I said – and eased the envelope out of my backpack. "There you go," I said – and threw them at his feet. Three glass beads rolled into the dirt.

"Clumsy fucker!" he yelled and fell to his knees to grab them.

It was enough. As his eyes went down, my right hand grasped the pistol butt – I sprang forward – and he looked up just in time to see the barrel of the Colt smash into his head.

He didn't even groan. He just went down and lay there, sprawled in the dirt – and bleeding from a four-inch gash above his left ear.

"Chelsea – run!" I yelled – but we were out of time. Van Rijder was over by the sliding gate and he was carrying a shotgun.

"Inside – NOW!" and Sulita caught Chelsea's arm and dragged her into the adobe hut.

I stood in the doorway and watched Van Rijder as he walked steadily towards us. With only a shotgun against us, we were safe inside the hut.

The adobe room was square and served as a nursery for baby crocodiles. There were four large tanks, each with three or four inches of warm water. As the occupants grew larger from tank to tank, I guessed the broods arrived at regular intervals.

"You cannot hide in there all day!" Van Rijder called.

"What's he up to?" I asked Sulita.

"He's gone to one of the other huts," she said.

"Do we know why?" I asked.

"Not yet," Sulita replied.

It was time to concentrate on Chelsea. "Are you truly OK?" I asked her. "Did he hurt you – harm you – touch you?"

"Did he fuck me?" and she looked at me with those doe-black eyes that always take my breath away. "No," she said. "He not make it work."

Big gun, but out of bullets. "We'll be out of here soon," I promised her.

"You said you get me for lunch," she smiled.

"May have to make it dinner," I said.

Sulita called me. "Come and look at this," she said.

From the safety of one of the other buildings, Van Rijder was throwing handfuls of rotting meat into the pond – then on to the ground – and then towards our hut.

"Want to make a run for it?" Sulita suggested.

I looked through the doorway. Something was missing. "Where's Rudi?" I asked. Van

Rijder with a shotgun was a risk. But Rudi with a Smith & Wesson was a threat. And now we had those bastard crocodiles!

"You should have caught the bus, David," Van Rijder called.

The first of the large brown logs had drifted over to the floating carrion. Two others were close behind.

"Ready for action?" I asked Sulita.

"Of course," she smiled and drew her own 9mm Colt from a shoulder holster. She looked at her watch. "We don't have long."

I removed the spare magazines from my backpack and stuck them in my trouser pocket – and was just about to throw the pack away, when I suddenly tossed it to Chelsea. "Put this on," I said. "It isn't much…"

"But every little helps," Sulita laughed.

Two large crocodiles had left the water and were making steady progress along the line of meat towards our hut.

"Why we wait?" Chelsea asked.

"Who wants to leave?" Sulita asked.

"What's the rush?" I wanted to know.

"You've got a plane to catch," came her answer.

"Then we'd better shift it."

"Put Chelsea in the middle," Sulita ordered.

"Praise the Lord and pass the ammunition!"

"Too damn true!" Sulita agreed. "Just keep shooting."

I stood in the doorway, flicked off the safety catch – fired two at Van Rijder's hut and watched them punch holes in the adobe wall.

"Go!" yelled Sulita - and we all started running.

One of the crocodiles was in our way. It saw us coming, reared its head and snapped its jaws. And that's the nearest I ever want to get to chain-saw teeth. Tigers are fine – but crocs should be avoided.

"Jump!" I yelled – but as we hurdled the back of the snarling monster, so the air was filled with the muffled *bark!* of a shotgun. Something like a hornet stung my shoulder.

"Fuck!" I cried, "the bastard's got me!" and in the shock of being hit, I dropped my gun.

"You'll live," Sulita promised – and let off two shots in the direction of Van Rijder's hut.

Then I saw the cowboy hat. Rudi was hiding in the shrubs about halfway between the nursery and the exit gate. I saw the glint of sunlight in the barrel of his gun – and I swear I saw the movement of his finger on the trigger.

"DOWN!" As we hit the earth, he fired – and the whine of spinning bullet sung in my ear as it flew away across the pond.

Rudi ran into the open and fired again – and hit Sulita.

I heard her scream.

"You OK?"

"Right arm – flesh wound," she called back.

"He can't get lucky all the time," I said. My shoulder hurt, I'd scraped a knee on the rock-hard ground – and was feeling pretty pissed-off with this sodding South African.

We were in a mess: Sulita was down – and Van Rijder was behind us, closing in with his shotgun. I needed that pistol – but was it close enough?

At this point, Rudi decided he was winning and went for glory. He posed like a mythical gunfighter and fired into the ground between us – probably to frighten us. Then he started moving towards us, psyching himself into killer-mode, getting ready to finish the job.

"She dies first" he was yelling. *"The cunt in fancy dress goes next – and you can go last!"* He was on another planet.

As he strode towards us, I could only focus on the barrel of his gun – and it was getting larger and larger by the second.

I saw a movement to my right. Chelsea was on her feet and pointing Sulita's Colt at Rudi. *"You no shoot Mr David!"* and she squeezed the trigger.

"Jesus fuck!" Rudi stopped – and looked at Chelsea.

"Now you!" Chelsea yelled. Left-handed, she tossed me the Colt.

If we had rehearsed the move for a month, we could not have done it better. The arc was perfect – and the Colt was in a sideways spin.

I caught it - raised it - filled the foresight with his body. Rats-in-a-barrel time! And when I squeezed the trigger, I hit him twice before he even knew I had a weapon.

He wasn't down and out – not yet. Although he was gushing blood all over the ground, he still managed to stagger as far as the water - where the crocodile was waiting for him.

With a giant swish of its massive tail, it knocked him clean off the ground. As Rudi hit the dusty earth, the creature eased itself around, grabbed a hold of an arm and dragged him into the slimy brown water.

Now my mind was in a total spin. Sulita was hurt – Chelsea was in shock – Van Rijder was less than thirty yards away – and Rudi was being eaten. But when you're up to your ass in crocodiles, it's hard to decide what to shoot at first.

Easy! Van Rijder had a shotgun – and he was close enough to do serious damage. So I stood up straight, aimed at his balls and shouted: *"Drop it – or I'll blow them away!"* then let one go at his head to suggest that I wasn't joking.

I looked to my right. Chelsea had ripped a length from her *Laughin' Pussy* shirt and was helping Sulita. They were OK. But when I looked to my left, Rudi had disappeared. "Tough shit, old son," I heard myself mutter.

Very carefully, Van Rijder laid the shotgun on the ground – then grabbed this tiny ladies' handgun from his sock and fired a shot at me.

Cheeky bastard! So I stiffened my arm to fire back, squeezed the trigger – but the mechanism hammered on an empty block.

"For fuck's sake ... NO!!!"

No need to worry. Van Rijder was away like a rat up a drainpipe... And by the time I had pulled a spare magazine from my pocket, replaced the empty one and cocked the weapon, the old South African was already out of sight, deep in the undergrowth. I picked up my own gun and started to follow.

"Leave him!" Sulita shouted at me. "Out of time – gotta go!"

"What hurry?" Chelsea asked.

"God knows!" I told her. "I do lunches – she does transport," and we hurried after Sulita, out of the crocodile compound, through both gates and out into the country lane.

"Oh shit!"

"What's wrong?" I asked Sulita as I closed the wooden door.

"It her," said Chelsea. She was pointing at a large navy-blue 4x4. Sure as hell, there was Yasmin, sitting at the wheel of the Mitsubishi, waiting for whoever came back with the diamonds.

I was still holding Sulita's Colt. I looked at the 4x4 – then sized-up Yasmin. I had no choice – and raised the gun, shoulder-high.

Sulita tried to read my mind. "Don't," she pleaded. "Leave her!"

"It has to be done," I said.

"NO!" Yasmin screamed in terror as she threw herself across the front seat, hiding from the line of fire. *"He make me do it!"*

"Sweetheart - I don't give a damn..." and *SMACK* - I put a bullet into her nearside front tyre. Job done – now she couldn't follow us.

"Time to go..." Sulita ordered and we ran back to the chicken run to recover the Jeep.

32

"Where are we heading" I wanted to know.

As Sulita had been wounded, we all agreed that Chelsea should drive. This suited me: I can't read Thai road signs.

"Ubon Ratchathani," Sulita pronounced it *Rat-cha-tani*, placing all the emphasis on the *tani* bit.

I checked Sulita's map: it was fifty miles to the south-east of Yasu. We were heading out of town, down a long straight road with farms and small plantations on either side. "May I ask why?"

"Because it has an airport," Sulita explained.

"And...?"

"We are going back to Bangkok."

"Why the rush?"

"So that we can arrange the hand-over before Villavito starts asking questions."

That made sense.

At Ubon airport, we borrowed a first-aid kit to patch-up our injuries. We packed our guns in my holdall and Sulita used her badge to collect the tickets for Bangkok. Now we were waiting in the glass-fronted *X-Press Boarding* lounge used by *Thai Air Asia*.

"Neat piece of resource work," I said.

"Some days we get it right," she smiled back.

Chelsea just sat quietly and sipped at a bottle of water through a plastic straw. "Nice to not move," she said.

I took the opportunity to text ahead to Viv: *All well – coming home* I told her. *Details to follow... love to Anni.*

Viv answered: *Singha's will be ready and waiting.*

Our 737 was parked on the tarmac in the summer sunshine – painted white and red, with the *Solatron* logo right along its fuselage.

"Come on, Cinderella," I said to Chelsea. "Your coach awaits."

"What you mean?"

"Tell you when we get to London," I smiled.

An hour later, we arrived at Suvarnabhumi. "Is that it?" I asked Sulita. It seemed out of balance: Tuesday's bus ride up to Yasu had taken the best part of a day.

"We could have taken the scenic route," Sulita smiled, "but Mr Sam is waiting for us."

"Mr Sam – he *always* waiting!" Chelsea smiled.

"So let's hope he's ordered afternoon tea," I said.

Our taxi pulled onto the forecourt of Bangrak Police Station and stopped in the shade of a palm tree. Sulita rang a bell and the side-door was opened from inside. "Let's go find the boss!" she laughed.

I nudged Chelsea's arm. "Last time we came, he wasn't happy," I grinned. "Let's hope he's in a better mood this afternoon."

She didn't get the joke. "He nice to me," she said. "But I not hit anyone."

Fair comment, little kitten.

At the end of the corridor, Sulita knocked on Sam's office door. This time, it was different. No more Mr Hard-Man.

"Come in," we heard him call.

Sulita opened the door. Sam was over by his desk. "We are so sorry about Jimmi," she began.

"Was it Schiller?" Sam asked her.

"Who else?" she told him.

"If you find his gun, you can check the ballistics," I said.

Sam accepted that. "But otherwise, OK?"

"We got there," I said, "but thank Sulita – she made it work."

Sam nodded. "No other problems?"

"Only Van Rijder," I said.

"He won't get far," Sam promised. "Anything else?"

We were standing round Sam's desk, still under the watchful eye of His Majesty, the King of Thailand. As there were enough chairs, we made ourselves comfortable.

"A scratch or two," I said. "Just wish you'd kept Rudi in jail."

"Don't we all," Sam agreed. "But Villavito has friends - did the Trekker man cause you any trouble?"

"Scared the pants off Chelsea," I said.

"*No he not!*" Chelsea objected. "Not let him touch me!"

"Yes, we know," I said to her quietly. "Figure of speech."

"Will I need to re-arrest him?" Sam wanted to know.

"Not any more."

Sam understood. "Can we leave it to the Yasu people?"

"They'll need to drag the crocodile pond," I said.

Sam shook his head. "Not our problem," he said. "But what about the Chinese diamonds....?"

"Here," and I pulled the two gold pin cushions out of my backpack and placed them on his desk. "The cause of all the fuss," I said.

Sam picked them up and checked them over. "It doesn't seem possible," he said, almost to himself. Then he noticed the decorative buttons. "Good place for a tracker chip - just in case..."

"In case of what?" I wanted to know.

Sam glossed over the obvious *just in case* – like me being dead - and came up with the flimsiest of reasons. "In case we lose them," he muttered. Then, more brightly: "Who wants coffee?"

"Darling, I have mango juice?" Chelsea asked.

"Of course you can," and Sam used his phone ask for them.

"What's next?" Sulita asked her boss.

"Has to be the handover," Sam replied. "At some point, you'll have to give Raphael his merchandise."

We paused for a moment as a young policeman in a well-starched khaki uniform came in with a tray of coffees and a mango juice.

"How will that happen?" I asked when he'd left Sam's office.

"Villavito won't to do it in the open," Sam replied.

"Why not?" I asked.

"Because he works best in the dark," Sulita explained. "Remember - at the end of all this, you're expected to drown in a canal."

Nicely put, sweetheart. "So we have to draw him into daylight?"

"That might save your ass," Sulita agreed.

While we sat round his desk, I tried to think of anything that could get me away from

195

the drowning problem. But nothing came up to the surface... and unless I could find a bright idea from somewhere, neither would I. "It's not all bad," I said at last. "If Villavito thinks we're coming back on the bus, we're fine until tomorrow morning."

"And if Van Rijder's been telling tales?" Sam asked.

"Unlikely," I said. "He was also after Anni's diamonds."

Sam placed his cup very precisely on the corner of his desk pad. "Does anybody know where to find these diamonds?" he asked

I shook my head. "Like the three-cup trick," I said. "They're never where they should be."

As our meeting broke up, it was agreed that Chelsea and I should go back to the Four Sons Village. It seemed safe enough.

"After all," I told Sam. "We've nothing to hide."

Anyway, we waited around in Sam's office while one of his techie girls stuck miniature tracer pins into the cushions – and then we took a Green/Yellow taxi up to Soi Rambuttri.

Sulita stayed behind. "But I'll be watching," she promised.

When we reached Four Sons, Viv and Anni were sitting in the shade and drinking Singha. "Anyone been worrying?" I called out.

A second of total silence – then: "*You still alive!*" and Anni – with tears running down her face – jumped to her feet and threw her arms around Chelsea.

"*Love you too!*" yelled Chelsea, hugging and kissing her sister.

"*Love you mak-mak!*" Anni cried.

They broke apart and Chelsea came over to me. "We go shopping now," she said. "Need new clothes."

I took my cue and gave her two thousand baht. "Enjoy," I said.

"Not enough," Chelsea complained.

"Don't push your luck!" I grinned and they scampered away, laughing their heads off. "That'll keep them busy for a while," I said to Viv. "What's have you been getting up to?"

"This and that," Viv replied, nodding in the direction of the fast-disappearing Anni.

"Not you and her..?"

"In your dreams!" Viv laughed. "But she's fun to have around."

We sat at the table and sipped our beers while I brought her up to date with the Yasu story – bus rides, Rudi, crocodiles and cute little cushions stuffed with Chinese diamonds.

Viv followed the story with interest. "...dragged into the water...?"

"Looks that way."

"Poor sod," Viv muttered to herself.

"Did she ever come up with the missing package?"

"No," Viv shook her head. "Virtually denies all knowledge."

"What about the escape route?"

"Now there, we've had a bit more luck..."

While Viv was finishing her report, I suddenly remembered that we still had the 9mm Colts. "Hang on," I shushed her. "Must call Sam," and reached into my holdall for my cell phone.

"Something wrong?" Viv asked.

"Right now, we have more guns than *Johnny Rambo*," I said, "and I don't want them lying around in a hotel bedroom."

"Call him now," said Viv.

I tried, but something wasn't right. I couldn't find Sam's number on my *Contacts* list. Then I realised: this was Chelsea's phone. I checked the holdall again – and this time, found the right one. However, as Sam wasn't in, I couldn't really leave a message. The hardware problem would have to keep for a while.

"What now?" Viv asked.

"Good question," I said and started playing around with Chelsea's phone. Out of interest, I checked her call log.

"What are you up to now?" Viv wanted to know.

"She's always phoning people," I said. "Would be nice to know how many husbands she has."

Viv laughed. "Having doubts?"

"To see if she's been calling Villavito," I said.

"Is that likely?"

"At times, he knew as much as I did."

"And you think it was her?"

"Let's find out," I said – and selected the *Dialled Numbers* option. *Nolli* I recognised. Several numbers that ended with a 4-4-2 sequence that reminded of something other than football. I couldn't nail it – not right there – but I pulled out my wallet and found the piece of paper that Nixie had given me.

"Come on, Sherlock... make with the case-breaker!"

Of course - third number down. Nixie!

"There..." and I showed Viv the evidence. "That's our leak."

"Has Chelsea been short-changing you?"

"Jeez – I hope not," I said. "Could be girlie talk – to Nixie."

Viv looked doubtful. "Can you be sure?"

"If she was ratting on us, wouldn't she use another phone?"

Viv thought about it. "OK, she's been gossiping."

"To all and sundry," I said. "She's a bloody chatterbox."

"Fair enough," Viv agreed. "But what can you do?"

"Use it to our advantage..."

33

While we were sitting on the Four Sons patio with a bottle of Cambodian red, I gave them Plan C, chapter and verse.

If my theory about Nixie was right, I could leak her something sweet and she'd pass it on. If Villavito found it irresistible, he'd have to come out of hiding to collect it.

"Like the mouse and the bar of chocolate?" Viv suggested.

"That's the idea," I said.

"It's a plan," Sam agreed. For Jimmi's *goodbye party*, he was wearing a peach-coloured shirt and his usual knife-edged slacks. "What will you be using as bait?"

Trust Sam to find the holes. "For a start," I said, "we have two very expensive pin cushions."

Sam shook his head. "Not nearly enough."

Some twenty other people were out on the patio but they were at the other end, near the bar and watching *Sleepy Hollow* with Johnny Depp and a cast of headless extras.

Sam was right. "We have Anni's diamonds," I said.

"Nice idea," Sulita agreed, "if someone would produce them..." and she looked across at Anni.

Anni said nothing. She just stared into her napkin and kept quiet.

"If we offered him Anni as well..." and for the next five seconds, there was silence. Nobody said anything. Nobody even looked at me. I was invisible, nothing more than a bottle of Cambodian red and a half-eaten lobster.

Sulita spoke first. "Glad I'm not your sister," she said, more to relieve the silence than to offer a compromise.

Chelsea took her turn. "You not do anything with Anni!" and she hit me with her rolled-up sweater.

Anni smiled a sort of *thank you* at her sister, took a firm hold of Viv's hand and shuffled a little closer to her spiky-haired minder.

Viv put her arm around Anni's shoulder. "It's OK, cherub," she whispered. "I won't let him hurt you."

Was there something going on between them? Did it matter? "The only one at risk is Villavito," I said quietly.

Sam shook his head in a no-no motion. Although he was with me on the *who-what-why*, he couldn't see the *when-where-how*. "Go on, David" he offered. "Tell us how to catch a tiger."

"No problem," I smiled. This was it. No need for smoke or mirrors. Just a simple revelation. "I'll just tell Nixie..." and I took Chelsea's hand and kissed it. "Thank you, kitten..." and I hugged her tight. "Now we can really screw that miserable bastard!"

Right on cue, my cell phone rang. Guess who... "Raphael," I said, "how nice of you to call!" and I signalled to everyone to keep quiet. "What's new?"

"Where are you?"

"At one of those roadside halts," I said. "Don't ask me where – I've no idea."

"Why so late?"

"Hold up on the road," I said. "We hit a donkey cart."

"Why the delay?"

"Our driver took fright and ran off," I said.

"Too bad," said Villavito. "I wanted to finish this tonight."

I just bet you did, concrete overcoat and all. "Should be OK for the morning," I told him. "Want me to call you?"

"No," said Villavito. "I will be in touch."

The very thought of being *touched* by Villavito sent a nasty shiver right down to my feet. "I'll be waiting," and I clicked [Exit].

"He's getting anxious?" Sam asked.

"Ripe for plucking," I said - and went back to the Cambodian red.

An hour later, Chelsea and I were up in my room. As Viv and Anni had set up camp across the corridor in 303, we'd been left to make the best of 302.

"Are you OK with this?" I asked her. We were now in back-packer land and it was not the greatest hotel room of all time.

"Am fine," Chelsea conceded. "This one got hot water!"

"Is that right?"

"Yes!" she laughed. "You come – I show you."

And she did. If the hot water was good, then sharing it with Chelsea turned into something well beyond my wildest erotic fantasy.

All it needed was a sponge, a bottle of bath foam - and the most beautiful girl in all

Thailand. Once you have assembled the ingredients, you just toss them into a free-fall situation and let your mind run wild. Believe me, this soapy joy was way above the entertainment in a Bangkok massage parlour.

We splashed, soaped and foamed each other and sponged every corner of the human universe. When we kissed, it was the top-ten, glad-to-be-alive, end-of-the-game, *ain't we brilliant!* kind of kissing that only comes from something special. Then she eased me into the corner of the shower, wrapped her arms and legs around me and left the rest to my creative imagination.

After that, we lay together on the bed, naked in the heat of the evening - not sleeping, not talking; happy to be with each other. But total contentment is a relative condition and it couldn't last.

Chelsea broke the silence. "Why you go see Nixie?"

It had to come eventually. "Good question," I said, turning on my side to gaze into sweet little face. "I think she's been twittering to Villavito."

She frowned and narrowed her eyes, trying hard to understand me. "What you mean?"

Yes, what exactly *did* I mean? Was it only leaking snippets to Villavito? Or was it more about a breach of trust? It would not be easy. It would not be fun. The sooner we started, the sooner we could kiss-and-make-up. So I rolled off the bed, picked up my backpack and found her cell phone. "You called her several times," and dropped it on the bed. "She's all over your Call Log."

She could hardly deny it. "Nixie my friend," she said quietly.

"You also called Nolli and Catti."

"Why me not?" she asked. "They all help find Anni."

"Yes they did," I agreed. "But someone spoke to Villavito. He always knew what we were doing."

"You think me tell him?" She wasn't angry. She was hurt.

"No, I don't," I said to calm her. "I think it was Nixie."

Chelsea sat up sharply. "What she say?"

Now it was my turn to *not understand*. However: "I think she asked you some very clever questions," I said.

"What she do?"

"Passed on your answers," I finished.

Chelsea thought about it. "Why she do that?"

"Because he pays her to?" I suggested.

"Why he do that?"

OK – from the beginning. Spell it out – spell it slow – and let's see if we can make it stick.

"Villavito wants three things from us," I said. "First, he wants those cushions with the Chinese diamonds."

"OK," Chelsea nodded. Even naked, she could still look serious.

I closed my eyes for a second and tried to forget those gorgeous little breasts with their chocolate nipples. "Second," I said, pushing on and hoping for the best, "he wants the package that Anni took."

Chelsea nodded again. "OK," she agreed.

"And third..." Always keep the best till last. "He wants Anni."

"Oh..." and that was all.

"*Oh* is right," I said. "But it may work in our favour."

"What you mean?"

"Thanks to you, Villavito believes what Nixie tells him."

"Why this good?"

OK, she may well be the most delightful creature in my universe – but sometimes, it's like swimming in porridge. "Because tomorrow," I said, "I'm going to sell him a dummy."

"What you mean?"

It was far too warm to answer any more of her questions. I sat back on the bed, wrapped an arm around her shoulder, pulled her close and kissed her. Now I can't be certain if it counted as a total *make-up* – or even as a partial *make-up*. But it was better than nothing.

Anyway, when we'd finished rolling around in the heat of the night, she smiled softly and gave me back her cell phone. "I not make call until you let me," she promised.

"Nice one, kitten." Some part of the message had found a home.

34

At around nine o'clock next morning, I met Viv, Anni and Sam on the patio for coffee. Chelsea and Sulita were missing.

"Anyone seen them?" I asked.

"Sulita is helping Chelsea to get dressed," Sam explained.

Cosy - when would it be my turn?

"They'll be along in a minute," he promised me.

I sat and watched Soi Rambuttri warming up for another profitable Friday. Stalls were being prepared; yesterday's garbage was being collected and a handful of tourists were checking the breakfast menus. Any second now, a large white Mercedes could ease its way round the corner and come looking for us. So what? We could handle it.

I found myself thinking of Day One, when I'd found her in a nearby street. She'd been wearing that beautiful scarlet T-shirt and her first concern had been for her watch... How long ago was all that? Just over a week. It seemed like a lifetime.

Sam broke into my daydream. "Anything more from Villavito?"

"No," I said. "But he'll rise from the dead at any moment."

"Any you have your stick of garlic ready?"

"And the silver bullets..." And I tapped my backpack.

"Do you need more ammunition?" Sam offered.

"Jesus Christ, I hope not," I replied.

Sam gave me a *been-there/seen-it/got-the-medal* smile. "Go on," he offered. "How many did you let-off in Yasu?"

"One magazine," I said. "Two full ones left."

Anni was munching her way through a bowl of muesli and took no notice of our conversation. Viv was with us all the way. It was time to change the subject. "What about Anni?" I asked her.

"No problem there," Viv answered. "She has a passport, and as soon as you give us the nod, we'll be off to Malaysia."

"Any special reason?"

"No visa required," Viv replied.

"Sounds good to me," I said. "Who provided the passport?"

"Don't ask," Viv shook her head, but smiled at Sam.

Chelsea and Sulita came waltzing down the flight of steps to join us. For her day out with me, she had chosen a slightly-modified T-shirt of the *Laughin' Pussy* design and a light blue anorak with a furry collar.

"Expecting rain?" I grinned, stoking the collar.

"Is monsoon season," she explained with a dead-pan expression. "Me no get wet."

"Not in that, you won't," I said. "Would you like a brolly?"

"I happy, thank you, darling" she said. "Me have mango juice?"

"Of course, sweet kitten," and I waved to a waiter.

After mango juice and another round of coffee, Sam got down to business. "What's your plan?" he asked me.

"If I leave now," I said, "I can be at the RiverSide in an hour."

"Sounds about right," Sam agreed.

"Give me half-an-hour to chat her up..."

"What you mean?" Chelsea wanted to know.

"We're going to tell her the biggest lie *ever*," I said.

"Oh good!" Chelsea laughed. "I come with you?"

"No, little kitten," I said. "I want you to step off the Klongsam Ferry at half-past eleven and walk up to the croissant shop."

She looked disappointed. "Yes, Mr David." She was being cheeky. "For you, I do it."

"Viv and Anni will wait inside River City – by the *Sala Thai*."

"And us?" Sam asked.

"Get ready to arrest the bastard," I said. "Let's do it for Jimmi."

Everyone was happy. All we had to do was make it work.

"See you by the cake shop, kitten," and I kissed Chelsea's cheek.

"Be careful, darling," she smiled.

"Trust me!" I waved farewell to the breakfast party and cut through the Soi Chana Songkram alley to head along Phra Arkit Road and Pier 13. Here, the ticket table was in the charge of two blue-shirted women. A handful of Europeans were hiding in the shade.

I paid for my ticket and went outside to enjoy the brilliant sunshine. You don't get days like this in Kentish Town, and I wasn't going to waste it.

The ferry arrived. I found a seat and let the journey take its course. There was no point in rehearsing my speech to Nixie. Just to let it happen.

As the ferry made it's way down-stream, I watched the familiar scenery – The Temple of Dawn - the Grand Palace – Memorial Bridge - Ratchawongse Pier – the Royal Seminary – a giant portrait of the King – River City. With a bit of luck, I could do this ride again tomorrow.

Then we reached Si Phraya.

Ten minutes of *take-it-easy* strolling to pass the Royal Orchid Sheraton and the River City shopping mall took me to the glass-fronted entrance of the RiverSide hotel.

"Good morning, Nixie! Make me something special, please?"

As ever, the Queen of the Beans was behind her counter, wearing her white apron with its rainbow neckband. For today, she was using an emerald green butterfly to tie-up her hair in an elaborate fantail.

"Mr David!" she smiled in greeting. "You come back?"

"Just called in to see you," I told her. "Am meeting Anni."

"Our Miss Anni?"

"That's her," I confirmed, and hung my backpack on a chair.

"Here?"

"No," I said. "In the precinct, where we met last week."

"That's nice." Nixie tapped the Colombian jar. "Is she OK?"

I nodded at her choice of coffee. "She sounds good," I said, "and I came to thank you for your help."

Nixie poured the beans into her grinder. "We are very happy that you find her," she said. "Where she hiding?"

I noted the 'we' in her sentence. "In Klongsam," I said.

For a moment or two, Nixie busied herself with the coffee-making process and when it was ready, she set up a tray with cup and saucer, a jug of cream and two sachets of sugar, one white, one brown. Then, as she filled the cup: "You find her diamonds?"

Nice one, Nixie! "That was my deal," I said. "Is he in?"

"No Mr Villavito today," Nixie smiled as she placed the tray in front of me. "When you want see him?"

"No rush," I said. "He'll call me." *As soon as you tell him*, I thought as I made the most of the brew.

We made small-talk: usual stuff: how was Chelsea? - where was she working? – why had I booked out?

"There was a fight in this massage parlour," I began - then checked my watch. "Forgive me, Nixie, but I have to meet Anni off the Klongsam ferry," and I kissed her cheek, dropped a 100-baht note on the counter and picked up my backpack. "See you soon!" and I set off for the precinct.

At the Croissant Café, Karina – still in black - was on duty.

I waved and said: "Good morning!"

Karina smiled and waved back. It's always nice to be recognised. I chose a table out in front. I wanted all-round vision: no blind spots, no dark corners. Viv and Anni were in sight: they were sitting at a table in the *Sala Thai*, drinking water.

But there was no sign of Sam or Sulita.

Karina came over to my table. She had a pad and pencil.

"Just a coke," I said – and she was back within a minute. "Thank you," I smiled.

From where I was sitting, I could see the causeway that crossed the stretch of fishing water to the cross-river pier. As I watched, a dozen or more people drifted past in ones and twos, all heading for the ferry. A ferry arrived – and a load more people scurried away from the pier, heading for the taxi rank next to River City.

I looked, but Chelsea wasn't with them. I placed my backpack on the table and waited. There was nothing else to do.

Two more ferries – then I saw her! She was still wearing the light-blue anorak. It was open and the *Laughin' Pussy* shirt was there for everyone to see and admire.

She smiled when she saw me and came up to my table and as she was supposed to be Anni, we made a *wai* to each other.

"Right on time," I said.

Then, as the crowd of ferry users melted away, we saw him, weaving towards us like an angry cobra, ready to strike. A moment later, a snub-nosed Smith & Wesson .38 revolver was aimed at my face.

"Raphael - I have them here," and I started to open my backpack.

"*All* my diamonds, David?" Always Mr Polite.

"Most of them," I said – and pulled out the two gold pin-cushions that held the dross we'd helped to smuggle from Laos.

"And what about Rudi?"

"He couldn't come," I said.

"Why was that?" Villavito asked me.

"He tried to rob you..."

He wasn't listening. "*I warned you,*" and waved his gun the way they do in cheap detective movies.

I put up my hands. "It's OK – you have the consignment..." and I pointed to the two little cushions. "And we'll soon find the missing package."

"You had your chance," he said. "Now it's my turn."

"Raphael – be reasonable!" I tried.

Too late... he raised the gun to shoulder height – changed his aim and fired twice. Both hit Chelsea – and threw her backwards like a broken doll. She hit her head on the edge of the veranda and just lay there, not moving – her blood spreading over the paving stones in a crimson flood.

Now the gun was pointing back at me. I could see his finger on the trigger. It was him or me. Which left no option. I had to kill him, there and then.... in front of everyone.

For the next two seconds, we stared at the twisted, lifeless body. Red mist filled my eyes... I picked up a chair - threw it at Villavito – then ran at him, aiming to hit him as hard as possible and as often as possible.

One! - Two! – Three! – Straight from the shoulder and right on target. *"That was Chelsea!"* I screamed as the blows went in. *"You killed her!"* I just lost it. I broke his nose, knocked out three teeth and felt his jawbone snap.

He collapsed, drew up his legs and tried to protect himself. *"You killed her!"* I yelled again - and kicked at his ribs... far too many times.

There was blood everywhere – on my hands, my arms, my shirt, my shoes and my trousers – and all over Villavito's head and shoulders.

I grabbed my backpack. Now the 9mm Colt was in my hand. Its catch was off. It was pointing at the gap between his eyes.

"Bastard!" I said. *"Now it's your turn...!"*

Before I could squeeze the trigger, someone grabbed my wrist and pulled the gun away from its target.

"*No more,*" Sam ordered. "*You've done enough.*"

"*He shot Chelsea,*" I yelled – and I pointed at the figure, lying in the gutter like some tossed-out piece of rubbish in a country lane.

"Yes," Sam agreed. "We know that."

I just stared at Sam in disbelief. "*And I want to blow his fuckin' head off!*" I was blowing hard and trying to catch my breath.

"Not here," Sam whispered. "Too many witnesses."

Now Viv and Anni were in my face. "*Is she OK?*" Viv yelled.

Anni made a dive for Chelsea's body – but Sulita caught her arm. *"Leave her!"* Sulita screamed. *"Leave her to Mr Sam!"*

It was enough to stop us all in our tracks. For a second, no-one moved. We just stood stock still and watched.

First, Sam slipped a pair of cuffs on Villavito.

Next, he asked Karina for a bottle of ice-cold water.

Third, he opened the bottle and poured it over Chelsea's head.

But if I was expecting some religious incantation, then I was in the wrong ball-park. Instead, the twisted little body gave an involuntary shiver. Then its arms began to twitch. Her head began to move - and two wonderful brown eyes looked up at me. Last of all, my Chelsea smiled!

"That sore..." she complained.

"Not as sore as he'll be!" Sulita told her.

Sam took her hand and helped her to her feet. "Now, we can take this off," and he slipped her arms out of the light-blue anorak.

"Shirt as well," Sulita ordered.

I should have known. Under the *Laughin' Pussy* shirt, Chelsea was wearing a Kevlar vest – with two .38 bullets wedged in its fibres.

Sam looked happy. Viv was laughing – Anni was crying – and somewhere in the background, Villavito was groaning.

"Did you have to hit him quite so hard?" Sam asked me.

"He resisted arrest, your worship," I said.

Sam just laughed. "One day, I must visit London," he said.

While Sam organised the removal of the bloody mess that we had once called 'Villavito', Sulita took Chelsea into the back shop of the Croissant Café to remove the vest and get the little kitten back into shape.

While all this was going on, Viv and Anni came to say *Goodbye*. "We'll be off," said Viv - and she put an arm round my neck to kiss me. "I'll send you an e-mail," she finished.

Then it was Anni's turn – but this was a two-arm job – and a smacking kiss, right on the button. "Thank you, Mr David," and she pushed a little red silk purse into my hand.

"What's this?" As though I had to ask!

"Take care of my sister," Anni smiled.

"Now I can afford her," and I waved farewell with the purse.

"Do we now get paid?" Viv called back.

"Who get paid?" It was Chelsea, all bright and shiny in that wonderful crimson T-shirt.

"Everyone," I said.

"That good" she laughed. We were walking in the direction of the gold shops in Si Phraya Road. "Now we go tell Nolli."

"Why?" Then I remembered... Nolli worked in a gold shop.

"I save your life," she smiled. "I shoot at man in silly hat."

"Of course you did," I agreed. "You were bloody marvellous!"

"What is she after now?" Sam asked me. Villavito had been wrapped in blankets and eased into the back of a police car.

"A new gold bracelet," I said.

"Which reminds me," Sam went on. "What about the diamonds?"

I handed him the two silk cushions. "For starters," I said.

"And the others?"

"Gone – gone for ever." I shrugged my shoulders. Not entirely true, of course. But they would be, very shortly.

Sam hadn't finished. "May I call on you this evening?"

"Any special reason?" I asked.

Sam was grinning. "Chelsea's UK Visa," he said.

"What about it?"

"Granted," he smiled.

"That's wonderful!" I could hardly believe it.

"You should take her away for a while."

"You know best," I agreed.

"Hotel this evening – about nine?" Sam asked me.

"You got it," I grinned. "And you can tell her yourself."

Chelsea touched my arm. "What he tell me?"

"That you are a very brave little kitten," I told her. I had my cell phone in my hand and was calling Ronni. *If you bring them to me* she had promised. "It's David," I said. "I've got something for you."

"What you doing?" Chelsea asked.

"Paying for the trip," I told her. "Then you'll get your *Thailand Honey.*"

[THE END]

209

About the Author

Leslie Cameron lives near Mouse Valley in southern Scotland with two rescued dogs and a bag of golf clubs. He has written all his life - and admits that essay-writing was his best subject in school. He is married, has two grown-up daughters and enjoys the company of his five grandchildren, aged ten to twenty. Leslie is a sports fanatic; follows cricket and football - and plays mid-handicap golf as often as the Scottish weather allows.

Thailand Honey is his third adventure into fiction - and he keeps in touch with his many friends in Bangkok by e-mail.